INK

Printed in the United States of America.
Title of a book: Ink A new Superhero is born.

First Printing, 2013

ISBN 978-0-9898130-4-4

Pen an Ink Publishing
4863 Rubidoux Avenue,
Riverside, CA 92504
www.PenanInk.com

INK

Thanks to my family, and friends, also Melanie Bettis, Angela Martin.

I would also like to thank Frank Hamilton, and Yusi.

For contact information write to: PenanInkPub@gmail.com

INK

Contents

INK

INK

On a dark moonless night, officer Paula Davis moved through the forest with her flashlight trained on the underbrush ahead. The beams of a dozen other flashlights cut through the humid, Kentucky night on each wall of the ravine, played over the moss-covered trunks of old-growth maples and dogwoods. Near the bottom of the ravine, Paula forged a path through the thick undergrowth, ferns slapped against her already-damp trouser legs and briers plucked at her jacket. She thought the group of thirteen was overkill for a week-old truck-jacking lead, when all that was stolen were two hundred cases of pen ink.

Her radio crackled with the slow, deep drawl of Buford Nelson. "This is Sheriff Nelson. Frank is about a mile from here, at the old Talbot place. The stolen pallets are outside, plus three bodies...all male." He sounded unusually grim. Paula unclipped her radio from her belt and raised it to her lips. "Roger, Sheriff." A cold knot of fear gripped and twisted her stomach. *Three bodies? Whoa! There had not been a triple homicide in Sutpen County since that Hobart boy went wild back in '68*, she thought. She swallowed, holstered her radio, and started south toward the former Talbot estate.

The other flashlight beams swung with her-Tom, Jimbo, Sandy, and Corliss. Hell, half the county force was out in the woods. Paula was not surprised Frank was the first on the scene. He had found the stolen truck, a hunter and a body builder, he also read detective novels in his spare time. Paula could see a flashlight going on and off in a coded message near the estate, and she ordered the team to kill their flashlights. It took a little less than ten minutes for the team to follow the light to reach deputy Frank Crofter, who squatted down near rusted-out wrought iron dual-swing doorway gates, his gun in his hand, and stared at the entrance to the estate. In the gloom, the Talbot estate looked like an open grave. A strange, blue-white light

INK

flickered from a shuttered window on the second floor of the leaning building.

Paula and the officers followed the deputy's pointing finger into the trees, and soon she could see the swinging heels of the three men hung from the branches of an old oak. Half a dozen plastic buckets sat beneath them to collect blood. Nearby were the stolen pallets, a heap of garbage, and a pile of old cigarette butts. The smell of rotting trash and stale smoke was thick in the air.

"Mother of God," gasped Jimbo Wharton, when he came up beside Paula. He was a huge man, six-foot seven, and pushed three hundred pounds. He stared wide-eyed at the corpses, like a little boy waking up from a nightmare. "What in the hell?"

"Quiet," Paula warned the big man with her all five-foot nine stature. She did not like any of this, for the obvious reasons, however, there was also something very wrong here. Something she could not yet put a finger on. The ropes creaked in the hot, sweating silence, mosquitoes buzzed and bit. Paula waited with the other officers in the dark until the sheriff and Dan Figgins emerged from the shadows on her left side. Dan, the office clerk, a potbellied little man with large, rimmed glasses and thinning black hair, kept his eyes on the bodies when he circled the buckets twice.

Paula watched Nelson, the tall, broad-shouldered sheriff of sixty with a head of cropped white hair and a formidable jaw, tuck his thumbs into his belt while they all gathered around.

"One of them bodies is Wayne Stone," said a voice from the surrounding darkness. The sheriff let that sink in. Paula knew Stone as a drifter who disappeared off the streets a week or so ago. "The others we ain't got shit on yet, but it is a safe bet whoever's squattin' in Maude's house has some answers for us. Paula, you are takin' Jimbo and Dan round back. Click your radio twice when you are in place. Frank, watch over the estate, but stay within earshot. The rest of you, with me." Nelson drew his gun, locked and loaded. "Understood?"

"Yes sir," said Paula, nodding. She turned, Jimbo and Dan followed. They set off along the remains of the wooden perimeter fence. Older than the county was the Talbot estate,

INK

some mining tycoon's retreat that was purchased in the '50s by the widow Maud Talbot and kept up by her family until 1979. Then they lost everything to her son's gambling. The family moved north with nothing left to their name. To the locals, it was still Maude's house, though, or just the Talbot place. Shame they let it stand there collecting moss. Paula slipped through a missing section of fence and into the overgrown backyard with its stagnant, crumbling pool and moldering gazebo, ivy spreading unchecked in all directions. Some of the windows were boarded up, and tiles were missing from the roof.

The back of the house itself was a few hundred yards off. The light oozed from the windows had dimmed a bit, enough that Paula could not be sure whether shadows moved across those windows. Six suspects, the report said, all armed, all male. They had accosted the trucker when he pumped gas, beat him unconscious, and taken his truck. That was where the trail ended, until a rancher found the truck ditched in a meadow a few miles from the highway. *Who the hell steals ink?* She thought.

Paula led Jimbo and Dan around the gazebo, staying clear of the house's windows, and then they crossed the weedy lawn in a short dash that left Jimbo wheezing and red-faced. The old porch creaked under the big man's weight, and Paula noticed ice on the slimy porch rails. She reached the door; fear raised goose bumps on her outstretched arm. The door knob she gripped was frozen enough that she knew she would lose some skin turning it. This was not good.

"Oh, Jesus," Jimbo whispered. Alarmed and annoyed, she looked back at him. He was pale and shaking. Dan, wide-eyed, told Paula they felt the same thing.

"All right," she whispered. Her mouth was dry as sand. "All right, on radio." She clicked the receiver twice. A moment passed, and sweat built up on Jimbo's brow. Paula started to think something might have gone wrong. Perhaps they did not get the message or maybe the radio's battery went dead.

"NOW," crackled over the radio from Sheriff Nelson. Paula kicked the kitchen door down and burst into the dusty, rotted house gun first. She could hear the sheriff and the rest of her fellow officers enter from the front and stomp around in the dark. One of the flashlights swept the kitchen doorway, then vanished. She clicked her own flashlight on, and raised it to her other outstretched arm, that was pointing a gun. Somewhere upstairs the sheriff gave orders in his slow, deep voice. Paula left the kitchen, crept through the cobwebbed dining room, with its table that had once seated Rockefellers and Hursts, stepped into the ruined foyer, and then climbed the grand staircase.

Behind her at the top of the steps, Jimbo puffed away; she stopped. The rest of the officers stood on the mezzanine, spread out around a large, empty doorway. Flashlight beams scanned the area where a lone candle flickered by a shuttered window. Shadowy figures sat on the floor in the center of a huge, bare room. An old-fashioned iron chandelier gave off the ugly blue-white light Paula had seen from outside. She inched forward toward Frank, who covered the sheriff's left flank.

"Ma'am," the sheriff said calmly, and then Paula could see that it was a woman who sat cross-legged on the filthy floorboards on which generations of kids had scrawled their graffiti. A child, maybe three or four years old, was nestled in the woman's lap. An older boy, about six or seven years of age, ran around them, directionless and bounced off walls. The sheriff's flashlight beam glinted off a knife in the woman's hand. "I am going to have to ask you again to put down that knife and step away from the children."

Squinting, Paula could just make out the bronze knife. Her wrists were dark with blood. *Shit*, Paula then realized, sickened. That was not graffiti on the floorboards. The woman had mixed her blood with the stolen black ink, and it glistened red from the floor to the walls, and even the ceiling. Droplets fell with a constant *PLUNK, PLUNK, PLUNK,* of liquid that struck the dry wood floor. It was difficult to pick out details, however, Paula thought she could see a smile appear over the woman's thin, hungry face when she looked up through matted hair at the sheriff.

"Put the knife down," the sheriff said again, "and step away from the children."

"It is too late," the woman said.

INK

And then it all came to life. The first thing Paula saw was the bear. It lurched out of the wall behind the woman like a drunk stumbling out of a closet, its body slid from a two-dimensional blotch to a horrifyingly real mass of hair, teeth, claws, and muscle.

"Oh shitting fuck," screamed Jimbo while the eight-foot-tall bear turned to regard them with dumb, unblinking eyes. It grunted deeply in its chest. It's rough breath was the only sound in the hall when Paula and the rest stared, transfixed by the impossibility of the scene before them. This was not happening. The sheriff opened fire. Two shots, one right after the other, and both hit the bear in the chest.

The great black brute towered and charged. Paula fired. She saw its paw catch Dan Figgins across the chest and tore him open like a cheap party favor when ten other guns opened up on it. A few shots hit Dan, one in the chest another in the head, however, he was already dead. Paula fired steadily, she breathed rapid and shallow. The bear bellowed and swung a paw for the sheriff, that clipped his shirt when Frank pushed him out of the way. The bear claw slashed into Frank's ribs, and then the bear's teeth sank into Frank's throat.

The creature lifted him right off the ground and shook him violently, like a dog would shake a rat in his jaws. The sound of his neck when it *SNAPPED* was enough to set Paula's stomach churning, and her mouth tasted of bile. She collected herself, choked down the awful taste, and fired again. The bear dropped Frank, and a lengthy string of blood flew from its mouth to slap against the peeled wallpaper. It swung a claw at Tom and let out a long, piteous groan, and then stepped aside to avoid the boy, who continued to ran around oblivious. Then it stepped towards Paula in the left corner of the room, and sank.

The rotted wood collapsed beneath its colossal weight and the beast descended slow, then plunged through the floor like a toppled monolith, into the basement with a cacophony of splintered wood, twisted steel, a thunderous growl, broken bones, and torn flesh. Sandy shook and screamed at Frank by the doorway, while Jimbo in the right corner said "fuck" repeatedly to no one in particular. Tom laid a few feet from

INK

Paula, practically torn in half, however, somehow alive, while the sheriff, bled from two gashes across his chest, slumped against the wall. Shaking, Paula turned towards the woman.

She was stark naked, and Paula could see then she was covered in tattoos. From her ankles to her throat, she was a mural of entangled illustrations, the only bare spots were two identical strips on her wrists, cross-hatched with scars. Paula stared. "What is this? What the hell is this?" The baby in the woman's arms, then squirmed and cried. *What kind of baby would a woman like that birth? I should kill them both,* Paula thought wildly. *We should burn this place to the ground and salt the earth. Nobody should ever come back here.* The woman pressed her palm to the wall and pulled a gun, an old Colt .45, from the ink-smeared wood. *It is magic,* Paula thought, her breath steamed in the frozen air.

The woman's first shot caught Floyd Fern right in the teeth. Paula fired at the woman however, was out of bullets. The second shot hit Sandy in the shoulder, that forced her head over heels down the stairs. Paula, ignored the danger, the smell of gunpowder and blood, the screams of the injured and dying, charged with fury and slammed into her like a runaway freight train. The gun thundered again, then hit the floor while they wrestled. She grabbed the woman from behind and placed her in a lock, placed as much pressure on her shoulders as she could, while Jimbo backed away with the squalling baby in his arms.

The woman fought like a tiger, swung arms, pulled hair, and bit. The patterns on her bare skin rippled in the blue-white light. She screamed when Paula forced her to her knees and cuffed her. The little boy ran towards the hole left by the bear when Paula picked him up. The child looked about four years old; he stared at her with the bluest eyes she had ever seen.

"It is all right," she lied. "You are gonna be fine." She placed him on the floor then knelt down in front of him. His eyes vibrant, even so, they were vacant, something was wrong with the boy. Paula took out her belt radio, despite the fact her hands shook.

"This is Officer Paula Davis," she said, her voice a throaty rasp. "I have men down at the Talbot place." She did not let go of the boy's hand.

INK

"What?" Crackled over the radio.

"Jesus Stan, just send a fucking ambulance. Send two, and send the coroner."She ignored Stan Coyle's reply, when it blared over the radio and just stood there, shaking, while the tattooed woman raged and Jimbo helped the sheriff back to his feet. In her ears, her own breath was as loud as a storm. *I will remember this until the day I die,* she thought.

Crime scene investigation from State did not find any bear in the basement. They did not find any Colt .45, or any bronze knife. They did find many weird paintings, paint canvases soaked in blood, an encrypted laptop with a thumb print lock that did not recognize the woman's thumb, about four thousand dollars' worth of acid and coke, and some baby formula. Paula helped them comb the site over and over until there was nothing left to find. The woman was one Jessica Crawford, widowed, thirty-three, of Austin, Texas, where she had worked as a scientist until 1982. Her children were not registered with that state or any other state, and they vanished into the system.

INK

INK

A few years later, the blonde haired, blue eyed boy watched the movie <u>Rio Bravo</u> on television at an orphanage in Austin, Texas. Everybody said he was the most volatile child they had ever seen. It was true too. So they would leave him alone as much as they could. He liked to watch television and most days, they would find him in front of it. The large communal room had seated fifteen, however, he was the only one in there usually. The boy had thrown a chair, at an older larger boy who kept talking during a movie. After that, most the kids would avoid him. He was lying on the floor with his head propped up on his hands, when a large black man, in his thirties, entered the room.

"Stop watching television Jason. Go play with the other kids," he said.

"It is a John Wayne movie, Mr. Abraham Moses, sir," said Jason.

Surprised that Jason used his full name, he answered in kind, "I don't care, Mr. Jason Crawford. You watch too much television. It is not good for you. Get some exercise," said Moses, and switched off the TV. Then he pulled Jason to his feet and walked him outside.

Fifteen kids were on the grass, ran around and played games like tag, leapfrog and hopscotch in the front of a Victorian-style home with a wraparound porch. A baseball came near Jason and he picked it up.

"Jason!" said Chip, an older boy, with red hair and freckles. His hands in a catch position. He was playing with Tom, another older boy, who was scruffy, barefoot, with dark, thick hair and a big nose, and wore hole-riddled coveralls. Jason handed the ball to Chip.

"Moses kick you out again?" Chip asked.

"Yeah."

"You wanna catch frogs?" Chip asked.

INK

"Okay." Then Chip, Tom and Jason walked down by a tree-line. They walked along the path, near dried banks of a creek that the sun turned into a patchwork of cracked mud. The fast-moving five-foot winter creek became a trickling three-foot stream in the summer. The smooth surface mirrored the tall rose gum, silk oak trees, and sky. Pink, green, black, and blue-ringed dancers, club tails, darners, arrowheads and spike-tailed dragon flies, skimmed the top of the creeks surface. Butterflies flew by, while tadpoles swam freely in the shallows. A brown-and-black spotted southern leopard frog leapt on a rhyolite rock, and failed to mimic the grayness of its color.

Jason's head of blond hair rose above the rock. He lunged to catch the frog when it jumped up into his hands.

"I caught one!" said Jason, and turned to Tom, who was farther down the creek.

"You always git'em," said Tom. "Can I have it?"

Jason handed it over to Tom, and felt good about it. He had promised Tom he would give him a frog.

Chip ran up. "You said you would give it to me."

"I will get you another one," said Jason.

"No, I want that one," said Chip, and tried to pull it out of Tom's hand.

"Don't," said Tom, trying to avoid Chip.

Jason restrained Chip's wrist with both hands. Chip broke the hold, and then punched Jason in the face—which caused Jason to crash into Tom, who lost his balance and fell into the creek, which freed the frog. The three began to fight each other. Jason punched both of them to the ground, and then ran off on the dirt path.

"Let's git'em," Jason heard Chip say and ran as fast as he could. A snake had slithered onto the trail. Without missing a beat, Jason ran around it.

"DIAMONDBACK!" he yelled as a courtesy to all in the area. There was half a mile of rose gum and silky oak trees that lined the path. Jason ran to a ninety-nine-foot blue quandong tree with a rope tied to one of its branches. He gripped the end of the rope, like he had done so many times and swung to the other side of the creek so fast that his hands slipped down; the

INK

first few layers of skin on his hands burned off on the fibers. With his adrenaline pumping, he would not notice the injury until later. He hit the ground running.

The rope swung back across the creek. Chip arrived, and then Tom; both wet and angry. Together they clutched the rope and swung across, the branch bent rigorously under the combined weight and then snapped, which plunged the boys into the three feet of cold water. They slowly swam to shore.

"You fat ass," said Chip.

"You are the fat ass," said Tom.

"Leeches," Chip yelled. And both raced out of the water. When they reached the banks, they pulled off the Leeches, and were forced to strip down to their underwear. That got them far more angrier, and as they walked the rest of the trail—told one another how they would beat Jason up when they caught him.

Jason dodged the trees, and weaved through the shrubs all the way to the orphanage. Moses kept vigil over the ten other kids that played on the front yard, while he sat on a rocking chair just outside the front door.

"Slow down, Cowboy!" said Moses, when Jason leapt up the three wooden steps to the porch. Moses sprung out of the chair and picked him up.

"Why you runnin', boy?" He asked.

"I like running, sir," said Jason, out of breath. Moses put him down.

"You will fall over. That is how you get them holes in your jeans. Slow down," Moses said, and pointed to Jason's pants and the holes around his knees.

Chip and Tom snuck up on Jason, then waited until Moses went into the house, and they both ambushed Jason. Chip and Jason traded blows when Moses heard the commotion from inside the house and ran out, and pulled Jason off Chip with a little too much strength. Jason hit his head on the wooden steps of the porch, Moses became alarmed, and ran over to him.

"You two go to the office," he said to Tom and Chip.

Jason felt woozy. His head bled, when his world swam back into view. Moses picked Jason up. Through bleary eyes Jason kept brawling, and punched Moses in the face with all his might, nonetheless, it was as harmless as a fly landing on a tree. Moses admired his tenacity.

"Good to have you back, Cowboy," Moses said, in his deep voice.

Later that month, Jason watched <u>The Good the Bad and the Ugly</u>. Moses came into the room and switched the TV off.

"Go and have a bath right away," said Moses. Jason ran up the stairs and into the bathroom. *Bath in the middle of the day? Strange,* he thought, however, did what he was told. He had a quick bath, then Moses dressed him in new pants, shirt, and tie.

Am I in trouble for watching television? I did not do anything wrong, Jason thought, and waited outside Moses's office, like he was told. He had visited the room twice before for brawling. When the door opened, he entered, and Moses introduced him to a couple who sat in his office.

"This is Cynthia and Mitch Morgan." *They were both skinny, and asked a lot of questions,* Jason thought; he was anxious, fidgeted in his seat, and thought about how much time had elapsed. He wanted to see the TV movie.

"The Morgan's would like you to live with them; you shall have your own room. How do you feel about that?" Moses asked.

"Okay," said Jason nonchalantly. "Can I go now?" He would have said anything to get out of there and go back to the TV.

Moses allowed him to leave, and they all worked out the details. Jason was disappointed, because he ran into TV room only to catch the ending of the movie. Two weeks later, Moses had him pack a bag and walked him out to the Morgan's, who stood by a white Mercedes Benz sedan. Moses carried a small backpack with Jason's belongings and passed it to Mitch. From behind her back, Cynthia presented Jason with a small guitar.

"This is for you, sweetie."

"Oh, wow." Jason's eyes widened in happy surprise. "Thank you, ma'am" he said, and sat in the rear seat of the car. He strummed his new guitar while they drove off.

INK

His new home was not far from the orphanage; he had his own large bedroom with a walk-in closet in a Victorian-style house, however, his tenancy there was short-lived. After a few months had gone by, they took Jason into a high-end jewelry store. Cynthia held up a diamond necklace to the light, while Mitch distracted the sales clerk by pointing to another piece. Cynthia dropped the diamonds into the sleeve of her fur coat and pulled out a fake copy from the other sleeve. Jason saw it all. Then they took him out of the store and shoved him into the back seat of the car for the drive home. Tired, since they had dragged him around all day, he fell asleep.

Then one night, while Jason plucked to learn his guitar, Cynthia made macaroni and cheese in the kitchen, and then placed it on the dining table. The strummed guitar agitated her. She snapped, went over to the sofa where Jason was, snatched the guitar, slammed it over Jason's shoulder, and smashed it to pieces.

"Get out!" she screamed, "Get out and do not come back!" She threw Jason out of the house. It was dark, cold, and Jason wore jeans torn at the knees, a gray t-shirt, and new sneakers. He saw the dirt road into town, and held his shoulder where the guitar had hit him. "We have the diamonds, we do not need him anymore!" He heard Cynthia scream from within the house, Jason decided to walk to the orphanage because the drive there did not seem long.

It was fall, and the trees stood firm, with a beautiful display of yellow, orange, and red leaves, that were visible even in the moonlight. The maples, oaks, gum, and other species usually came to their peaks in late October. A few miles into his walk, he could see a billboard advertising cigarettes in the distance, towered high above the road. He was on the right track because he had seen it from the car rides. Boredom set in quick, so he kicked small stones on the side of the road, to keep it at bay. *Wow, this is long,* he thought. It always seemed a short car ride. When he passed the billboard, the glued cigarette poster shimmered, moved, bulged, and then slowly protruded out, stretched into the shape of a face. The face consumed the entire billboard, and then came to life.

It blinked, then turned to observe Jason, and watched him walk along the road. Jason was unaware; he had found an empty soda can and kicked it down the road. Then headlights appeared behind him. When he approached a dirt road to turn onto it, the face on the billboard saw the van. It sped towards Jason, the headlights shone onto its target. When Jason heard the van pull up beside him, it was too late. The van door opened, and one man dressed in black jumped out and seized him. Jason kicked him in the shin, and ran off. Then another man exited the van and raced after Jason, and caught him after a short while.

Jason stomped on his captors foot, punched and kicked. However, both men picked Jason up and threw him into the van. He brawled with them until a chloroformed handkerchief covered his face. Jason woke up on the ground, between oak trees on the outskirts of the orphanage, and did not know how or how long he had been gone. Frightened, he hid behind a tree and searched the area. When he saw the lights of the orphanage, he ran to it as fast as he could. Moses was on the porch, slouched in the rocking chair, asleep; his blanket had fallen to the ground. Jason quietly picked up the blanket and placed it over Moses before he slipped into the house. Moses opened his eyes, aware of what had just happened.

He treaded lightly and quietly through the house until he stepped on the stairs and they creaked. *Stop,*he thought and stepped off the stair and onto another one. Then he reached a door, slowly turned the knob and opened it to a dormitory. With white walls, a window on the right side, that let in the moonlight, which revealed a row of ten wheel-away beds on each side of the room. He searched and found an empty bed, and slid in quietly. To his left, he saw Chip, awake, looking at him.

"I knew you would be back, Cowboy," Chip said. "Everybody hates you." Jason exploded out of the bed and punched Chip in the face, which thumped him unconscious.

"Go to sleep," Jason mumbled.

INK

He slowly slid back into bed and rested his head on the pillow. He looked at his rope burn scar, on his palm. Tears began to form in his eyes, as he started to believe Chip.

Then it became worse. The next foster parents were ranchers who would shove Jason in the middle of a cow pen, dressed in jeans, chaps, boots, a vest, and a cowboy hat. A bull calf would bash Jason to the ground. The grizzled cowboy rancher would run over to him, pick him up, and yell in his face, "DO YOU WANT TO BE A COWBOY?"

"Yes, sir." Jason would always say, when he held his chest in pain, and gasped for breath.

A few months later, Moses was standing on the porch of the orphanage, and gazed over the kids playing in the front yard, when a beat-up red pickup truck drove up. The kids ran into the house in fear. The cowboy leapt out of the truck in a hurry, went to the passenger door, and opened it. He dragged Jason out, who only wore tighty whitey underwear and cowboy boots. Then he snatched a plastic shopping bag full of his clothes from the back of the pickup and slammed it into Jason's chest. The bag fell to the ground, because Jason was too afraid to move. The cowboy then stuck a cowboy hat on him, marched back into the truck, and drove off.

Moses smiled sadly, "Hello, Cowboy."

Jason would not look at Moses; he gazed at the ground, and believed he had done something wrong again. His eyes were red like he had been crying, and scratches and bruises covered his body. Tom, Chip, and some of the kids inside the house watched out of the windows and made fun of him in his underwear.

Jason saw them point and laugh at him. When Moses noticed what was going on, he rapped on the glass and yelled, "Get away from the window!" The kids scampered and promptly complied. Moses walked towards Jason, and then stopped.

"This orphanage is not big enough for both of us," said Moses. *Those are fighting words,* Jason thought and gazed up at him. He wiped away a tear and tilted his cowboy hat. Moses and

Jason observed one another intensely. Jason pulled an imaginary cigar from his mouth and dropped it to the ground, and then snuffed it out beneath his boot. Moses drifted his shaking hand toward an imaginary gun on his right hip. Jason placed both his hands by his underwear because he had two imaginary guns.

"Fill yer hands," Jason quipped.

They glared into one another's eyes, and hunted for the one who would move first. They drew together and made the sound *BANG* in unison. Moses smiled, twirled an imaginary revolver, and said, "I think I got you that time."

Jason shook his head. "No sir, I shot your pistol out of your hand before you could get a shot off."

"Alright, I guess you can stay," said Moses, when he placed a hand on Jason's shoulder and steered him into the orphanage.All the kids in the orphanage had their quirks, and Moses knew he could manipulate Jason with a cowboy quip or move.

INK

Jason lay perfectly still on the workbench. When he moved, Mao hit him. Mao hit hard. Once Mao started, he had trouble stopping, so Jason lay on his stomach and concentrated on not moving. It was not easy with the needles in Mao's electric tattoo pen. The iron jabbed little spots of fire up and down his back. *Do not be a baby,* he told himself savagely, *you have done this before.* The workshop was hot; a single fan blew in the air from the dusty window, however, moving the hot air around did not help any. Oily rags and crumpled sketches covered half the floor. A canvas-shrouded Harley, half-gutted, leaned against a rack of rusted shelves. It was a hell of a way to spend your tenth birthday.

"You know what this shit is?" Spouted Mao, his stale, smoky breath hot on the back of Jason's neck. The needle stitched more fire into his skin while the big New Zealander worked. He sat beside the workbench on a padded stool, the stump of his right leg up in a special sling. His prosthetic leg leaned up against the bench, just below the clip-lamp he had trained on Jason's back.

"No," said Jason, and took a shallow breath. Sometimes Mao told a pretty good story, when he was sober. He had not seen him drink that day. *Maybe this will not be so bad.* Mao flicked ash from his cigarette into the heavy glass ashtray behind the fan.

"No, what?"

Jason squeezed his eyes shut, furious with himself for forgetting.

"No, sir."

He could almost see Mao's eyes, amber with flecks of gold floating in his irises, tensing, narrowing. Any minute he might start in on Jason. *Stupid, stupid.*

"Sorry, sir."

Mao must have been in a good mood. He did not hit Jason, he just lit another cigarette and blew smoke out his nose. He had a big flat nose, all blotchy with broken veins.

"It is the ngū," he said after a while. "You know what that is, dumbshit?"

"No, sir." It felt good to have a break from the needle.

"It means squid." Mao took the needles out of his iron, flicked it off, and dropped the needles into a bowl of water-alcohol solution. "My grandpa had an idol of one with him when he came over here, after your war. He said we were like the ngū. He lives in the ocean because Tawhiri, the god of storms, drove him there with his creator, Tangaroa. Tawhiri's own brother. Just like your war, yeah?" He did not wait for an answer. "We fought Tojo for you. Now we are here in your country. Texas." He spat the word like a curse. "So hot my balls stick to my boxers."

It was night out, however, the heat was terrible. It was always bad in the summer. The big islander was quiet for a while. He just sat there and smoked in the stagnant heat. He scratched absently at his stump, then retrieved the needle cluster, dried it with a rag, and slid it back into the pen.

"Tangaroa made fish," he said, when he bent over Jason's back, and the pen buzzed back to speed in his hand. "Lizards and shit, too. They ran away, though, onto land. The ngū stayed with their father, but he gave his ink to the Maori so we warriors could tattoo ourselves."

Jason flinched when the needle touched his skin. That earned him a slap across the head and five minutes of screaming about how ungrateful he was, and about how the state could just come and take him back to the boy's home in Austin. *At least he was not drunk,* Jason thought, and blinked back tears while Mao finished the tattoo with much cursing and muttering. When it was done, he told Jason to stay where he was for an hour, buckled his leg on and limped out of the garage, and back into the house. Jason heard Mary's voice for a split second before the door slammed shut.

When he was sure Mao would not come back, Jason jumped down from the padded table and went to the cracked, dirty mirror on the shelf behind Mao's half-built Harley. Three years with Mao had taught him that the big man had to be obeyed, however, only when he was around. Mao was so sloppy, he would never notice things out of place, and he did not check in often, once he would decide to plant himself somewhere else.

He would probably go drink anyway. Jason thought, and turned his bare back to the mirror then craned his neck around to see Mao's latest work.It was a fantasy sword. Its long blade stretched all the way down his back, and the point stopped at the top of his butt. The spread, clawed wings of a bat at its safeguard and a light-blue sapphire, set in gold at its pommel, reached the nape of his neck. The blue sapphire reminded Jason of the eyes of a lizard. It was too vibrant and all-knowing for the rest of the sword.

Dinner that night was rice and fish. Mao ate on the sagging couch in front of the TV and watched Cops, while Mary cleaned up in the kitchen. His leg was off and a beer was close at hand. Jason, still not allowed to put a shirt on, helped with the dishes. Mary was a short, thin woman with skin like light coffee and a huge mane of curly black hair. She did not talk much, however, when she did, her voice was almost too quiet to hear. Jason loved the way she smelled—like clean towels and soap—and he loved her floral dresses and her dirty old aprons. Mao hit her a lot.

"Jason, sweetie," Mary said in her soft, quiet voice. She set down the tray she cleaned in the sink. "You go ahead to bed."

She had a big, dark bruise on her left cheek. "I will finish up here and you can help me with the shopping tomorrow."

"Yes ma'am," said Jason, and put the dish in the drying rack.

She kissed the top of his head. "Happy birthday, little big man."

Jason's bedroom was crammed behind the pantry. It was tiny, just large enough for a cot and a flimsy IKEA dresser. He turned back the covers when he saw the cupcake on the dresser. It was a big one, chocolate-frosted with a peanut butter cup on top. It appeared fancy, with its waxed wrapper and swirled frosting. Jason was hesitant to bite into it. He carried it to his bed and stared down at it for a while before he saw the guitar wrapped up in newspaper and tucked carefully behind his bed. His heart stopped. Other kids in the neighborhood received whole cakes and parties on their birthdays, nevertheless, he would not have traded Mary's cupcake and the guitar for anything.

He took a bite, and it felt like heaven in his mouth. Excited, he set the cupcake down, and unwrapped the guitar with trembling fingers. It was an old worn acoustic with a bent neck, most likely found in the trash or at a five-and-dime store, still, it felt bright and shiny-new to him.

"Ten's too young, Mao." It was Mary outside in the hall.

"He eats my food. He sleeps under my roof." The thump of Mao's fake plastic foot on the floorboards paused. "He can earn it."

Jason took a bite of the cupcake. It was rich and sweet, better than anything he had ever eaten.

"The checks," Mary said.

"He doesn't earn those! I do. Out of the goodness of my fucking heart I took him in, and you knew this was coming. Stop trying to protect that little shit."

"They will kill him!" she cried.

There was a loud smack, a cry, and then a thump. *He has her against the wall,* thought Jason. *If you were a real man, you would go out and stop him. Kill him, maybe. John Wayne would do it.* He was not John Wayne though. He knew that, so he sat in the dark and ate his cupcake while tears rolled down his cheeks. Mary sobbed outside in the hallway while Mao did whatever he always did. It made his breathing rough. Whatever Mao would do to him, it could not be worse than this. The cupcake tasted like ashes in his mouth.

Mao's hand shook sometimes, usually after he did not drink for a while. When his hands became bad and he had a big tattoo client, someone with a heavy street reputation, he would practice on Jason to calm his nerves. He did it more and more these days. Mao's squid ink illustrations were all over Jason's body; he

INK

would display him as a portfolio to potential customers. Jason had a shark on his right calf, a throwing ax on his left thigh, and a Shaolin monk throwing star on his shoulders. He had a dagger on each forearm, a whip on his right bicep and a chain on his left bicep.

A lit cigarette with smoke billowing on his left breast. Two 1870s Colt Peacemakers with long barrels on his lower stomach, linked to rose flowers, that were tangled up in barbed wire, which framed Jason's abdomen. Mao always forced him to wear long-sleeved shirts so the police and the social worker would not ask questions. Jason did not know why Mao bothered with the social worker. Toby was a big, fat man with long brown hair he wore tied back in a ponytail. He did not seem to care what shape Jason, Mary, or the house was in when he came for his six-month inspections.

The man they sat with in Mao's favorite bar, McGill's, seemed a lot like Toby, only fatter and with shorter hair. His name, as his knuckles announced, was STAN FROG.

"He is tall," said Frog. He ate barbecue chicken wings, tearing the meat off the bones with his big, square teeth. There was sauce all down his chin and the front of his wife-beater. Around them, the bar was quiet and empty, except for the old man who polished glasses by the tap.

"I will be thirteen next week, sir."
Mao smacked Jason on the ear. "Nobody asked you, dumbshit." He had lost weight since the cancer, nonetheless, he was still dog-mean and stronger than he should have been. Jason had hoped the cancer would kill him, and that all the cigarette burns he had endured would invoke karma when the tar filled the islander's lungs and choked him to death.

He should have known better. "Sorry, sir," he said, and looked down at his shoes. That cancer killed itself, going after Mao.
Frog spat out a bone. "Big for his age. Can he take a punch?"

"Yeah," said Mao. "He can take a punch. We had him in Nunez's thing when he was ten 'til...I dunno, late last year.

October. Hell, he almost killed this big nigger bastard twice his fuckin' size before the cops shut it down. Didn't do half bad."

Except for the cracked skull, Jason almost blurted out. Instead, he bit his tongue until it hurt. Mao's temper was worse since the chemo, mostly because he was not as good with the needle anymore and the gang bangers were going elsewhere for their ink. Anything, even another fighting ring, was better than brawling the other kids at Nunez's on Fridays, in the big unfinished basement under the Real Tapatio Mexican Restaurant. Some of those kids had been half-starved and kept in cages.

"So, you want him?" There was greed in Mao's eyes, and he struggled to hide it.

Frog took another wing and sucked the meat off it. He considered Jason with his small, watery eyes.

"Yeah," he said after a short pause. "Yeah, I will take the boy. He will train with my people...and no fucking him up! I want him ready to fight when I call and tell you he is fighting." He downed half his glass of beer in one swallow, then wiped his mouth on the sleeve of his Hawaiian shirt.

"Sure, Frog," said Mao with a big fake smile. "Sure."

They shook hands, and Frog passed Mao an envelope. Mao stood, gripped Jason by the shoulder, and steered him out of the bar into the blazing heat of Austin in May. Fat black flies flew by, buzz in the heavy air. They walked in silence toward Mao's battered Ford Pinto. When they reached it, Mao's hand tightened like a vise on Jason's shoulder.

"You are not going to fuck this up for me," he growled, and shoved his mouth close to Jason's ear. "Do you understand me? Say you fucking understand me, dumbass."

Jason nodded. "I understand you, sir."

Mao shoved him.

"Get in. If I had wanted a bitch, I would have taken your sister."

Jason stumbled, and caught himself on the hot fender of the car.

"Sister?"

"Get in the fucking car."

INK

Mao hauled himself awkwardly into the driver's seat, his haggard face flushed and screwed up in concentration. The scars from his lobectomy showed right through his sweat-soaked shirt. Jason hopped in. He closed the passenger door.

"I have a sister?" Jason leaned in to ask, and was met with a slap in the face.

"Shut the fuck up!" said Mao, while he drove off. "I have business to think about." The way home, he stared at Mao's profile—the thick chin and lumpy nose, the wild dark hair, and red cheeks. He hoped Mao would talk more about her, however, he never did. *Is she younger or older? What color is her hair? Eyes? Is she tall? Does she know our mom and dad? Do we have both the same parents?* Jason's head drowned in questions. Nevertheless, the thought that he had a true family, and not just these foster families with ulterior motives, brought a smile to his lips. Mao slapped him in the face.

"What are you smiling at, numbnuts?"

"Nothing, sir."

Jason stopped smiling. Mao never smiled or was happy and would get angry when he saw someone else who was. Jason was forced to gaze out the window, to try and hide from Mao, his uncontrollable smile. Because he kept thinking, *I have a sister.*

The trainer was a quiet, whip-thin woman named Sadie. She had iron-colored hair and a fierce, infrequent smile that seemed to come out most often when someone got hurt. When Mao came to pick him up the first day at her gym, she had beaten Jason so badly he could hardly limp out to the car. That night, Mary helped him out of his blood-crusted shirt and dabbed antiseptic on the worst of his cuts while he watched <u>True Grit</u> for the hundredth time. John Wayne's character, the drunken federal marshal, Rooster Cogburn, rode toward a band of outlaws with the reins in his teeth and a pistol in each hand. "Fill yer hands!" Jason shouted in unison with John Wayne.

He dreamed that night of a house in the woods where shadows stalked him in the wallpaper, slid like ghosts between stenciled flowers and trees. When he woke, he was so sore he could hardly get out of bed, still, he forced himself to play a few scales on his guitar. He did it quietly, cloth stuffed into the body of the instrument, and hid it before Mao stomped into his room and dragged him out to the car. That day was better, however, just a little. The one after that, Sadie stopped whaling on him and started to teach him how to hit. "I just had to make sure you were no fuckin' pussy," she said by way of an apology. "I don't fuckin' train pussies."

He had his first fight six weeks later in a vacant lot outside the city. The only light came from a ring of smudge pots positioned just outside the circle. The rules were no weapons, hair pulling, eye gauging, strikes to the groin, last man standing wins. Jason stepped into the ring sharper and smarter than he had gone into Sadie's gym—his fists taped, his jeans cut off at the knees and hemmed to fit closer. Never let anyone get their hands on you, Sadie had told him. Grappling is where you get killed.

The other, who pushed his way through the dark, faceless crowd and into the circle of smudge pots, was a lean Cuban guy—maybe fifteen or sixteen—short and springy. He bounced on his toes and stuck up his fists. There was no ref to call the match, so Jason put his up as well. They circled for a few seconds until the shouts and curses of the crowd drove them together like magnets. Jason jabbed left, ducked under a clumsy haymaker, caught a right across the jaw, and then the rest was flying fists and smokey outlines.

Afterwards, Frog gave Mao a greasy bag full of bundled fives and tens. Mao was in a good mood the whole drive home and swigged from a flask of Jack Daniels. In the passenger's seat, Jason tried to rub some feeling back into his battered hands. There were other fights that year, and more the next. If he lost, Mao would not let him have any dinner. He lost some, however, won more.

When he was fourteen, Frog put him up against a huge Texan named Bill Bones. They held the fight at a deserted warehouse on the Houston Wharf. Mao, limping, dragged Jason through a grungy, unused car park. Rusty ghost ships that once transported cargo awed Jason with their silent bulk. He dragged Jason to the door of the warehouse, *KNOCKED!* five times, paused and then *KNOCKED!* again five more. A viewer on the door slid open and two large, bloodshot eyes peered out.

"Fighter," said Mao. The bloodshot eyes scanned them both; Jason still impressed by the ships.

The door opened to a large bodyguard type—the owner of the bloodshot eyes. About forty people, men and their girls, made bets, swilled cheap beer, and scored a little crystal meth off one of the wannabes slinging in the bathroom. Jason was taller now, pushed five-nine, and ropy with muscle. His dirty-blonde hair was cropped short. Frog pulled Bryan, a flashy, slick promoter type who wore a gray suit, over to Mao and Jason.

"This is him?" Bryan asked, with an expression of disbelief. "You sure he is twenty-one?"

"Yeah. What are you, a cop?" Mao asked, and limped forward in a threatening way.

Frog placed a hand on Mao's chest, and stopped him. "Whoa, whoa, whoa. Yeah, he is. I swear! I have seen him. He is good." Bryan was not convinced, however, they all walked towards the ring.

INK

INK

A painting on the floor rested against the wall. When Jason walked past the painting, it came to life and a hand clutched his ankle. Jason was startled. He kicked at it with a snap reflex, and pulled his leg away from it. The hand held a smoking cigarette retreated into the painting. Jason looked around to see if anyone had seen what just happened. No one had. He sniffed cigarette smoke that wafted into the air before it dissolved, and squatted to look at the painting closer. It was of a female bullfighter smoking a cigarette, with a red rose in her hair and Day of the Dead makeup on half of her face. Her jacket collar covered most of a skeleton-hand tattoo on her neck.

The girl is pretty, thought Jason. She was sexy, with a do not-give-a-shit attitude, ominous and foretelling with the Day of the Dead makeup—Female beauty and death, erotic and disgusting. He was mesmerized until Frog yelled out, "FIGHTERS READY?" Jason stood up and went over to his opponent. There were shouts, jeers, and applause.

Bill Bones was built like a neo-Nazi dumpster: three hundred pounds of fat and muscle with biceps like hams and a huge, taut belly crisscrossed with scars, his left pectoral muscle tattooed with a swastika. He wore a pair of ripped khakis, and a leather bracelet on his right arm with an acid-etched image of a hammer on it, and nothing else. His tiny brown eyes were set very close to each other above an oily, blackhead-studded beak of a nose and a small, mean mouth. Someone blasted a Cult song just when Bones stopped circling. For some reason, Jason imagined the fighter with Day of the Dead makeup on. "You are dead meat, faggot!" the fighter said, and then he skipped forward and swung. Jason jerked back just out of Bones' reach, and his arms went up automatically. The gargantuan man moved quicker than someone half his size, with fists flickered like pistons.

INK

The crowd screamed as one, and cried out for blood. *Jesus, he is fast,* thought Jason, when he ducked under a vicious right. Bones came on like a madman, with a grunt added to every jab. The first punch he landed sent Jason careening back, stumbling away from the advancing Bones with stars that flashed in his vision. He shook it off. *Ouch, that hurt.* He then saw Mao's face in the crowd when he circled. *You want to eat tonight?* Then Jason's onslaught began, even so, nothing Jason did slowed the titan. He hammered at Bones until his knuckles bled through his bandages, and his fists felt as heavy as lead weights. Bones only grunted and kept on swinging punches—mechanical and grim. Another right cross to the jaw left Jason staggering, both lips split and bloody, however, he managed to stay just ahead of the bigger man. His arms burned with the strain of holding them up, his ears rang with the wild shouts of the crowd, and he was half-blinded by blood from a cut above his right eye.

The huge man snorted like a bull. Jason brought his hands up, gritted his teeth against the deep burn in his shoulders and biceps. Blood trickled down his wrists and over his tattoos. He relaxed into one of the defensive stances Sadie had drilled into him. Bones charged with an animal roar, together they went down, and rolled on the stained concrete.

People shouted. "FREEZE! EVERYBODY FREEZE!" Officers burst in from all directions with guns drawn. Sam Hopkins, a forty-five-year-old, six-foot, wide-shouldered, long-faced law man yelled out, "Freeze! Texas Rangers. Put your hands up!"

"Oh," said Mao, his eyebrows rose in surprise. "Fuck!"

The crowd viewed their abrupt entrance in stunned silence. Frog glared over at Mao suspiciously. The Rangers took up strategic positions around the crowd, and blocked the entrance and exits.

Jason was on top of Bones and punched his face with lefts and rights; Bones' blood sprayed in all directions, however, Jason did not know or care. Bones fought back so Jason kept at him with lefts and rights until he could hear his own grunts, and became machine-like. Dick McGregor, an athletic twenty-five-year-old Irish officer, tried to pull Jason off Bones until an elbow smashed him in the nose. Two other officers had to jump on Jason before they finally stopped him. All the participants were lined up against a wall, frisked, then dragged into vans, and hauled downtown.

Sam Hopkins took a swallow from his water bottle. They were in his office now, and he sat behind a clean, organized desk at the police station. "We understand you are his next of kin. He gave us your name. Very intelligent, but he is psychologically damaged."

"Are you a psychologist?" Moses asked, standing on the other side of the desk. He wore a dressing gown, pajamas, and slippers.

The officer grunted, "I am studying at the moment."

"He almost killed a man," said Officer McGregor, who stood near the door with his nose bandaged.

Moses turned to him and asked, "Did Jason do that?" And already knew the answer to the question.

"Yeah."

"What are the charges?" Moses asked.

"There aren't any. No one is pressing charges," said McGregor.

Hopkins interjected. "His parents are abusing him."

Moses arched an eyebrow, "Foster parents! Abuse?"

Hopkins shrugged his shoulders. "Come take a look." They all stood and walked out of the office. All involved in the illegal fight were being booked or sat around waiting to be. Officer Hopkins led when they snaked their way through the reception, people, and hallways.

"When can I take him?" Moses asked.

"I just need a signature and he is all yours," said Hopkins, and handed him a release form on a clipboard.

Moses signed it while they walked through to the holding cells, and then Hopkins pointed at one of them. In the cell were five men, bandaged in different ways, and appeared like they had recently been in a fight.

INK

"We had to stick him in isolation," said Hopkins, when he walked to another cell. "He kept beating up people. If you cannot get him to channel his anger, he will kill someone."

They stopped, and Moses peered into another cell where he saw a lone prisoner with a tattoo of a fantasy sword running down his back. Jason gazed through a barred window to the blue sky outside. Officer McGregor rapped on the bars with his baton. "Someone is here to see you, boy." Jason did not turn around. McGregor rapped again, louder this time.

"Hey numbnuts, do I need to come in there?"

McGregor stepped forward, however, Moses held him back.

"Cowboy?"

Jason recognized the voice and he looked over his shoulder to see Moses.

Oh, my lord, so many tattoos, thought Moses. Jason walked over and stopped near Moses. "I have a sister?" he asked.

Moses saw some fight bruises on Jason's face, however, he had also seen that his innocence was gone. "What the hell did they do to him?" Moses asked sheepishly.

"His foster parents tattooed him to make him appear older so they could get him into outlaw bare knuckle fights," said Hopkins.

"Apparently, he lost a lot of fights," McGregor chuckled, when he unlocked the door.

"That's a lie," said Jason and spat in McGregor's face. The officer stumbled back, spluttering, "Little shit, I am going to fuckin' kill you!"

Jason smirked when the cell door opened and goaded McGregor with his hands. "Bring it on, pig."

Hopkins seized McGregor by the arm and forced him away from the cell. "Get out of here."

"One day, boy. One day!" McGregor snarled when he shrugged free of Hopkins hold, and stormed out.

"Yeah, one day this!" said Jason, and grabbed his crotch while Officer Hopkins pushed Officer McGregor out of the holding area. Moses chuckled on the inside.

Jason relaxed. "How you been?"

INK

"Better than you," said Moses. They both smiled. Jason scowled at Moses in silence for a minute. Moses knew what Jason was thinking; all those years in the orphanage had brought them close, real close. They became like father and son.

"I was going to tell you, but you kept coming back to the orphanage, and I just figured you had bigger problems," said Moses. Jason opened the cell door, to stand face-to-face with Moses.

"A sister is not a problem," said Jason, while they exited the holding area.

"You're right," said Moses, and led Jason out into the lobby of the station. Most of the people from the fight remained there, some in cells—others interviewed and processed, however, wherever they were, they saw Jason leave.

"See you around, Cowboy," said Frog, when an officer uncuffed him.

Jason did not respond. He felt used, lied to, and awful, even though, he had become accustomed to those feelings by now, and refused to pay them any mind. He hung on Moses every word.

"When Child Protective Services took you both in, you were split up. She went to an orphanage, and you went to a hospital. You were high on some kind of drugs, covered in ink, and had syringe marks all over your arms. They believed you would die. You were in the hospital for two months before you arrived at an orphanage."

Both of them stepped out of the doorway and onto the sidewalk. The cloud cover blocked the moonlight and the night seemed darker than normal. It was hot, and the mosquitoes swarmed thick around every lamp post.

"You went to two other orphanages before you came to us," said Moses. "Your paperwork went missing and we received you from the previous orphanage with only a name, no papers. Hell, we were not even sure if your name was correct. We didn't know you had a sister until four years after you arrived." Moses stepped into his run down, light blue, Ford F 150 pickup truck, and Jason sat onto the passenger side.

INK

"Within her first few weeks at the first orphanage, Lauren was wanted by a very well-to-do, educated couple that went on to adopt her."

"Lauren, good name," said Jason. "Where is she?" He had to ask.

"I don't know, and if I did, I couldn't tell you anyway because of privacy laws. I could be fired for even speaking of her," said Moses, when he drove off.

Jason respected Moses position. Moses was an honorable man, the one man who had taught him what it meant to have respect, integrity, honesty, and loyalty.

"I will find her myself," said Jason, while he gazed out the truck window at the dark, moonlit night.

As Moses drove back to the orphanage, he thought, *Jason being back would not be good for him or the orphanage. This would be his fourth time returning. He would be one of the older orphans, and Jason always fought.* Then, he remembered Oleg Crichenko and made a U-turn. He was a Russian man who emigrated from Moscow, and had opened the only gym in town many years ago. Oleg invited the townsfolk to its grand opening with a BBQ. Moses had made a mental note to himself when he noticed the fight trophies covered in dust, laid on the floor of the gym, forgotten like so many dreams.

Jason had been brawling a lot at the orphanage that year, and Moses believed that those two could be a good fit. However, the fourth set of foster parents had taken Jason just days before the BBQ. Moses realized then that Oleg could be the only one to help Jason if he could convince Oleg to take him. It was past 10 p.m. and the front door of the gym was locked, nevertheless, Moses could see silhouettes pass by through a window, deep in activity inside. Therefore, Moses rang the doorbell.

When Oleg went to the door, he stood by it for a moment, reluctant to open it, with pursed lips. *Only bad things happen after ten p.m.,* his mother would say, even so, he relented when he realized it was Moses. Jason saw a broad, solidly-built man in his fifties with muscles bulging beneath his gym clothes. He invited them into the office. Moses told Jason to wait outside the office.

INK

They closed the door and sat at a stylishly ornate desk swamped with paperwork.

"I am hoping you can help me and the orphanage. I have this fighter out there with no direction. Would you consider teaching him how to fight?"

"Sure, anything for you and the orphanage. Have him here for training Tuesday and Thursday, four to six p.m."

"Well, I was hoping he could stay here. He is a good kid. Just had some bad luck," said Moses.

Oleg beheld Moses thoughtfully, and then answered, "This is not a halfway house. I have no time or patience for kids."

"You would get a check from the state, like child support. Try him. If you don't like how he works, send him back to the orphanage," urged Moses, and noticed dust on the desk light. "He can work for you dusting, sweep the floor, clean the bathroom, file this paperwork you are drowning in, and do the stuff you don't have time for. It does not have to be permanent."

Oleg sighed. "What can I do?"

"Teach him to fight. He is good at it. Develop him. Ever since I have known this kid, he has always liked to brawl. If he does not learn control, he will kill someone. He beats up all the kids in the orphanage, even the bigger, older ones. Just try him."

Jason stood there by the office door, until he saw a boxing ring in the center of the gym and was fascinated. He walked around it and noticed the details on the mat, the ropes, and the padded corners. This was a professional fight arena and Jason stood in awe. A much older fighter stepped into the ring and began shadowboxing. The fighter beckoned, and Jason entered. They began to spar. Then the fighter put Jason in a judo hold.

Oleg and Moses came out of the office.

"Sorry, Moses, I just cannot have a kid around here."

"I understand." Moses noticed Jason in the ring. "Cowboy, what are you doing?"

The fighter chuckled, and tightened his hold.

"Cowboy is losing," he said, just when Jason tripped and flipped the taller, older fighter, with a take down. Oleg raised an eyebrow.

Moses shook his head. "Get over here."

"I will take him," said Oleg, to a smiling Moses. "Kid just flipped a two hundred pound, twenty-eight-year-old."

Jason exited the ring and went over to the corner where Oleg and Moses stood.

"This is Mr. Oleg Crichenko. Do everything he says. I will check in with you next month.Do not mess with him. He is a UFC fighter and ex-KGB." Moses hugged Jason, then left. Jason could see Oleg was a fighter. The physique, the flat nose, and the tiny scars on his face were dead giveaways of a life spent fighting. Oleg pointed to a blackboard. In chalk, was a to-do list on the left side—laundry, sweep, mop, dust.

"You do those chores, you eat. Follow me." They walked over to a dusty locker room with a shower and basin. It was a large area with three bench seats, enough lockers for forty-five members, weight scales, and a stack of books in one corner of the room.

"That is where you sleep." Oleg pointed to a broken-down sofa with an orange blanket near the books.

Jason scrutinized the older man. "You a UFC fighter?"

Oleg nodded. "That is right."

Jason searched his green eyes, then swung a left punch and a quick right. Oleg avoided both punches with very little movement. Jason was impressed, and thought *Oleg would not be expecting the same combination.* So he tried the same combination. However, Oleg did expect it and this time hit both fists with his forehead. Jason yelped in pain, fell on the sofa, and held his fists.

Oleg pointed to his forehead and slapped it with a finger. "This is the strongest bone in the body. Do not ever use the same combination one after the other." He noticed Jason's tattoos. "It is always the same with you young men. Where did you learn?"

"Texas," Jason grunted, and spoke into the sofa.

"This is Texas. Is that where you got all the tatyrovka? These tattoos?" He appeared disdainful when he examined the throwing star on Jason's shoulder. "Real men do not do this shit."

INK

Well, thought Jason and levered himself up into a sit position with his arms, *I did not have much choice.* "That is your thinking," he said instead. "My business."

Oleg frowned, then nodded. "Fair enough." He turned and left.

As Jason stretched his fingers, and tried to subdue the pain, he noticed a book in the stack titled *Cooking*. He took the book and flip pages. Then after some time, he noticed a picture hung on a wall. It was a painting of men playing soccer, in blue Italian jerseys, against yellow Brazilian jerseys. The painting shimmered and protruded out of the frame, which exposed detail to the painting. The Italian player headed the ball at goal, and the name on the jersey read "Rossi." The canvas took the shape of a face, and then it came to life. It blinked, then turned and looked at Jason.

He was slack jawed. Goose bumps rose on the back of his neck, and he was stymied by what he saw. The goose bumps traveled down his arms, and he shook it off. He went up to the painting and looked at it straight on. When he came closer, the animated face viewed Jason up and down then tilted. Scrutinized the room, then withdrew into the painting, which turned into two men wrestling. *Is this really happening? Or is it all in my mind?* He thought. It had been a long day. Jason placed the book on the floor, switched off the light, and placed the orange blanket over himself when he laid on the sofa. The street light came in through the window, and illuminated the painting. Jason tried to fall asleep, however, he watched it. Frustrated, he pulled the painting down and turned it around so it would face the wall. Then he felt comfortable enough to fall asleep, and he did.

INK

INK

Tranquil nights were a constant in the affluent part of Morristown, Vermont. The most expensive, exclusive subdivision was a gated community with beautiful homes on half-acre lots with manicured lawns. Jason's sister, Lauren, lived in a two-story, Cape-Cod-style house in this subdivision. Her bedroom was immaculately clean with a Barbie doll in one corner of a bookshelf filled with books. Lauren, a skinny brown-haired girl in pigtails, raised her head from the viewfinder of her telescope.

"Look," she said, "a shooting star!"

James Maylor, a balding, short, pudgy man, raised his eyeglasses and gazed into the viewfinder. "What is the constellation it is crossing, Lauren?"

She paused.

"If you get this right, I shall purchase that chemistry set you asked for."

She smiled, because she knew the answer. "Ursa Major."

"Good girl," he said, and hugged her. "It is late. We had better get to bed before your mother gets upset." Lauren hopped into bed, and hugged a stuffed teddy bear.

"Love you, sweetheart," said James.

"Love you too, Dad."

The lights went out when he exited her room, and made his way down the hallway to another bedroom. His wife, Alison, a pretty woman whose beauty was fading, read a periodical on medicine in bed. James sat down on the edge of the bed.

"She is amazing, honey. She remembers everything. We should consider higher education for her."

Alison turned a page. "Perhaps in the chemistry field?"

James nodded. "The field has served you and I very well."

INK

Alison set down her periodical. "She is just a little girl. Let her find what makes her happy."

"Science makes her happy." He hopped into bed and she turned off the light.

Lauren was in a printmaking class. She worked on her tile for hours, longer than anyone else in the class did, and her red rose surrounded in grass did not come together. *I took on too much,* she thought, frustrated. *This is nothing like sketching or watercolors.* She had a lot of work to do with oils, however, this class made her forget about that. She picked at her half-finished work, dissatisfied with the chunky, inexpert lines she had cut into the soft tile. Still, she thought, when she glanced around at the other students, *I might as well finish.* Her teacher, Mrs. Fenwick, made her rounds between the tables and stooped over to inspect Lauren's work.

In another fifteen minutes, Lauren would have a passable excuse for a rose, in the midst of a green grassy patch. She sighed and pushed a loose lock of hair back from her face. Mrs. Fenwick did not wax enthusiastically, however, she did pat Lauren encouragingly on the shoulder and told her she was "getting the hang of it." When the bell rang, she stuffed the tile into her notebook, swung her backpack onto her shoulders, and joined the herd of eleventh graders headed for the parking lot of William McKinley Memorial High School. She was exhausted after a spent night writing a paper on Roman plumbing innovations for Mr. Burk's class. When she walked amidst the throng of people, the sea of bobbing backpacks and swaying ponytails was almost hypnotic to her.

Most days, her father walked her back and forth the mile distance from school to home, however, he was in the city for a dentist appointment, and her mother was out at her laboratory working on a new project. That was fine with Lauren. Another walk full of questions about her day was the last thing she wanted. She just wanted to go home, nuke something, eat, and collapse. She popped her iPod's ear buds in and chose some David Bowie, when she walked past the bus and the queue of

INK

people formed at its doors, and out to the sidewalks on Maple Street. She shoved her hands into the pockets of her jacket.

The leaves turned yellow, red, and flaming orange. Lauren liked Vermont in the fall; summer was too hot, winter was brutal, and spring swarmed with flu, still, fall was clean, cool, and quiet. A few people ran around and snapped pictures of leaves and bought decorative jugs of maple syrup, however, the tourists did not really bother her much. She liked Vermont better than Nevada. Her family had lived in Nevada for three years before the move, and sometimes she still dreamed of that endless red desert.

After she walked for a few minutes, Lauren realized she was being followed. He was some thirty feet back, a slim, dark-haired Latin man in his early twenties. He wore a black suit and stylish shoes. His glasses had thick, black plastic hipster frames. A sudden breeze blew his unbuttoned jacket open to reveal a heavy, functional Beretta M9 in a shoulder harness. Lauren had never seen a gun in person before, and she shivered at the sight of the Beretta. Fear struck her now, however, she did not want to show it so she pulled leaves off branches, tried to make eye contact with people on the street, smiled, and combed through her pockets, in an attempt to stay busy so she would not think about it.

Her hand closed around the keychain in her pocket with its ChapStick-sized vial of pepper spray. *He is never going to get close enough for me to use it,* said a small, strident part of her fear-paralyzed brain. *This man could shoot me in the back of the head dead before I realized it. Maybe I am overreacting. If I stop walking, he will pass by.* She stopped. He got closer, and then he came purposefully toward her. The street was then empty of people and cars, silent except for the ubiquitous drone of the autumn cicadas. Bowie was in her ears, and still belted it out. The man smiled and drew his gun. Lauren panicked and bolted for the trees.

Past the thin tree line was the junior high soccer field, and past that the motor pool where the school district parked its buses. Someone would be there. Someone has to be there! The crack of a gunshot tore through the cicadas' buzzing. She gave a yelp, hit the grass, and landed on her back. The impact smacked the air from her lungs in an explosive exhalation that left her blank and gasping, like a fish caught out of water. The sky was cold and blue in the gaps between the trees limbs. She pushed herself up onto her elbows, her head swam when she managed to draw a ragged breath. The man strode toward her. Closer now, he appeared menacing.

The muzzle of his gun yawned like a bottomless pit. He had a slim black cell phone in his other hand. The hit man tried to take his shot, stepped to the left to get a clear line of sight on Lauren. She raised her hand in the direction of the gun in disbelief and shock. *Who is this man? Why does he want to kill me? What did I do? I am going to die.* The thoughts raced through her head in a fragment of time. The bullet exploded from its barrel, hit Lauren's hand and bounced away. He kept shooting, and the same thing happened, as if she were surrounded by a force field. Bullets ricocheted in all directions, and Lauren felt afraid, confused, amazed, and strong, all in one moment.

Another man in his forties, dressed in a dark suit, took a shot at her would-be assassin from a nearby tree, however, missed. The assassin shot back at him, the bullet whacked his gun to the ground, ricocheted, and lodged into his thigh. The assassin forgot about Lauren and ran over to the man who shot at him. He placed him in a choke hold and dragged him toward the road, where a big black sedan pulled up to the curb. A short, Japanese man, in a loud Hawaiian shirt, was in the driver's seat. The assassin slid neatly in through the open back door, and dragged his captive in with him. Then the car peeled away from the sidewalk.

Seven people were scattered on the street. They heard the commotion, and one of them pulled out a cell phone and made a call. Lauren brought her hands to her face, to inspect them for bullet holes. *You are on crack,* she told herself. *Someone stuck crack in your energy bar, or else you just lost it like Melissa Carr in eighth grade, or...or...or...or you are a superhero with magical powers, able to stop a hit man from sticking two bullets in the back of your skull,* she thought. She shook her head at the strangeness of it, gathered up her stuff, when a crowd surrounded her with questions.

INK

The police found her halfway home. It was Officer Bradley Church, one of her dad's friends. He assisted her into the police cruiser, then sped her all the way to the emergency room with the lights and siren on. She sat numbly in the back seat of his cruiser, when he shouted into his radio. He turned frantically to ask her, "You okay, sweetheart?"

"Yeah, just some scrapes," she said.

They examined her at the hospital. Afterward, her mother was there sobbing and hugging her closely. A little later, Officer Church gently questioned her in a private room, just off the visitor's waiting room. She knew her story was strange and her answers were completely garbled. She had a hard time keeping her thoughts straight when every inch of her wanted to tell them she had stopped the bullets with her hand.

"How could he miss? Witnesses said that was point-blank range," Church asked, curiously, and then walked out the door.

Lauren was in the room alone trying to remember the sedan. The door flew open, and in walked Church with a high cheek-boned woman in her thirties, she wore a black overcoat. The woman was followed by a handsome, all-American marine in his early twenties. The woman flashed a badge and an ID card crammed with serial numbers and codes.

"Agent Caitlan Decker," she said, and placed the badge back into her coat pocket. She was tall and slim, with wiry hair and an easy smile. She jerked a thumb over her shoulder at the marine in her company, a stocky, square-jawed, authoritative appearing man with a typical jar-head-type buzz haircut.

"That's agent Cole Braxton. We will take it from here, Officer."

When the two agents entered the room, Officer Church muttered to Lauren, "I shall get a hold of your dad." Then he promptly exited the room. Agent Decker took her seat with relaxed grace. She arched an eyebrow at Lauren, while Agent Braxton shut the blinds and stood at attention by the door, like he was guarding the president. There was no other way to describe it. He did not merely stand, and he did not lurk, or loom, or hunker down; he took up position as if he expected a black-ops raid on Maplewood General Hospital. *This is crazy.*

INK

Someone just tried to kill me on the street in broad daylight, thought Lauren. *What is next?*

Decker leaned back in her chair. The picture of relaxation. "Hi, Lauren. How are you feeling? I understand you had a close call."

She talked through the sedative they had given her earlier, Lauren answered, "I am fine." And tried her best to play it cool. "Is something wrong?"

"Fine?" Agent Decker's eyebrows rose. "I remember the first time someone took a shot at me. I was not fine. Tell her, Special Agent Braxton."

"She was not fine," Braxton said flatly.

"That is right," said Agent Decker. "It was an Italian death squad outside of Rome. One of them blasted two bullets in my back while I was coming out of an espresso bar. If I had not had this on me, I would not be here right now." She slid her hand inside her coat and produced a felt-padded marble coaster, and slapped it down on the table. Cut expertly into the white marble was a lean black Doberman pinscher at the center of twenty or thirty rings of cramped, unreadable text. Lauren swallowed.

"There are a few things you should know before we leave this room, Lauren." Agent Decker's tone was gentle however, firm. "I cannot legally detain you, but I am betting you want to hear what I have to say. Am I right?" She did not trust herself to speak, Lauren nodded. *It is not even English,* she thought when she inspected the coaster. *It is more like hieroglyphics.* Decker leaned forward and clasped her hands together on the tabletop, right beside her coaster. Decker continued, "First, and I do not like being the one to inform you of this if you are not already aware of it—do you know that you are adopted?"

"Yeah. They told me when I was five," answered Lauren.

"Alright, good. Do you know you have had a top secret government SSA agent tailing you since you were four years old?"

"Since I was four?" Lauren almost choked, "Is that who—what?—"

"Perfectly legal," said Agent Decker, matter-of-factly. "Consent from your guardians and the state, yeah. Can you guess why?"

Lauren swallowed, and tried to regain at least a little composure. She might have been eleven, however, she was very mature, and had even jumped two grades through sheer nail-biting hard work. Still, she did not have to act eleven in front of a federal agent and a handsome marine. In fact, she could just play it dumb like she did not have a clue and probably get away with it. She blew out a long, slow breath.

"Because of the hit man?" She asked.

"Bingo," said Agent Decker. "Now, you can tell local police that he missed you from point-blank range, but do not try to sell your story to me."

"Your tail did a great job keeping me from getting shot." Sudden irritation pricked through the layers of icy fear built up around her addled thoughts. "Who was the hit man?"

Decker paused, while a speculative stare came over her. She fished around in her pocket for a pack of cigarettes, withdrew one, and lit it.

"Our man could not get to you in time," she said at last. "Let us leave it at that. As for the person, that was Ricardo Costa, a Brazilian hit man. He is bad news. At least fourteen confirmed hits, and those are just the ones we know about."

Lauren's heart skipped a beat. She licked her dry, chapped lips and tried to think of something besides the apparently top-notch hired gun that just missed killing her.

"I do not think you can smoke in here."

"Yeah, they can throw me out," said Decker. She blew a smoke ring and grinned. It was hard not to like her. "Anyway, Ricardo's bad news, but you and your family do not have to worry about him right—"

"What is going on anyway?" Lauren cut her off. "Why did that guy, Ricardo or whatever his name is, try to kill me?"

That silenced Agent Decker for a moment. She stubbed her cigarette out on the table and stuffed the special coaster back inside her overcoat.

INK

"First, we are Symbolists. Give me the rose tile you are making in printmaking class." Lauren furled her brow and thought, *Symbolists? How did she know about printmaking class? Or the rose tile?* After her initial amazement, she pulled the tile from her bag and handed it to her.

"What is a Symbolist?"

"I shall show you."

Decker took off an opal broach on the lapel of her jacket, pulled Lauren's hand, and pricked her index finger with a pin.

"Ouch," said Lauren.

Agent Decker then guided the dripping blood onto the rose image on the tile when she continued. "Second, the one thing I know is that you can do a brick more than I can." The rose sprang to life, to Lauren's utter amazement, and it extended a full foot from the tile. Lauren thought, *the flower was not real*—they had forced her to swallow a sedative earlier that she did not want, and she believed it kicked in. She struggled to make sense of any of it, while they constantly demanded her attention.

"Third, now that they know you have the power, they will come after you again and perhaps try to kill your parents. You will need to come with us to our secured compound for you and your family's safety." She paused, bit her bottom lip to allow the gravity of the situation to set in. Lauren believed the flower was an illusion, or she was having a nightmare until she touched it. "This is real."

"Fourth, does the name Fergus Blackwood mean anything to you?"

"No. Should it?"

"I guess not," said Decker.

"It is beautiful," said Lauren, and guided her finger over the thorns, on the stem.

"He is your grandfather. Want to meet him?" Agent Braxton asked.

Decker's expression at Braxton was surprise. Lauren wondered why that was. Braxton had not spoken until spoken to. Then she thought, *Perhaps Braxton said too much.*

"I'm Lauren Maylor."

"You're a Blackwood," said Decker.

"Okay. So what?"

"Some Blackwood's have been known to be Symbolists," said Decker.

Am I a Symbolist? Thought Lauren.

INK

INK

A small four-man black submersible vessel slowly surfaced from its watery depths within the confines of a secret mountainside port cavern. The room was vast, with hanging twenty-foot stalactites that dripped water into the dark pool beneath. At one time, it had been a busy submarine base, originally built by NATO, who spent 357 million dollars on its construction. Its fortified caverns were built to withstand heavy artillery shells and explosives, with tunnels darting in all directions. When the war ended, there was no use for it, and the constant maintenance rendered it a liability. It was decommissioned, and nineteen years later, it was placed on the market and sold for 17 million to an anonymous buyer.

Ricardo and his assistant, Kiko, stood at dry dock, patiently waiting, when the submarine drifted in. Kiko hooked a rope to it and hauled it into its mooring, where he tied it off to the dock. The hatch opened, and the lone occupier, Karen Smith, a stunning, six-foot-tall, older Victoria Secret model type, stepped onto the dock. Ricardo held her arm for support, so she could steady herself; her high-heeled stilettos clacked with each step. She handed Ricardo a briefcase, and he passed it on to Kiko. Her style was suitable for a nightclub, however, appeared completely out of place in that setting. Her white skirt opened to expose her leg, and Ricardo glimpsed at a tattoo on the outside of her thigh. Even though it was written in Kunstler script and difficult to read, he could just make out the words *Home Wrecker*.

"She has the power," said Ricardo, and steered her into the blinding light of the main passageway, Kiko followed.

"I knew it. She has Durga, the power of the Hindu princess," Karen said.

"I took a hostage," Ricardo said, quick and abrupt, like he was annoyed.

INK

"Why?"

"He is SSA."

"How do you know?"

"He was protecting her."

They turned into a passageway with multiple entrances to tunnels.

"That does not necessarily mean he is an agent."

"I figured you could use the blood if he was not," said Ricardo, then stopped at the entrance of a dungeon.

"Always thinking of me." She smiled and tapped him on the cheek. "My good boy!"

Kiko opened a medieval-style solid-wood door to enter a dark cave, where the captive was bound to a wooden chair.

"This is Symbolic Sector Agent Michael Vailer," said Kiko. "He was trying to protect Lauren. Ricardo shot him in the leg and dragged him into the car." Vailer was beat-up, had a red wad of material shoved in his mouth. Under Vailer's chair was a white bucket, half-full of collected blood. Vailer was glad the visitor was female, however, did not show it. He had a swollen black eye, a cut above it, red bruises on both cheeks, and a cut lip. Karen approached Vailer, who tried to wriggle loose from the bindings tied around his wrists to no avail. They were tied so tight, they cut off his circulation. He sensed that this visit was not going to be good. Karen walked around the chair, studied him, then pulled out the red wad of material, that gagged him with her black glove.

"Have you been taught not to talk?" Karen asked softly, her blue eyes glinted through her eyeglasses.

Vailer remembered that phrase vividly, as though from a former life. The torture club at SSA he attended for two years. It was there he learned to suppress the pain and never admit anything. He faced the very thing the SSA had warned him about. Never get caught—and if you did, the torture club would consider you dead and out of the game. The game was built on suffering and pain management. How many times could you be slapped or punched in one area. Last person standing was the winner. He never won.

INK

"We respect each other," said Karen, bent over a little, and smiled with her red lipstick.

He was attracted to her.

"Speak to me," she said, "No?" Then she raised her hand, and Vailer prepared himself for the slap. *WACK*. He felt his face explosively turn, bent him forward, and then the sting tingled in his cheek. Ricardo and Kiko stood on each side of her, smiling.

"Very good," she said softly, and when she raised her hand again, "Now we duel."

Vailer could not do anything to defend himself. Before he could move, she hit him again. The pain was intense, so all-consuming that he no longer knew where he was. His head was surely going to burst. Then she stopped.

"Painful?"

Vailer did not answer. He was going to die, her conscious less blue eyes told him. There was nothing he could do about it, except perhaps manipulate her to kill him instantly. He was not going to say anything. He was not going to obey Karen. He was not going to beg.

"I asked you whether it is painful," she said, and sounded annoyed. She went to Kiko and opened her briefcase, took out two gold plated knuckledusters, and slid them on over her black gloves. Vailer had to think fast. What was the best way to die? It needed to be instant and not slow and torturous. In his helpless state, the only weapon he had was his mind. The psychology classes he took at the SSA taught him that to ignore a woman would place most of them in a rage. He felt this was his only weapon.

"Answer me!" Karen ordered loudly.

He smiled. That was all it took; she flew into a rage, and punched him with lefts and rights. The chair fell back and he landed on the floor. She followed him to the floor and frenziedly continued with the bloody assault until she was out of breath. She stepped away, and bent over to focus on breathing. She had overexerted herself. His face was a bloody pulp. Ricardo and Kiko did not smile anymore. They had never seen Karen go into this type of rage before.

INK

"Pick him up," she ordered Ricardo and Kiko. They snapped into action, and lifted Vailer with the chair up onto its legs. There was no hope for him, and no help on the way. She raised Vailer's face. "You will not answer me? Perhaps another little dose of pain?" She flashed a knife and waved it in front of his face. "Let us see if you can ignore this!" She stuck the knife deep into his shoulder.

The sharp pain surged through him. He felt his heart rate increase to circulate what little blood was left in his body. His respiration also increased to get more oxygen into the red cells that were left. With the adrenaline release, he felt himself start to sweat profusely. His body temperature plummeted, and his blood pressure along with his breathing became slow and irregular. The pain and loss of blood shut down parts of his body, while he tried to hold on to consciousness. The SSA had taught him the signs of shock, and he felt it coming on. *Good*, he thought. If he could go into shock, death would not be as torturous and painful. The plan was working; all the signs of shock were there.

She then pulled his hair to lift his hanging head, so they could be face to face.

"Where is the SSA compound?"

He was on the verge of death and knew it. All he needed was one more stabbing, one more punch, any flick of pain and the shock would kill him. Therefore, he mustered what little strength he had to produce a defiant smile. The smile was full of blood, with teeth missing. She studied him for a bit, and noticed the sweat and heavy breathing.

"He is near shock and wants me to kill him quick. He is SSA," she said to Ricardo. "Bleed him slowly."

"No, no!" Vailer finally spoke.

"Where is the SSA compound?"

He did not respond. She shoved the red gag into his mouth abruptly.

"Ricardo, did the paintings go out?" She asked.

"Of course," he replied.

"Come into the print room when you are done," she said, and left the room.

INK

Ricardo helped Kiko tie a rope to the chair, then Kiko went to the right side of the cave to a winch, hooked Vailer onto it, and slowly raised him into the air. Then he brought over an orange bucket from near the winch and replaced the one under Vailer; it was three quarters full. He opened a cabinet near the winch. In it were several used needles and a clear blood transfusion tube. He took one of the needles, attached the tube, then stuck it in Valier's foot. Blood started to trickle through the tube and into the bucket. After inspecting his work, Ricardo clutched Valier's head and raised it up to make eye contact with him.

"Adios, amigo," he said, in mockery, and then exited the dungeon. Kiko took hold of the full bucket of blood and followed. He locked the medieval dungeon door, and then caught up to Ricardo who walked down the hallway. They let themselves into the print room, turned right, and saw Karen sat at a table with her arm resting on it. A needle was in her vain, held by Frank Burns, who also held the attached tube to an intravenous bag. Karen's blood trickled into the IV bag. Burns had come back from the war with shrapnel in his leg and a great dislike of governments.

When Karen had noticed his paintings in an art gallery, she offered him a life of anarchy. He jumped at the chance. Granted, she held a gun to his head at the time and told him his other option was death. Frank liked the quiet life and to paint. He could churn out one painting a week with a print poster for billboards. Customers would acquire his work on the Internet. The first paintings were free of charge, as long as the customer paid for shipping. All the rest of the paintings cost $30. He did not have to liv off his paintings, so he could sell them cheap. His works were featured on more than 70 percent of the billboards in the United States. He was the go-to person in the commercial world of advertising, however, free is rarely free, and all his work came with a sinister catch.

Kiko carried the bucket to Frank, when he was dipping a piece of canvas into an open-top wine barrel filled with blood. Frank hung the blood-soaked canvas on a clothesline where ten other canvases were drying off. The excess blood dripped into a

INK

pan beneath them, then trickled back into the wine barrel. Kiko poured the bucket of blood into the barrel. It then became three-quarters full. Frank would bring the dried blood canvases to Karen, who would dip a brush into her own blood on a china plate, and then brush the canvas with one stroke from bottom left to top right.

Once the canvases had dried, Frank would mix paint with ink, then create countrysides, English fox-hunts, a bunch of top-hatted lords, dandies on big high-stepping horses, their hounds milling all around them, beaches, cities, portraits, and other images.

"We are running low on paint," said Frank anxiously.

Karen and Ricardo evaluated the stockpile. Three forty-four-gallon drums remained on a pallet with room for six. Four empty pallets leaned up against a wall next to it.

"I will take care of it," said Ricardo.

"Take Kiko and get ink as well," ordered Karen.

Ricardo and Kiko exited the room. Frank went over to a wall.

"Karen, these are dry. Can you see if they work?" Frank asked, and pointed to two city skylines paintings on the wall.

She rose up from her chair at the table, walked over to the paintings, and stopped in front of one. She paused. She did not like doing this, however, knew it had to be done. She held the frame of the painting and slowly stuck her face into the painting. Half her head disappeared into the painting. The adjacent painting began to stretch until a face protruded out of it. Frank could see the outline and then the details of Karen's face. He held up four fingers, and then placed his hands in his pocket. The face withdrew and she pulled her head out of the painting and stood near Frank. She swayed a little, like a person does when they are dizzy, paused for a moment, acquired her bearings and said—

"Four fingers."

INK

Jason called his new home "the Longhorn Gym" after a year of living there because it was in the town of Longhorn, Texas, and that is what Oleg called it. It stood on a hill surrounded by ranches, overlooking the town. Two other gyms in town catered to everyone, with aerobics, yoga, spin, Pilates, step classes, and juice bars. This was a man's gym. It had none of those classes because it had no female members. Punching bags, boxing gloves, hand wraps, bandages, gauze, safety gear, and weights were strewn all over the room, constantly being used by ten to fifteen fighters a day. With a vending machine that dispensed protein shakes, or water.

Most of them were cowboys from the surrounding ranches. Some would ride up on horses, tie them up to the porch, and then work out. Oleg designated Jason to fill troughs with water for the horses to drink from. The town folk all agreed that the gym was trouble. Something strange and horrible had happened in the town—something that the older inhabitants still talked about when topics for gossip were scarce. The year before, on a hot summer night, a gym member was at a bar drinking and playing pool. His opponent lost the game for $50 and did not want to pay up. When the member called him a welcher, his opponent swung at him with a right cross. The member ducked the attack, and then punched him straight in the face.

His opponent fell back and hit his head on the floor, which killed him. The member was charged with manslaughter. The gym and Oleg had been charged as accomplices. The jury gave the member a twenty-year sentence, however, dropped the charges against Oleg and the gym. The local and state news ran with the headline, "The One-Punch Killer," and coverage of the court proceeding caused a spike in business in the following years. All the bad boys from the surrounding cities came out.

INK

They all wanted to be trained by the person who could teach you to kill a man with one punch. On a local scale, though, the incident tarnished the gym, and its members had since been considered trouble by the town folk.

Moses helped Jason build a kitchenette with fridge and microwave. He enrolled Jason in home schooling, so the few hours on a computer a day would free Jason up to sweep the floor, mop, dust, do laundry, and clean the showers. Jason learned to cook meals from a Cookbook, read whatever book he could find, and did what he was told for the first six months. All the while, he watched Oleg train different fighters, and practiced the different moves he saw when he was alone. When Oleg asked Jason why he had removed the paintings and pictures from the gym, Jason responded, "I can't sleep. They look at me."

"Even during the day?" Oleg asked.

"Yes sir. They bother me."

Then one day, Oleg noticed peach fuzz had started to grow on Jason's face. He thought to himself, *if he did not teach him something, Jason would mop floors for the rest of his life.*

"That is enough for one day, go hit the showers," said Oleg, to the fighter he was training. Jason set the mop down and scurried over to pass Oleg a towel; he stood outside the ring like he was not allowed in it. When Oleg said, "Come in," Jason felt a tinge of excitement because this was the first time the boss had asked him to step into the ring. So he did. *This arena is hallowed ground. Legal, government sanctioned fights took place within the ring.* He placed one hand on the rope, slowly, like he was savoring the moment. He stepped onto the mat and pulled himself up. *No running and hiding from authorities once you were in here. It was the last bastion—the only arena left in the modern world where men can still be gladiators.* Jason slipped between the middle and top rope. He felt privileged. Then he stood in the center of the ring. Calmness came over him. He felt home.

"You want to learn how to fight?" The calmness left Jason. Oleg was the only man in the gym. The happiness was short lived, with the belief that he would go toe-to-toe with the much larger Russian man. He told himself, *I am not afraid of Oleg, but the man has skills.*

INK

"Yes sir," Jason nodded.

Oleg placed him in a clinch hold, quick as a snake. Jason thought, *that was fast. Uncalled for, but fast.*

"This is a boxing clinch. Try to get out of it." Jason tried, however, had no luck. "Very difficult to get out of," said Oleg.

Oleg taught Jason boxing in the first year. He picked it up in no time, and he wanted to fight. Oleg would not allow him to fight in competitions, saying his bones were still growing and it would be unhealthy for him at his age due to the high injury rate with young competition boxers. Annoyed, Jason went to the town library to do some research on low-injury fighting. He sat at a table with a book, to read statistics on sports injuries, when he felt someone to his left. He turned to see a girl in pigtails, sundress, and stood beside him, barefoot. She had a sunflower in her hair.

"Hello. I am Emily," she said.

"Where are your shoes, ma'am?" He asked.

"By the door," she said, and pointed at the entrance door, "I like the feel of carpet on my feet. I'm not a ma'am. I'm a girl. What are you reading?" Jason did not get much reading done. *She talked a lot and asked many questions,* he thought. She introduced him to her friends; Amy with fair hair and eyeglasses, and Carmelina who had just moved from Italy. Carmilina had dark features, was shy and spoke little English. From that night, Jason found himself in constant girl talk when he went to the library. The girls would come to the library every day after school. Their parents would use the library as free childcare and would pick them up at closing time at 9 p.m.

Jason was home schooled, and visited the library once a week for books. He made sure to go when he knew the girls would be there so no weekends. Surrounded by adults every day, the girls were the only people his age. He was learning about girls too—how they thought, what they felt, and how they would manipulate. The girls did not do much reading and always talked about the same thing—school, friends, make-up, music, TV, and boys. They always spoke to Jason like he was just one of the girls, however, hearing about periods and menstrual cramps was just confusing to him.

INK

When Jason asked Oleg to teach him taekwondo because of its 14 percent injury rate, Oleg knew he had someone special. Nevertheless, Oleg still refused to teach him. He wanted to see how badly Jason wanted it. After being bugged for months, Oleg knew he had to teach him when Jason added taekwondo to every sentence.

"Mop the floor."

"Yes sir, with taekwondo."

"Are you growing a beard?"

"Yes sir, with taekwondo."

"Do you want a cheeseburger?"

"Yes, thank you, with mustard and taekwondo."

In the first year, Jason won the state taekwondo championship with little challenge. Hunger was Jason's motivation and, even though Oleg gave him all the food he wanted, Jason's wiring was different from anyone else's. He had been raised to believe that if he did not win his fights, he would not eat. The hunger pains of his childhood would come to the surface, when he feasted his eyes on his opponents across the ring, and when that happened. He would brutalize them. The fortunate middle-class kids whose parents could afford to send them to taekwondo lessons were no match for his vicious upbringing and natural aggression.

Some of his opponents left the ring crying. Jason lived in a fighting gym every day, and learned by observing older gym members fight. He lived and breathed fighting, while most of his opponents would have taekwondo classes twice a week. When the members needed an opponent, they would use Jason so they could practice moves on him. For the most part, Jason was no match for their strength, however, he outmatched them in endurance, and memory. His technique developed rapidly. Seven days a week, 365 days a year, one member after the other, earned Jason nicknames like "Energizer Bunny," and the "Cowboy."

Once Oleg had taught him wrestling moves and holds like: the Polish Hammer, Cross Body Block, Sharp Shooter Scorpion Death Lock, and the eighty other moves of the sport. He earned the new nickname of "Rubberband Man," because he learned to contort his limbs to slip out of his opponent's best wrestling

INK

holds. He practiced with older gym members, and learned the type of technique, strength and patience it took to wear down an opponent. The wrestling state title came in only a few months.

Gym members became proud of him and would give their Cowboy hats to Jason. One of the members even gave him a guitar that he would practice on, especially when he had trouble sleeping. Oleg would not allow him to defend any of his titles, telling him he must learn all the fight disciplines to be a good fighter. Their objective was the state titles. When he won the title, Oleg would teach him a different style of fighting. There was no money in junior competition—only titles and trophies. Oleg would not waste his time and money for little reward. Karate came next, and then judo, jujitsu, and boxing again.

The KGB had taught Oleg death strikes that would kill a person instantly, and he passed them on to Jason so the boy would know what a death strike looked like, along with defensive moves for each of them. Jason focused on his skills without television, football, or any other interests; he was consumed by fighting. It became fun for him. He would read books on *Wrestling*, *Martial arts*, Boxing or any other book on fighting he could find. The town of Longhorn did not interest Jason; the few times he did venture out were with Oleg for some supplies, or when a gym member needed help wrangling cattle on his ranch. That is where Jason learned to ride horses. He even rode a bull once, however, believed fighting was safer.

The titles and trophies meant the world to Jason. They gave him confidence, purpose, and a tangible reward. Jason would polish them all the time. Then one day, while he mopped the showers, he heard a *THUNDEROUS* sound from a distance. When it came closer, the sound became louder, reverberated the surrounded air and the walls of the gym. He investigated the sound which led him outside. A customer had ridden up on a blue motorcycle.

"What is that?" Jason asked.

"Harley Davidson Night Train, cowboy," said the member, when he unhooked his gym bag from the rear of the seat before he walked inside. Jason studied it, saw the sun bounce off the chrome, and knew he had to get one. He would polish his trophies less and less after that day. He had that Harley on his mind so he went to the library, and photocopied pictures from a book to hang on his wall. At the library, he saw Carmelina at one of the computers. Once he had his pictures, he said hello.

"Jason... I thinka... we can finda... your sister," Carmelina said in broken English.

"Come. Che cosa ha trovato. (How? What did you find?)" Jason asked, in Italian. They both were teaching each other the others language.

"Looka. I founda this. All da cities have a... county registrar's office... it a lista all da peoples of da city... you justa type in da name and see if it... come up, but not all da county registrars are... online. Somea... you have to walk inside... and ask for da search."

"Carmelina you are so intelligent," Jason said, while he searched the names.

"I founda... no listing for da Lauren Crawford in thisa... cities. But...foster parents could hava changed her nama." While Carmelina spoke, she handed him a piece of white paper with a list of cities, written in blue ink pen. Then Emily and Amy came up on their right side, and interrupted them.

"Jason, we need you. Come along Carmelina," said Emily, while she pulled Jason by the arm, and dragged him out of the library. Carmelina and Amy followed.

"Amy has a date and you need to get her ready," Emily said, when she steered them behind the library to a brick enclave of a storeroom doorway. The group would go there sometimes to drink hot chocolate from the vending machine because no food or drinks were allowed in the library. The enclave visits would become longer and longer. The girls would paint their nails, and Emily tried smoking a cigarette once, however, did not like it. It gave them shelter, though, more importantly, privacy.

"Ready for what?" Jason asked.

"Kissing," said Emily "Go on Amy." Jason looked at Amy. Emily tried to convince Amy, and then Carmelina, however, both were shy and would not kiss Jason. Then Carmelina said, "Youa kissa." Emily said, "If I do it, you have to do it." The girls agreed and Emily moved closer to Jason. She closed her eyes and puckered her lips. Jason did not move, and after a while, Emily opened her eyes and said, "Jason kiss me. Put your lips on mine." She clasped his head and kissed him. Jason never closed his eyes, and when their lips separated, he wiped his lips with the back of his hand and said, "Yuck. That was wet." Emily said, "Don't be a baby. All the adults do it. It is supposed to be a little wet. Now you try Amy." She pushed Amy until her face was inches away from Jason's. They slowly eased their lips onto one another and kissed.

"Jason, close your eyes," said Emily, so he did. Then Emily pressured Carmelina to kiss him, however, she would not. Emily had to place her hands on the back of their heads and physically bring them together. Then they all did it again and became comfortable with each other. In the week that followed, they heard all about Amy's date, and that her date did not even try to kiss Amy. She did not care though because she did not like him anymore.

That night, they all learned how to French kiss, and Jason's trips to the library became more frequent. One night the girls could see Jason was sad. He had found out the Harley he wanted cost fifteen thousand dollars, and there was no way he could come up with that kind of money. So Emily asked him, "Do you want to make out?" So they did. Then Amy and Carmelina took their turn with Jason. *My lips hurt,* thought Jason, while most trips to the library ended with kissing.

Soon the girls would take Jason into the enclave individually and hands began to feel genitals, when puberty hit the girls faster than it hit Jason. He would learn later that the girls agreed to a 30-minute time limit with Jason so they could see what a penis looked like. One night, Jason struggled to sleep when he heard tapping on the window. When he went to investigate, he saw Emily in her pajamas. He opened the window and pulled her inside.

"I snuck out," she said.

Jason was confused and asked, "Why?"

"I wanted to see you," Emily said.

"Okay," said Jason. She lifted the blanket to his bed slid in and said, "I am cold. Come cuddle, keep me warm." He hopped in and hugged her. They would always cuddle in the enclave when it was cold, and did not think much of it. They faced one another kissed, and that night they had sex. In the morning, Emily was gone and Jason started his day as normal: breakfast, home school on the computer for a few hours, chores, and then training.

INK

Jason did not see the girls until a week later when Amy came to the gym in the afternoon. She played hooky from school. Oleg was training Jason when she walked in. "I need to see Jason," she said, to the three gym rats near the door who had stopped training.

Jason stopped swinging punches at Oleg's padded hands, "Amy?"

"Can I see you for a moment?" She yelled out.

"Sure. Give me a minute, Mr. Oleg." Jason followed her out of the gym and towards a few shady trees, while Amy made small talk until the trees surrounded them. She asked, "You had sex with Emily? She told Carmelina and me."

"Oh," he said and was taken aback. Not sure what to say next.

"It is okay. We share everything." She tried to calm him, and said, "I am next."

"What?" Jason asked.

"I want to have sex with you next. That is how it goes—Emily, me, and then Carmelina," she said. Jason thought about it.

"Okay, but it will have to be quick. I am in training," he said, and raised his boxing glove covered hands, and then laid on the ground. She laid on top of him and they had sex. It was so fast that Jason kept his boxing gloves on. When Jason returned to the gym, two gym rats hi-fived him, and asked, "Is that your girlfriend?" Oleg was training another fighter, and Jason walked over to him.

"Sorry sir, I didn't know she…, " stumbled out of Jason's mouth. When Oleg stopped training the fighter, and cut him off.

"I don't give a fuck. This is a man's gym. I want no women coming here. I have known so many men whose dreams have been destroyed because of a woman. You cannot have it all. Sacrifices must be made for your career. If you want to be a champion fighter, you cannot have a girlfriend."

"Yes, sir," said Jason. "I want to be a champion fighter."

"You horney, go get laid. Take care of it. But no girlfriends. This is a rule. No women or no career. Understand?"

"Yes, sir."

"Go clean the bathrooms. I am too angry to train you now," said Oleg, and went back to train the fighter, however, he was secretly proud as could be. Jason's shoulders dropped, as if he lost a fight. Disappointed, he moped around all day and no one talked to him. Messing with Oleg's time, which all the fighters' strived for, was the wrong thing to do. He thought *it best to warn the girls to stay away from the gym.* That same evening he went to the library, and Carmelina was the only one there from the girls. He explained the situation to her and she understood. Then she asked questions about Jason having sex with Emily. When he said, "It was fun," she said she would like to try it. So they went into the enclave and had sex. They were standing up having sex in a corner, when Emily and Amy interrupted them.

"What are you doing?" Emily asked, intensely. Amy was gob-smacked.

"We're having sex," said Jason. Carmelina was embarrassed, so she stopped and pulled her panties up and school dress down. Jason turned to talk to the girls with his erect penis out. All the girls had seen his genitals, and he had seen theirs so dressing was not a priority.

"You had sex with me this morning," said Amy.

"You slut. You knew I liked Jason," said Emily.
Innocently, Jason said, "And now it is Carmelina's turn."

"He has had sex with all of us," said Emily.

"So, I have kissed you all as well," said Jason.

"This is different, Jason. I do not want to be your friend anymore," said Emily.

"Me too," said Amy, and both of them left. Carmelina followed them.

"How is this different? It is like kissing. We were having turns. Its Carmelina's turn." A stressed Jason pulled up his pants.

INK

He was confused, frustrated, and angry, while thoughts raced through his pubescent brain. *How can they be angry with me? I did what they wanted. They do not want to be friends, okay. They were just manipulating me to do what they wanted. That won't happen again.* He put on his shirt and walked home—angry at them all. Jason decided he would not go to the library when the girls were there, and he never did. He went when he knew they would not be there—on weekends.

Sleeping was a problem at times. Energized, and restless, it would be hours before the comfort of sleep would befall Jason. Some nights, the Harley pictures on the bedroom wall made him think about the Softail model he wanted—how he would customize it, and how he could make money to purchase one. Or practice fight moves, on imaginary opponents in the dark. With state championship titles in taekwondo, wrestling, kickboxing, jujitsu, boxing, and karate at sixteen and a half, he matured quickly. Because he never shaved, his full beard made him look like he was in his twenties. The large state of Texas seemed too small for his talents so they started to travel out of state. They took titles in Oklahoma, Utah, and Arizona.

Traveling across those highways, freeways, and streets, he would always see Harleys, and would name them when they thundered by: Roadking, Deuce, Softail, Dyna, Electra Glide, and Sportster. Then one night, while headed home from a fight in Tulsa, they stopped for some food at a truck stop. It was Friday night, and the place buzzed with truckers, travelers, and teenagers on their way into the city. Jason sat on a bench outside the diner, took off his cowboy hat and picked at his chips. A Harley rode up and parked nearby. The rider went into the diner. Oleg could see Jason eyeing it.

"What's the model?" Oleg asked.

"That is a 2002 Fatboy."

"Engine size?"

"Fifteen-eighty-four."

A man swaggered over to them; he was in his thirties, wore blue denim jeans, a brown shirt, and a bone hat. He placed his hands on the table and said, "Excuse the interruption folks. My name's Jim Malone. Which one of you likes to wake snakes?"

Jason and Oleg looked at one another with that "what is he talking about?" look on their faces. They understood each other without saying a word.

"You can make $500." Jim Malone stated. Jason raised an eyebrow.

"Wake snakes?" Oleg asked.

"Cause a ruckus. Got a fighter named Buck round back who is all hat and no cattle. Fighter didn't show."

"I will do it," said Jason, before he knew what the man was talking about. "Are you looking for a fighter?"

"As white as the driven snow."

"I do not think it is a good idea," said a worried Oleg.

"If I am ever going to have one of those"—he pointed to the Harley—"I need to start making some money."

"Okay," said Oleg, and they followed the cowboy to the back of the truck stop where all the trucks were parked.

"Be careful. There are no rules out here. Everything goes in these bare-knuckle fights," warned Oleg, when they made their way through the trucks. "Can ya tell us anything about who he is fightin'?"

Malone scratched his head and said, "Reckon he's bigger than all hell, and will beat ya like a red-headed stepchild if you let him."

A group of trucks had formed a circle that made up the ring. Spectators stood in front of the trucks, splitting the intense bright-beams from the headlights. A tall, lanky, bare chested Indian, displayed red and yellow war paint on his face, and a long ponytail, stretched his arms in the center. Some spectators, mostly truckers watched him. When he saw Jason take off his shirt, he swung punches into the air.

"These fighters are unpredictable. Put him down quick," said Oleg.

The fight started with the Indian doing acrobatic roundhouse kicks, cartwheels, and swung wildly with haymakers. Jason never had a wild opponent like the Indian, and panicked. He moved his entire body out of the strike zone at first; once he had measured the Indian's speed and accuracy, he had the confidence to tilt his head left and right slightly to avoid the strikes.

"Your boy there looks as nervous as a cat in a room full of rocking chairs," said Malone to Oleg. Using one heavy right punch, Jason thumped his opponent to the dirt. Out! Dust billowed up through the shards of light, fragmented by the audience in front of the trucks' bright hi-beams.

"Your buck is as lucky as a blind man crossing the street," said Malone, when he counted out money to Oleg. Jason walked over to Oleg, who handed him $500 in cash. That was the most money Jason ever held in his hand. He was excited until he heard, "Like to try me on, kid?" He turned to see a huge-bellied trucker, who wore a stained wife-beater. *This guy won't have much endurance,* thought Jason. He gave the $500 to Oleg and then said, "We have a winner." He stepped back into the ring. The trucker took off his shirt and exposed his fat belly to the crowd, who were disgusted. And they let the overweight trucker know with comments like, "Put your shirt back on," "Kid's going to beach this whale," "That belly's going to show up on a radar," and "Put that thing away. It's hurting my eyes."

Jason made one thousand dollars that night. He did the math. With 15 nights like that he could buy his Harley. With the taste of that easy money, he was hooked. He bugged Oleg every week for them to travel. Oleg resisted until Jason offered him 50 percent of his winnings. They went back to Oklahoma for more fights with Jim Malone, who gave them underground locations in different states—Texas, Utah, Arizona, Colorado, New Mexico, and California. Oleg would sign Jason up for official league matches that would lead to championship fights. Then he only allowed Jason to prizefight on the way home from winning those matches. Oleg would say, "Learning is more important than money at this stage of your life." He would not allow Jason to fight in national competitions because, as he said, "There was more money to be made with less recognition."

In the years that followed, the titles went by the wayside, while the prize-money fights took precedence. Jason kicked the shit out of truckers, cowboys, roughnecks, day laborers, rednecks, businessmen, hillbillies, or any crazy person willing to step into the ring with him. Wherever he went, he stopped by the county registrar office to search for Lauren Crawford, in a determined pursuit for the sister whose existence Mao had revealed. Once or twice he found a nibble—a Mary Crawford out in Georgia, and a Elizabeth Crawford in Ohio. However, one turned out to be Filipino and the other was dead. To his dismay, there was never anyone named Lauren Crawford. *She is not dead,* he told himself. She was out there somewhere. He could feel it, along with a slight developing depression caused by the fruitless pursuits, over the past years of searching and fighting with only trophies to show for it. However, he kept at it, and saved his money.

Then came the day he and Oleg walked into a Harley Davidson dealership. Jason carried a black backpack, and his boots clacked on the white tile all the way to the showroom. There was a polished blue-and-chrome Road King, a gun-metal-gray Fat Boy, and a metallic black Night Train. Jason picked out the details, and was awed at the chrome exhaust pipes, crinkle black engine, exposed belt drive, and chrome velocity stack until a stranger interrupted him.

"See anything you like?" The stranger asked. He wore a black western shirt with the sleeves rolled up—that showed off a menagerie of tattoo's, boots, blue jeans, and had mutton chop sideburns.

"Yes sir. I want that," said Jason, and pointed at the Night Train model.

"Good choice. I can help you get it. I'm in sales. Chuck." said Chuck in a cool, laid-back way. He stuck out his hand and Jason shook it. "I like a man that knows what he wants. Follow me, and we will fill out the paperwork." They all went into his office, and Jason emptied the content of his backpack onto the desk.

"There is fifteen thousand dollars," said Jason.
Chuck was impressed with the pyramid of cash on his desk. He typed into a calculator and then said, "With tax and license fees, the total comes to sixteen thousand, seven hundred."

"What?" Jason asked, confused. He had never purchased anything before. Everywhere he went, Oleg took care of the financials. This was his first purchase, and it seemed like it would not happen.

"I will get the balance," said Oleg, and handed over a credit card to the salesperson. He ran it and filled out the transfer of ownership papers.

"Thanks, boss. I will pay you back," said Jason.

"No need kid. You earned it," said Oleg.

"What is your license number?" Chuck asked.

"I don't have a license," said Jason.

"It is going to be a little difficult to ride without it," said Chuck. He and Oleg laughed. In Jason's excitement, he had never applied for a motorcycle or automobile license. They had the motorcycle towed to the gym, and the following week Jason acquired his learner's permit. He was sixteen, and rode all over town, with the wind in his face and the first euphoric feeling of freedom. He wore sunglasses and a cowboy hat on his back, held by its strap round his neck, white T-shirt, blue denim jeans with a hole in the left knee, and cowboy boots. Oleg gave him a few days off and he rode until his ass was sore. He then would find a diner, bar or roadhouse and would eat or drink standing up. Then he would ride some more.

On a Saturday afternoon, he cruised onto the footpath of the library, flicked the kickstand out with his left boot, and parked his shiny new Harley. He unhooked the books from the rear seat and then entered the library. He dropped the books into the return slot and then went to find some more books. What he saw stopped him in his tracks. It was Emily, and his eyes met hers. He checked the clock on the library wall. It was 3 p.m. on a Saturday so this was out of the ordinary. *Holly crap,* he thought. She was sitting with Amy and Carmelina at a table full of books.

Jason noticed Amy and Carmelina talking, like they were asking a question. When Emily did not respond, they both eyed Emily, and saw she was focused at something by the door. All three then saw Jason. Years had passed and he would see them around town sometimes on the footpath or in cars, however, very rarely. *Wow, all three are beautiful, attractive southern bells,* he thought, nevertheless, turned around and exited the library. He would not allow them to play with him, like they did in the past.

As much as he wanted to be with them, he would show the girls there is a cost to manipulating people. His response would show them that cost. He wanted nothing to do with them. *Why were they at the library? Its Saturday. They know it is my day.* He sat on his Harley, the mirror on the handle bar reflected the library and the girls watched him through a window. He stuck his sunglasses on, and then rode off—his hat fell into place. He loved those girls, however, did not know it. And the rest of the female population was going to pay for it.

INK

DURGA

CHAPTER NINE

One of the first things Lauren learned from her grandfather was that you shall get what you pay for with Symbolism. Dab a little blood on your totem, and it will not last long. Splash it with a gallon, and you can pretty much write your own check. The second thing she learned was the stronger you were, the less blood you needed to use. She also learned that no one was stronger than her. Her blood, infused with power by whatever her birthmother had done to her in an abandoned house in the backwoods of Kentucky, was more potent than any other living Symbolist's. The compound swarmed with thirty-three peacocks and seventeen vibrant geckos that Lauren created in her first year. Her love for animals necessitated a visit to the Director's office so she was restricted to one animal per tile.

"You need to create a protector tile," said Director Heliodoros, with a Greek accent. He was a distinguished man in his 60s, with a head of grey hair. "Which animal do you choose?"

"Lion," Lauren said. *That was quick, like it was automatic. I do not know why I said that. Why a lion?* She thought, and noticed the Director beheld Fergus. *They know something—what?Did I say something wrong?*

"Is that okay?" Lauren asked in an insecure way.

"That is acceptable," said the Director. "Why a lion?"

"I am not sure. I just said it."

The Director leaned back in his chair and reached behind to a bookcase. "The Hindu Princess Durga rides on a lion, and we believe you may have those powers." He took a book from one of the shelves and placed it on the desk in front of her. "Read this." The cover was titled *Durga*, with a painted picture of a beautiful, mystical, powerful woman with ten arms, riding on a lion with a bushy mane, and an army of followers behind the lion. Lauren was in awe. She picked up the book and took it to her apartment to read.

She thought that Fergus Blackwood did not really give a shit about anything. When she met him, he was a crabby, unpleasant old man with an unintelligible Scottish accent and maybe eight hairs left on his spotted scalp. Now, six years later, he was older, less pleasant, and his last few hairs were gone altogether. *At least I can understand him now,* thought Lauren. She sat in her grandfather's dark, cramped apartment kitchen at a table where he would teach her the lessons of Symbolism.

"Your script is as sloppy as a ten-penny whore," he would growl, and jabbed a knotted finger at the tile she was inking. He pronounced the last word *hooer*, like he stretched it between pinched fingers. "You think you can call up your beasties with this tripe?"

The Script, the language the other Symbolists used to describe and refine their creations, was Lauren's only stumbling block. Learning its nonsensical grammar was an ongoing struggle, even after six years of continuous memory exercises. She trained with Agent Decker and her grandfather and made progress with her lion tile, scripting "protector" beneath its image. This lion tile was the one that would allow her to leave the compound or transfer to another compound or country.

The lion took a lot more time than the other tiles, however, it was almost done. She spent days to create each and every detail under her grandfather's careful direction, squinted through a magnifying glass until her eyes ached and her hand was cramped and trembling. She obsessed over it. Then it was just a matter of getting it to do what she wanted. Simple commands like kill and defend me was easy—so easy they could be enforced without Script. However, something like, sniff out the lost child in the city, was a lot trickier.

It was complex stuff, and that is what made Lauren stand out from all the other Symbolists. As a rookie, she synchronize ten peacocks to do a Tamasaburo Bando kabuki dance on her first tile. All other Symbolists, teachers, and management took notice. She could make her seventeen geckos perform gymnastics, acrobatics, flips, handstands, somersaults, and floor

INK

routines. They could also do pommel horse moves on rocks, and dismount from bonsai tree branches. Later, management discovered the geckos would also mischievously steal jewelry, trinkets, tiles, and food, and hide it all in Lauren's room. After Fergus made her recreate her Script, the geckos merely hunched around her on fence posts and rocks, their eyes dull and lifeless. Fergus read through her new Durga tile. The circles of Script were much more complicated than anything he had seen before and at least three times the length of other protector tiles.

"You shall amount to little and less if you do not get this babble into your thick head," said Fergus, his scowl deepened the already severe lines at the corners of his eyes and mouth. In his slacks, button-up shirt, and old sweater vest, he seemed like Mr. Rogers's evil brother. "Why have I been wasting my time for all these years if you are going to bunk up what your mother could do at eight?" He asked rhetorically.

"I am tired of hearing about her, Gran." Lauren crossed out a spiral whorl of Script, and then carefully modified another so that the "nyel" became a "mimyr," and clarified its meaning to better describe the roll of the protector lion she had painstakingly etched into her thin tile. "I know she could summon up air strikes and swarms of locusts and whatever the hell else she wanted to, okay? So just drop it. I am doing my best." She ran a hand through her hair, which was longer now than it had been in high school. "Okay?"

Lauren's mother never could do those things, however, Fergus said those things to motivate her. "Aye," the old man snorted, "Have it your way, spoiled girl." He leaned back in his seat and crossed his skinny arms over his chest. "When you meet your first Illustrated Man, though, you shall want to be able to get your thoughts down quick and clean. You will want to be able to depend on what you have made." He slapped a finger on the table, his rheumy old eyes fierce. His scowl deepened, and he gave a disgusted wave. "We are done for today."

Lauren did not need to be told twice. She dusted her wet ink with sand and hurried out of the apartment, down the narrow iron-grate stairs, and out through the ink-reeked studio into the blistering sunlight of the compound. Absentmindedly, she stuck her ear buds in and cranked Fleetwood Mac up to a truly ridiculous volume to drown out the thoughts of the day. Even in her thin, cotton t-shirt and light cargo shorts, she perspired by the time she made it across the hundred yards of bare rock and sand to the dormitory building, where she had her little studio apartment. It was next to Decker and Ditta, Lauren's best friend.

Ditta was almost as skilled as Lauren. A Swedish girl from Symbolic royalty, her parents, grandparents, and great-grandmother had all been Symbolists. She was skinny, lanky and her white hair was buzzed down to a stubble. She lounged like a crocodile outside her door in a canvas lawn chair, wore an undershirt and a pair of knee-length soccer shorts. Decker stood next to her. Ditta pushed her sunglasses up onto her head when Lauren approached. "Hey, Supergirl," she said, with a lazy grin. "How'd it go with the Lock Ness Monster?"

Lauren stopped and made a face. "Not great. He is riding my ass about my Script."

"Yeah," said Decker, nodding, "It does kind of suck."

"Thanks. You have been a big help."

Ditta's smile widened when she replaced her sunglasses, laid back, and stretched her long, lean legs. "Braxton is not getting the transfer."

"Management has big plans for him. The city needs him," said Decker.

"Then I would like a transfer to the city," said Lauren.

"I wanna transfer too so I can get out of this desert," said Ditta.

Decker asked Lauren, "How do you know he wants you there? Have you two even kissed?"

Lauren ignored her, climbed the stairs to her apartment, and entered. Which had a tiny kitchen with dishes piled high in the sink, a living area and a bedroom that was bare except for a bookshelf, a narrow single bed with the _Durga_ book laying on it, a nightstand with a lamp, an alarm clock, and a framed photo of her adopted family. Seeing the picture sent a pang of loneliness through her heart. Near it was another photo of Lauren, Braxton, and Ditta out in the barren desert, with their arms out in a "Nothing out here and nothing to do" gesture. She placed her stuff on the bed, then sat down and unlaced her shoes. The A/C was already on, and it was cool inside the bedroom.

I should keep working, she thought, and glanced half-heartedly at the family photo again. She picked-up the frame and pulled the back off, and a tile fell out. It displayed seventy-seven red-winged blackbirds and its range of Script. She had started this before she was restricted to one animal per tile, and every now and then she would continue to work on it. She figured she could send some of the birds out and keep an eye on her parents. Once Braxton had been transferred to the city, she worked harder to finish the tile.

They had kissed once, even though Braxton had explained to her that he could be sent to jail because she was under age. It was also illegal for the military to fraternize with Symbolists, however, there was a movement to change that law; with servicemen constantly assigned to escort Symbolists, the two groups had more than enough opportunities to make the law hard to enforce. Management had scientific proof that Symbolists' offspring were more skilled and had more power in the blood than the offspring of couples in which only one member was a Symbolist.

Reluctantly, Lauren peeled off the wax paper that covered her tile and slid down to the floor for more work room. She had spent years taking her time, a little bit here and a small amount there. Decker gave her the idea of a flock of scavenger-spies, a little villain trick some of the Symbolic Sector Agency's more senior members used to keep tabs on known unaffiliated Symbolists. There were international councils that would come down on criminals like the hammer of God if things grew out of hand domestically. So the SSA kept a close vigil over all Symbolists in the world.

Still, Lauren knew they had not plopped their base of operations in the sunny California desert for their health. Something big was going down, and had been going down for years. Two Symbolists had turned up dead in California, just since she came to the compound. This was a lot since the total Symbolist population in the United States was something less than a thousand. She had been allowed off the agency campus, a big dusty compound built on a low, rocky ridge, maybe ten or fifteen times in her six years there and never without a guard, a vial of blood, and a few choice tiles. Someone was messing with big juju in the Sunshine State.

She kept the lion tile around her neck wherever she went, and figured she could summon the lion inside two seconds from there. Some of the other Symbolists she had met, both the agents who staffed the little outpost and the civilians who came through to visit or lecture, thought animals were minor league. Agent Decker could produce a loaded and extremely, viciously functional AK-47 out of thin air with a thumb-sized votive card illustration, six drops of blood, and two lines of script. An English diplomat, who had stayed for two days had arrived in a self-propelled mini-plane, he had conjured from a blueprint practically black with Script.

That was pretty A-list stuff, however, Fergus said once Lauren had a firm grasp of the archaic sub-language, she would be able to do pretty much any damn thing she wanted. Of course, he phrased it much more...creatively, still, the prospect was exciting. Nevertheless, things seemed a little more urgent these days, which forced Lauren to make the blackbird tile a priority. It would be finished soon.

INK

On a cloudless, sunny day, a Hummer drove up and parked in the gym's parking lot. A slick suited man stepped out of it, and then walked to the front door. Jason's Harley was parked by the door, its front end customized to a more vintage-looking springer fork setup. When the man walked in, he saw ten gym members working out, and two men sparing in the ring. Oleg went down to the mat, of the ring, in a judo hold. Oleg slapped his opponent's arm, and the younger man released his hold. Oleg stood up, "Good! If you come from the side, they will not be able to defend against that." His opponent positioned himself for another attack when he heard something he had not heard in years and was a little stunned.

"Jason Crawford," the slick suited man yelled, and realized quickly Oleg's opponent was the only one standing there searching. Jason was then in his early twenties, however, the facial hair made him appear like he was in his thirties. He almost froze at the sound, his heart skipped a beat. He turned to find Frog.

"Mr. Frog," he said, turned back to Oleg and swung a right, and continued training.

Frog took a minute to soak it in. He could not believe the drastic change in the boy he employed once. His appearance was more like a titan. With muscles bulging out of every part of his body. Jason positioned himself for another attack when he heard Frog say, "Cowboy! I can get you Maddox. I manage him."

"Why would I want to fight Maddox?" Jason asked, and continued training without missing a beat.

Frog grinned, and said, "The fight's in Vegas. Cactus Casino is sticking up a hundred-foot billboard on the strip. You are going to be famous."

"I do not care about fame," said Jason.

"You can get a shot at the title with this one under your belt."

"I have enough titles."

"Big money."

"I do not care about money," said Jason.

"How much?" Oleg asked.

"Five hundred thousand," said Frog.

"Get out," said Oleg.

Four of the members stopped their training and surrounded Frog in an intimidating way. Frog was concerned, however, smiled his salesmen grin.

"You heard the boss," said one of the gym members.

Then fear gripped Frog, while he stepped back towards the door. "We are all fight friends," he said, when the four advanced, and forced him slowly out. Then Frog yelled out, "I can get you a picture of your sister from Mao."

Jason turned in his direction and rested his arms on the ropes. Now he was listening. "Hold up," he said. Frog was almost out the door. The four stopped advancing and stood there. Frog's speech became rapid fire.

"His challenger, Sam Hall. You know him. You fought him before he went UFC. He was injured in training. We spent a fortune on promotions. You have a bunch of state titles. We thought it would be a good match up."

"Tell me about my sister!" Jason said, urgently.

"Mao has a picture of her from the orphanage. I can get it for you."

Jason turned to Oleg and said, "We have to fight Maddox."

Oleg frowned. "You are not ready. Your head is all wrong." He turned to Frog and asked, "Who is we?"

"Maddox likes the idea," said Frog. "Giving a chance to an unknown, you have many titles."

"So get my head right," Jason said to Oleg. "We can get a title shot with this."

"You will have other opportunities," grumbled Oleg, while he unwound the tape from his hands. "Do not let him manipulate you. Maddox is nine years older than you, stronger, and he will eat you alive."

That hurt Jason and he thought, *What an awful thing to say.* He had never heard Oleg speak to him like that. Oleg would always say Jason was the best fighter in the world. "If the boss says no, it is a... no," Jason dropped his head.

Frog shrugged when he said, "So I guess you don't care about finding your sister." He raised his arms, and expected a beat down from the four, when he realized it had been a stupid and risky thing to say.

Jason raised an eyebrow and eyed him. The four surrounding Frog turned to Jason with a look that said, just give the word and he is a dead man. However, Jason did not and said, "I will do it."

"Hey!" Oleg yelled, and then took a softer tone. "I do not think you know what you are getting yourself into. Once you do this, you will only be able to fight in a few places."

"She is my sister. I have to find her."

"This is not good...UFC is international. Everyone will know your face. No one will want to fight you anymore. Your opportunities will dry up."

"She is the only family I have, and I do not know what she looks like."

Oleg felt Jason slipping away, and did not like it. He left the ring in a huff.

"It is on the 25th of September. I will send the contract over," said Frog, when he exited.

Jason placed his arms on the top rope of the ring, and hung his head down between them. A sweat droplet from his forehead fell, and he saw it hit the mat. Ten years had passed since Oleg said, "No women, or no career." Because of that rule, he was at the top of his game. Now and then, mostly after fight competitions, there would be girls he would have fun with in dressing rooms, bathrooms, apartments, and homes, however, it was all about sex—getting what he needed at the time, and then back to training. He became disciplined for many years, no women, on the other hand, this was his sister.

Divided highway lines on the road sped by, when Jason cruised on his Harley. Cacti stood stoic, in the barren landscape of the desert, while Jason thought to himself, *there is so little movement out here. Where are the coyotes, bobcats, antelopes, and eagles?*

INK

Then he saw a large bird on the road. When he rode closer, he could see it was a vulture. Its claws dug into the mangled meat of road kill, as it tore the flesh from the bones with its beak. When Jason rode near it, the vulture flew away. Then Jason passed it. His mirror reflected the vultures return to it. *Road kill looked like a coyote,* he thought.

He would pick out the different kinds of cacti and recite their names to himself while he rode along. *Barrel cactus, crimson hedgehog, pancake, prickly pear, saguaro cactus.* Up ahead, he could see a parked vehicle, with its hood up, and wondered if the occupants were having car trouble—or maybe a setup. He read about car-jackings all over the country on deserted highways, and the stories of dead bodies found in the desert. With suspicion falling onto the casinos, that dealt with gambling cheaters, drug dealers, and hookers on a daily basis. *Why risk it?* He would just ride on. Two women by the side of the car waved him down. *Damsels in distress. I have no choice,* he thought. He parked the Harley in front of the car, and turned the engine off. He lit a cigarette, placed his cowboy hat on his head, took a bottle of water from one of the leather saddlebags, that were draped over his rear seat, and drank. One of the girls walked up to him.

"Thanks for stopping. I am Angela and this is Chelsea," said Angela. She had long blonde hair. *Breathtakingly beautiful,* he thought. Chelsea was mulatto and equally pretty with long, jet-black curly hair. Jason stuck the empty water bottle back into the saddlebag. He could see a bulge in Chelsea's right sleeve jacket, that outlined the tire iron.

Angela said, "We broke a fan belt."

"Ladies!" he said, and tipped his hat. "Let's take a look."

Chelsea and Angela made way when Jason walked between them to the vehicle and peered into the engine bay. Steam slightly seeped from the radiator so he took off his shirt to wrap around his hand, and then slowly twisted the radiator cap. The steam poured out a little faster. Out of the corner of his eye, he caught Chelsea noticing the tattoo of the sword down his back and gave Angela a concerned stare. Angela tried to reassure Chelsea with a smile and leaned up against the car.

INK

"Hold that," Jason said, when he passed his cigarette to Chelsea. She gripped it between two fingers, and smoke overwhelmed her face so she waved it away.

Chelsea held the cigarette away from her, and said, "Okay. We tried calling, but there is no service out here."

Angela gave Chelsea a "Why-did-you-tell-him-that!" stare.

"We just wanted to lie out by the pool and have a few drinks," said Angela. Jason then placed his hand on Angela's leg. That is when Angela and Chelsea became concerned. Chelsea dropped the tire iron from her sleeve to her hand when Jason's hand went up Angela's pantyhose to a garter. He then ripped the pantyhose off her leg. Chelsea raised the tire iron above Jason's head.

"I would not do that. I do not need a tire iron," Jason said, when he tied the pantyhose around the pulleys of the car's engine. Once that was complete, he took the cigarette from Chelsea and puffed on it. "That should get you into town."

He walked back to his Harley.

"Wait. How can I thank you?" Angela ran up saying. He slid onto the Harley.

"I do not need thanking, ma'am." Jason took a puff and said, "Take care," and then rode off. Behind him, Angela observed his license plate number. It read TJF644, with some graffiti written in faded black marker pen, "fight or starve."

The main industry in Reno was "entertainment," when Jason rode into the city. He noticed empty office buildings and retail areas with vacancy signs. Streets were deserted, except for the occasional debris of tumbleweed that would cross. This was a ghost town. Many of Reno's strip clubs and gambling joints had aged so badly that they just appeared depressing. Nevada had the fifth highest suicide rate in the nation, and Reno ranked as one of the top ten depressed cities in the country.

Gangs had moved in, and the drug trade made Reno the meth capital of America. Jason remembered reading that somewhere, when he rode up to a dilapidated house in a slum neighborhood and parked the Harley. On the handlebars of Jason's motorcycle was a suit jacket, held in place with jockey straps. He took it off and slid into it. It covered all his tattoos. He checked his appearance in the mirror of the Harley. *A few creases on the jacket, but I look respectable,* he thought, when he walked up to the front door of the house. The house had an overgrown front yard. He *KNOCKED!* three times, on the door.

An elderly woman's voice responded. "Yes?"

Jason cleared his throat. "Sorry to bother you, ma'am. I understand Lauren Crawford may live here."

The door gradually opened to an elderly black woman, with gray hair and eyeglasses. She appeared fragile, when she peered over her glasses at him. Behind her, the hallway was large, long, dimly lit, and sparsely decorated with shabby carpet, that covered most of the wooden floor.

"Who?"

"Lauren Crawford," Jason repeated. "She is my sister."

The woman squinted at him. "Is she a white girl?"

Jason nodded. "Yes, ma'am."

"No. I am afraid you are mistaken, dear. Lauren Crawford don't live here…," she said. While she continued talking, Jason noticed a painting on a hallway wall behind her. It was a portrait of Martin Luther King Jr. The canvas slowly protruded out, stretched into the shape of a face, and then turned to stare at him. *Why does this happen? Why me? Am I losing my mind?* He kept his annoyance to himself.

"…I been livin' here for forty-three years. I ain't ever seen a white person living in this area."

"Okay, well thanks for your time, ma'am." Jason turned and walked away.

"You be careful now," said the old woman. "Those boys are up to no good."

She pointed across the street to eight black men who stood outside a liquor store. They were thug types with shaved heads, wore tank tops and jeans. One of the thugs stepped forward when Jason neared his Harley, however, did a double-take. Seemed impressed, he turned to talk to his friends. Jason sat on the bike, stuck a hand in his jacket, and pulled out a pencil and paper. A list of eight addresses were written on it, with a line through five of them. He then drew a line through the sixth

INK

address. The seventh address was 7294 Stanley Street Berkley, San Francisco. The eighth was 241 Exciter Avenue Oxford, England.

Night blanketed the desert. From miles away in the far distance, a single beam of light, shot straight up into the heavens like a beacon, announced to the world this is Las Vegas. At night, the light is so intense and powerful it has been photographed from space. Angela and Chelsea drove into the Las Vegas strip with the top down. Vegas neon lights bounced off the car. Police waited outside the Casinos for people to stumble out drunk. They would then arrest them. Scantily clad women starved for attention walked by, and boisterous teenagers, who were too young to get into the casinos, gave them all the attention they desired. Angela and Chelsea had been to Vegas so many times that they were immune to the promoters who handed out two-for-one deals at nightclubs, free entry passes to strip joints, casino fliers, and business cards of ladies who gave special "massages." Angela took a swig from her water bottle.

"What are you going to do? Give his license plate number to one of your cop friends?" Chelsea asked.

Angela shook her head. "No. That is unethical. You cannot use state services for personal use."

"Private detectives are expensive. Is he worth it?"

"There is another option." She nodded toward a casino billboard promoting a UFC fight between Jason and Brian Maddox.

Chelsea's eyes widened. "Holy shit. The guy's an animal."

"We need front row seats," said Angela.

"I was hoping we could go dancing tomorrow night!"

"You can go dancing; I am going there," she said, and pointed to the billboard.

Chelsea pulled out a cell phone and dialed. "What is the budget?"

Angela smiled and said, "Whatever it takes."

"You got it bad," said Chelsea, when Angela drove into a casino valet area, gave the keys to the valet, and walked into the lobby.

INK

INK

Fergus Blackwood puttered around in his kitchen. He set the kettle to boil and dumped a can of chicken soup into a pot. What he wanted was an éclair and a cup of coffee, with a shot of whiskey to stiffen it, however, two years ago, the chuckling, rosy-cheeked slip-of-a-whore woman doctor they brought in four times a year to check up on him had said no more sugar, no more coffee, no more drinking, and that was that. Fergus thought about killing her whenever she was in the camp—jabbing a pen in her eye, or slitting her throat from behind while she examined his blood work, however, he was old. His hand shook, and he was not ready to die yet. Not when he finally had one of Karen's children, anyway.

"You ever going to tell me? Who you think tried to kill me?" Lauren asked, while she sat at the table in her blue jeans and hoodie. She had spent the morning drinking coffee and reading a book called *Mastering Printmaking*.

"What? Oh," said Fergus darkly. "That. It does not matter; it was not anything important. Not now, anyway."

"It is important to me," said Lauren, shrugging. She kept at it.

Finally, Fergus said, "I think it is the Italian Mafia."

"Mafia?" Lauren asked sharply. "Why would they want to kill me?"

"No. Not kill you," said Fergus.

Lauren hesitated, then said, "That does not sound too convincing."

"No," said Fergus slowly. "Think, Lauren. If they do not want you dead, what is the purpose of trying to have you assassinated?"

She thought, *his first rule is that every positive has a negative, and every negative has a positive. What positive is there to the people who failed to kill me?* "Information," said Lauren impatiently. "Knowledge that they could not kill me."

"Good," he said. "Now try to sharpen your specifics."

Um, um,… I got zilch,… nada, she thought, and said, frustrated, "I do not know!"

"Have patience, it will come."

"Sometimes I just think I am dumb."

"Do not think that. Knowledge and wisdom take time. The weakness of youth is impatience," he said. "The assassin was sent not to kill you, but to see if you have the power. See, not all of the offspring receives it." He drank down his cold tea and set the cup aside.

"Why do they want to know if I have the power?"

"They use Symbolists to commit crime. They are as big as the Catholic church, and just as ruthless. Of course I could be wrong. People out there may just want to kill you."

"Thanks! Tell me about mother."

"No. It is a sad story."

"I had a dream last night. I was a princess and I danced with a bear."

He snapped to attention.

"Bear?" He said, alarmed. "Your mother had a bear," and reflected when the kettle came to a boil. He poured himself a cup, and then dropped one of the foul, grass-flavored teabags, that sodding bitch, doctor Beverly Crane, had ruled "acceptable" for his heart, into the steamed water. He blew to cool the hot brew. Lauren stopped reading and hung on his every word.

"Your mother was brilliant and beautiful until she ran off with that Pikey trash and joined his focking circus. That bear…"

He mumbled when he sat down at his kitchen table, and kept half an eye on the soup while he sipped his bitter tea. Light slanted in golden beams through the dusty blinds. He continued on his train of thought. "…she found it barely alive in Guatemala. Raised it up from a cub, she did. Was always playing with that beast. She gave it treats, and scratched its neck. It broke her heart to see it go. One winter, the bear caught a cold, and there was not a vet in Glenborough that would look at a monster like that."

"What happened to it?" She asked.

"It died, and some of her died with it."

INK

He put on a pair of quilted oven mitts and took the soup off the stove. He spooned himself up a bowl and sat down to eat.

When he saw Lauren twirl a finger through her brown hair, he began to lose his appetite. *Her hair is like her focking Pikey father's. Saints and sinners, damn that man to Hell,* thought Fergus. Anger boiled in his sour old stomach. He had lost his appetite, so he abandoned the soup.

"The peacocks and geckos—I have to admit, it was a clever piece of work," he said. "Subtle, versatile, a tad overcomplicated, still, remarkable for a beginner. I would never dare it; could not have done it in my prime."

"Could mother do it?" Lauren asked.

"Your mother—maybe with a little practice; she was good, real good 'til she came limping back proud as you please with the two of you and a great bloody dancing bear. The bear was like one of them grizzlies, however, black all over—black as night."

She stood up and said, "The two of us?"

Fergus took a moment, when he realized his slip of the tongue. His mind raced with thoughts. He had to tell her what everyone in her life had kept from her.

Lauren had heard many stories about her mother, even so, she would get different details each time she asked the people who knew her. So she always asked. She had dreamed of a bear, a great black bear, since she was a baby, however, also of a blurry image of an abstract that seemed like a pillow that the bear would play with. Then it came together as a blonde boy wrestling the cub, laughing innocently and joyfully. *I must have seen them when we were in Scotland,* she thought.

It is about time, he thought. "Yes, Lauren, the two of you."

"Wait. What?"

"You have a brother."

"I have a brother?" She placed a hand on the table for support.

"A brother named Jason."

She placed the other hand on the table. "Why didn't they keep us together?"

"A couple wanted you right away, but not him. They wanted a little girl. You were lucky to have those loving parents pick you in the first few weeks at the orphanage."

"Where were you and the rest of the family?"

"Your mother had changed her name. By the time we were notified, you had been with the family for five years. So we all thought it best that you stayed with the only family you knew. They would keep an eye on you."

"Why didn't they watch him like they watched me?"

"Human error," said Fergus. "His paperwork was lost at the orphanage."

"What about DNA?"

"They tested all the kids; they believe he was shipped off to another orphanage as soon as you both arrived there."

The whole thing felt surreal. Sometimes she forgot that Fergus was her grandfather. To her, he became more like a friend. The only one to tell her of the long-lost brother she had never heard so much as one word about. *Why did not Fergus tell me before? The Director must have known. Someone should have said something to me before now.*

"I am going to find him," she said, and started to pace. She seemed like she would walk through a wall to keep that promise. "I need to talk to the director. I have to get out of here."

"Stop, Lauren. Your emotions are getting the best of you," said Fergus. He stood up and placed a hand on her shoulder. "It has been discussed. The Director believes it is in the best interests of all, that if he is alive, he finds you. You know it is not safe for you out there, and you could led the killers to him. Then they shall kill the both of you."

Why is he being like this? Lauren wondered, when she watched her grandfather. *He is not a sad old man; he is a fucking hard-ass sexist bastard. Is he just glad he has a male heir?*

"How is he supposed to find me in here?" She asked, and raised her hands.

"Girl," Fergus said, "This place is not as invisible as you think. Besides, you could spend years searching for him. It is for your own good."

INK

Lauren sat down with him, still, her head was buzzing. *I will not be stopped. One way or another, I will find him, and no one would tell me different,* she thought, while Fergus continued to talk. Nevertheless, she realized Fergus was right; if she stepped outside the compound, there would be a good chance the killer would find her.

"Walk with me," said Fergus.

The two of them took a walk together into the rec room of the cafeteria building, or the Cantina, as the agents called it. He talked all the way, and Lauren listened, still, her mind raced with thoughts. Two men played eight ball, and two others were playing Ping-Pong. Board games were stacked on flimsy steel shelving near two black sofas. Fergus still had the cup of tea in his liver-spotted hand, however, it had gone cold while he talked. They were in the middle of the Cantina when it hit Lauren.

"Oh," she heard herself say, her voice distant. It came to her. She knew how she would find her brother.

"Now is not the time. Maybe someday—"

"I need to use the bathroom. Goodnight, Granddad." She cut him off, and ran for the door.

"Girl has a bladder the size of a fly," he said. She was out the door and raced towards the end of the building, down the narrow iron-grate stairs, and out into the night of the compound. She raced across the bare rock and sand to the dormitory building, where she entered her apartment, snatched the framed photo, pulled the back off, and held up the tile. It was the first time the tile had given her joy, and she smiled. Carefully, she stuck the tile in her jacket pocket and then left the apartment. She made sure no one saw her, when she stealthily managed to navigate the three floors of the complex, up onto the roof. She searched around and saw no one, and then pulled out her tile. She stuck a pin into her finger, and it bled onto the tile.

"Find my brother, Jason," she said, and stretched out her arm with the tile in her hand. Red-winged blackbirds majestically protruded from the tile, came to life, and took flight. Against the Californian smog covered, red desert moonlight, they fanned out

in seventy-seven different directions, and seemed like a swarm of
bats.

INK

CHAPTER TWELVE

Electrodes flashed and sparked, which illuminated the laboratory. Vials and containers of eerie, glowing liquid bubbled and spat. A large Ouija board was on the floor. On the right of the room, was a refrigeration system. On the left, was an autopsy suite with two exam tables, and at the end, was a door and elevator next to a spiral staircase. Animals were in cages on both sides of the room. There was a bear, bat, raven, owl, black and white cats, a dog, hare, hyena, and leopard. In fish-tanks were snakes, spiders, toads, tortoises, lizards, salamanders, and squid; it was a small-scale zoo.

On benches were IV bags full of blood, ink, test tubes, Bunsen burners, and potions boiled. Word had spread very fast that Karen Smith was seen in the building. Her imminent arrival made Cohen, the resident scientist, uptight and irritable. His hands shook while he tried to measure liquid into a test tube. Coke-bottle eyeglasses perched on his long nose, while he wore a white lab coat and high-top Converse shoes, in his attempt to "fit in."

Cohen's assistant, Vernon, seemed downright alarmed when he was informed that Karen would arrive shortly. Vernon cleaned the lab from top to bottom. He polished the Ouija board and hastily cleaned the animal cages. When he awaited her arrival, he checked his notes. "Does my coat appear clean?" Vernon fretted. "I have been wearing this all day. I shall change into a clean one. You had better put on new clothes. Your jacket has a crease in it." Vernon changed into a clean lab coat.

Cohen had rarely seen Karen, however, understood she was in command. Anxious about how annoyed she might be for the lack of progress, he tried not to think about her. Cohen's last encounter with Karen had ended with her criticizing Cohen's work in front of the group. In addition, she had scolded him for the lack of progress on the X-one-nine project. Cohen ran his index finger nervously over his mouth.

"Do you know how long she shall be staying?" Vernon yelled across the room. "No," said Cohen. He did not want to think of that. This could be uncomfortable. If she stayed long, they would pass one another in the halls and dine at the same table. How would they work together? She entered the room, with Ricardo two steps behind her. The animals instinctively backed away from the imposing woman, and a deathly quiet swept through the laboratory. Several of the animals ran to the back of their cages in a frenzy.

"...Kiko is placing the toner in the store room —," said Ricardo.

He was cut off by Karen, who asked Cohen, "Where are we on the X-one-nine?" When she walked up to him.

He stopped pouring liquid into a test tube. "We have not discovered the reactor yet," Cohen said.

Annoyed, she asked, "When was my ink fed?" Standing amidst the broken and twisted carcasses of animals near the Ouija board.

Cohen squirmed when he said, "Eleven days ago."

A cute, fluffy white kitten was missing its right front leg. It lay wounded on an experiment table. It had electrodes attached to it and wires extended into the missing leg stump. She clutched it by the neck while it struggled in vain.

"Why are you not fusing?" She lifted the kitten off its feet by its throat. The cat cried out when she squeezed its neck. It scratched at her black glove until they heard a gruesome *CRACKING* sound. The kitten went limp. Karen tossed the dead cat at a painting of animals. It bounced off and landed on the floor near a deceased toad that lay upside down by a red-winged blackbird and a mouse. She eyed Cohen.

"Show me the codes and dosage."

Cohen scurried to get the information from Vernon, who had it in his hand. Nervously, Cohen presented it to her and stood back. Karen read it and then backhanded Vernon, who crashed to the floor in a disheveled heap.

INK

"I ordered six milligrams of fibroblasts, not five point seven. Science is measurement! How many times must I say it? Check twice, pour once!" Karen turned to Cohen, who backed away from the outraged woman, tripped on a chair, and fell to the floor. She bent over, her white miniskirt rose up, and flashed a red G-string. There were tattoos on her lower left cheek and one on her lower right cheek. Combined, the tattoos said, *Pay Me*. Vernon's eyes almost popped out of his head at her sexy ass. He thought to himself, *Was Karen a call girl? Maybe when she was younger*, nevertheless, that excited him to know she had a dark, wild and perhaps debaucherous past. He felt privileged, like a preteen seeing up the teacher's skirt. Not only did he see her ass, however, knew she had a tattoo on it.

"And that is why we are behind. I am surrounded by incompetence," she said.

Cohen nodded reassuringly. "There has been some progress."

"Yes," said Karen. "We have found nine hundred seventy-eight ways it did not work. If I had never lost my notes in the fire, I could be summoning anything from the ink by now. I would also have no need for you two morons." She took a deep breath and thought of the time she spent working with the ink, the science and the black magic. The intricately refined organizational mechanics, over a hundred chemical compounds, ninety-four organic herbs, and twenty-three magic potions, along with thousands of in-process experiments, all gone in one fire. Her countless decades of research in the printmaking, biological, academic, and industrial for this elaborate yet complex piece of work was essential.

"Perhaps, Cohen, your talents lie in the construction of biological terror with the ability to destroy." She forced Cohen down over a bench, attacking, with the needle of a syringe, at his cheek, near his eye.

"I find your lack of progress disturbing," she hissed. "This is the second time it has troubled me." She considered Vernon, and smiled at him. "Vernon, want to head the X-one-nine project?"

"Y-y-y-" he stuttered, "y-y-y-yes bo—"

INK

"Get it out, you stuttering fuck! See, Cohen, I can easily replace you." She nearly jabbed the needle into Cohen when she noticed Vernon had wet himself.

"It would be faster if we could test on humans. By using a steroid enhancer, we could increase the male's occipital lobe to two times its normal size," Cohen said, in an attempt to save his life, while he trembled in fear.

Karen snapped upright. "To harvest more brain cells!" She grinned, like a shark. "Exactly. That will reactivate human brain cells stored in the cerebellum."

Vernon cleared his throat. "G-g-g-genetic engineering to increase brain mass violates the Harvard Genetics Compact. Not to mention the Chimera policy."

Karen squirted the green slime from the syringe at him, and he quickly moved to avoid it. She rolled her eyes. "The ship is in international waters. Speak when you are spoken to, you stuttering fuck."

Cohen swallowed. "It is an international law. It is illegal, that's why I haven't tried it."

Karen's smile faded. "Are you having a crisis of conscience? Listen, doctor Frankenstein, if it was not for me, you would not be practicing science at all. You would be back in jail." Cohen moved around the table away from her, still, she got back in his face again.

"I just wanted to make sure, you knew all of the facts," said Cohen.

"You may be doing the work, but I am in command. I do not care how you do it, just get the results." Karen then eyed Ricardo and ordered, "Bring in our favorite guinea pig."

The packed auditorium buzzed in anticipation. Brian Maddox was the most talked-about and celebrated fighter of the season. Not to many knew about the kid he was to face, however, everyone expected Brian to destroy him. They called Brian "the Bomber," because he would rain his fists like bombs onto his opponent. CEOs with hookers, gangsters, fathers, and sons filled the auditorium. The few women held onto their dates for dear life. Cheers and applause rose from the spectators. They clapped extra loudly when Jack Travis, a famous country singer, led his long red-haired girlfriend to the front row seats. The microphone descended from the ceiling to a bald man with a natty bow tie who stood in the center of the ring. For a little man, he had a booming voice.

"Ladies and gentlemen! Our main event! Standing at six foot one, with a thirty-inch reach, weighing two hundred twenty pounds, fighting out of the Crichenko Fighting Gym in Longhorn Texas with state championship belts in boxing, karate, judo, jujitsu, taekwondo, wrestling, and now making his UFC debut, Jason 'the Cowboy' Crawford!" Country music with a twang of hard rock began to play. From the shadows of a tunnel, Jason emerged in a white robe and cowboy hat, followed by Oleg, Moses, and some of the regular members of the gym. He scanned the faces in the crowd like he was searching for someone. He shook hands, hi-fived some of the audience members, entered the ring, and scrutinized the crowd. Chelsea and Angela sat in the front row; they saw a shark tattoo on his calf muscle and an axe on his left leg. He saw them and tipped his hat. Angela blushed for no apparent reason. The crowd chanted, "Cowboy up."

Jason saw Mao with Frog in a corner and they walked over to him. Mao handed him a picture.

"Good to see you son," said Mao. Jason saw the picture. It was a black-and-white of a young Lauren, wearing an overcoat, held a doll, and appeared uncomfortably squished. Jason's arm was around her, in a protective manor. It was taken in front of the orphanage.

"Where is Mom?" Jason asked.

"She died two years ago," said Mao.

Jason calculated that Mary would have been 49 years old. He then suspected Mao had killed her from one of his beatings, and then covered it up. Jason studied him, and could see guilt in Mao's eyes. *The husband, he should of protected her and she should have left him after the first beating,* he thought. Both were at fault, however, she was the only mother he ever knew—the only woman who showed him kindness.

INK

"Come near me again, and I will kill ya," Jason said, to Mao. The response from Mao was an expression that insinuated, "After all I did for you?" Then Mao turned and walked out of the ring.

"Cowboy up!" swamped the auditorium from passionate fight fans that read/watched UFC, MMA and underground fights, those who knew of Jason's capability. Still, the majority of the crowd yelled "Bom---ber." Stretching it (Bom-Cowboyup-ber) in a calculated shelling fashion. In the back row, a large white hat partially covered Karen. Ricardo was on her right side, and Kiko flanked her left.

She leaned towards Ricardo and whispered, "He has gotten bigger. We will need some more men."

The announcer proclaimed, "His opponent stands at six foot four, with a thirty-two-inch reach, weighing two hundred sixty five pounds, fighting out of the Bomber Fighting Gym in Phoenix, Arizona with a fight record of twenty-seven and one, Brian 'the Bomber' Maddox!"

Jason's song faded, and a Metallica song began. Maddox made his way to the ring; he had on a black robe with a hood, and he focused on Jason without acknowledging the crowd at all.

Jason gave the picture to Oleg, who passed it to Moses. A smile appeared on Moses' face before he slipped it into his pocket. Jason stripped to only his white trunks and met the referee and Maddox in the center of the ring. Maddox stared down Jason.

"The guy's as big as a dinosaur." Angela said.

The referee warned, "I want a good, clean fight. Shake hands, go back to your corner, and come out fighting."

Jason walked to his corner.

"He's bigger than you, so keep moving," muttered Oleg. The bell rang.

"Just stick and move," said Oleg, when Jason walked into the center of the ring. "He's gonna get killed." Oleg said to Moses, who stood by with a spit bucket.

The fighters met in the ring and started to feel one another out. They clenched together in a wrestling move. When Maddox head-butted, Jason landed on the floor.

INK

The referee stopped the fight. "Illegal head butt. One point deduction, Maddox." The fight restarted and Jason avoided Maddox, while he tried to get his bearings. The punches landed by Jason barely affected Maddox. The bell rang. Both fighters went to their corners. Oleg nodded. "Your movement is good. A few more rounds and he is yours."

Jason rubbed his hands together. "My punches aren't doing anything."

Oleg shook his head. "That is what he wants you to think. They are hurting him."

"You think?" Jason asked.

"Oh, yeah."

The bell rang. Jason hopped off the seat full off energy and continued the fight pumped-up. Moses looked at Oleg. Then Oleg shrugged his shoulders like "I don't know." Jason landed a kick on Maddox's right thigh. Maddox punched Jason across the face at the same time. Jason flew through the air, and landed on the floor of the ring. The crowd cheered. Maddox raised his arms like he had won. Jason lay on the ground near Oleg, groggy and blinking.

Oleg leaned over to him. "Are you okay?"

Jason sniffed and spit. "Yeah, nothing is broken."

Oleg growled, "I am going to throw in the towel."

Jason smiled through bloody teeth. "No, no. I have him right where I want him."

"You are on your back!"

"I know. I am resting."

"When you are done resting, we have a fight to finish."

"What is the rush? I am having fun," said Jason, when he slowly got to his feet. By now, he was injured and the referee directed him to his corner to patch a cut above his eyebrow that bled profusely. The trainer worked on the cut, and patched it. Oleg got in Jason's face. "Use your ground game now. Keep moving and you will not get tagged like that again. Stay away from his right."

Jason went back to fighting. He proceeded with caution this time. Maddox became frustrated and swung arbitrarily. He followed Jason around the ring.

INK

Moses scratched his head. "What is he doing?"

"Setting him up," said Oleg.

Maddox stopped and taunted him several times by sticking out his jaw. Jason anticipated a taunt, and punched him on the chin with a right. Maddox stumbled. Blood poured down into Jason's eye, and blinded him temporarily. Jason avoided Maddox's right cross. When it went by, he seized Maddox's neck and pulled himself onto Maddox's back, and locked the bigger man in a choke hold while he locked his legs around his waist. Maddox was in trouble. He tried to pull Jason's arm off with both hands, using all his strength, however, no luck. Then he flipped Jason over his head.

Jason's locked legs around Maddox's waist kept him from flying off. The bigger man then fell onto his back, which slammed Jason onto the floor. Jason hung on. Maddox could not breathe and lost his strength very fast. The crowd yelled, "Cowboy up" in thunderous unison. The fight clock waned down—three seconds, then two, and then one. The bell rang and Jason released him. Maddox held his neck, and breathed feverishly when he stumbled to his corner.

A glossy commentator spoke into a microphone, "Saved by the clock. Excellent fighting from Crawford. Great fighting from both. That last move, the rear naked choke hold from the Cowboy, came out of nowhere, but Maddox is fighting better."

Another commentator chimed in and said, "Maddox was lucky."

The first commentator snorted derisively, "Are you crazy?"

In Jason's corner, Moses refreshed the bandage on Jason's cut, while Oleg spoke strategy. "You have to attack now. Hit the body. Do not let him breathe. Be fast. Use the combinations. Try to keep him off balance. Change it up. He is struggling to breathe."

Maddox was slumped in his chair and held his neck. His trainer talked, yet, did not get any response from him. The bell rang. Both fighters met in the center of the ring again. Jason was on the attack, and connected with punches and kicks. He swept the legs out from under Maddox, that crashed him to the mat. Jason went in to finish Maddox, however, was kicked in the face, landed on the mat, and gasped for air. The referee stopped the fight and stood both fighters up.

The referee gestured abruptly. "Illegal move, kick to the face. One point deduction, Maddox."

The fight resumed. Even though both threw jabs, at one another, neither landed any punches. Then one of Jason's punches landed, hitting Maddox in the head and he fell forward onto the mat, face first. Jason went to his corner. Maddox did not move. The referee raised Jason's arm in victory. Oleg hugged Jason.

"Eat me alive, hey?" Jason said to Oleg, with a I showed you attitude. Maddox's trainer called out in panic. Two emergency medical technicians ran into the ring to revive him. Jason, concerned, went to the fighter's side.

INK

INK

In the morning, Jason was in his hotel room, and strummed a guitar, while he sat on a sofa. Last night's fight had left him with a black eye and a cut above his eyebrow. There was three *KNOCKS!* on the door. He opened it to Angela.

"Ma'am…" Jason said before he was cut off.

"Have you seen this?" She asked, and stroked his bruised face. "Nice shiner."

Angela held up a newspaper and gave it to him. The front page headline "Brian Maddox Dies." She entered the room, followed by Chelsea, who pushed a room-service cart with food.

Jason stared at the headline. "Maddox is dead?"

"Yeah, 3:47 a.m. I hope you do not mind I took the liberty of ordering breakfast," said Angela.

Before Jason could close the door, Oleg ran in. "You see what you have done?"

Jason dropped the paper. "I just heard…"

Oleg growled, "You killed Maddox."

Angela pleaded, "I can help…"

"Shut up, bimbo. This will ruin me," Oleg said, while he held his head in his hands.

Jason ran his hands through his hair and said, "I aimed for his cheek but I caught him high."

"The punch hit his temple," said Angela.

Oleg punched an unsuspecting Jason, and he landed on the floor.

Angela scowled, "Stop that or I shall call the police."

Oleg stood at Jason's feet. "I told you this was a bad idea. You are fired. I do not want to see you around my gym anymore." He stormed out of the room.

"Are you okay?" Angela asked, when she pulled Jason up by the hand.

INK

"I have had better mornings," said Jason, while he held his jaw.

"You are going to need help. I am a lawyer." She placed a business card on a table.

"How?" Jason asked.

"Blood clot, brain hemorrhage," Angela retorted.

Chelsea poured some coffee from the cart.

Angela exhaled and said, "I shall need to see your fight contracts. There must be a disclaimer. We also have the one punch murder defense to fall back on."

Jason took the business card off the table and wrote something on it. "Why do you want to help?"

Chelsea interjected, "That is what I would like to know. We are supposed to be on vacation; hanging out by the pool, working on my tan, drinking, meeting guys, and dancing the night away."

Jason went into the bedroom.

"Karma," said Angela. "If it were not for him, we would not be in Vegas. He helped us when we were stranded out in the desert. Now we can help him." She snuck a peek inside Jason's bedroom and saw his naked butt while he tried to pull up his jeans, hopped on one leg, lost his balance, and then fell over. Angela laughed.

Chelsea whispered to Angela, "And the fact that you want to jump on his penis has nothing to do with it?"

"That is silly," said Angela.

Chelsea said, "Its Karma alright… Karma over here." She pointed to Angela's crotch. Chelsea and Angela struggled to keep from laughing. Jason came out of the bedroom with his leather saddle bags slung over his shoulder.

"You want to help? Find out where Maddox's widow lives and text the address to this number," said Jason. Then he gave Angela her business card back with a phone number scribbled on it.

"Ungrateful pig. We just ordered breakfast for you," said Chelsea.

Jason was annoyed and stormed towards her. Backpedaling, she fell over the sofa. Her head on the floor, and her back was on the sofa. Jason walked around the sofa and eyed her, red in the face with anger.

"I've already had breakfast. Be respectful and you will not find yourself in these positions," he stated, and then exited the room.

Chelsea's legs dangled in the air, over the back of the sofa.

"Angela, can you help me?"

Jason exited the hotel into the blast of the Vegas sun, squinted to protect his eyes, and searched for his Harley. He was a little frazzled until he found it parked near the valet. An attractive reporter shoved a microphone in his face.

"Mr. Crawford, how do you feel about the death of Brian Maddox?"

Jason walked toward his Harley. "It is a tragedy that should never have happened."

Another cute female reporter asked, "Did you know Mr. Maddox personally?" When more of the press pounced on him.

Jason shook his head. "No. I admired him from afar."

A slimy reporter pushed his way through all the others and said, "Stop with the fluff questions. The state may press murder or manslaughter charges against you."

Jason started his Harley, and then lifted his voice to be heard above the rumble. "Everyone has a job to do."

Jason rode out of the casino between the spraying water fountains. He rode through the city, and then out southeast to Henderson. He took a brief pit stop at Kingman, and ate lunch—a steak sandwich and a beer at a truck stop. Filled his tank, stuffed two large bottles of water in his saddle bags, and then headed back out. It was not long before he came upon a road sign partially covered by a cactus tree that read "Entering Arizona." Jason cruised past it. The day light combined with the Arizona smog and haze turned the color of the sun red, as it set on the horizon. Fatigue started to set in when he saw the "Entering Phoenix" sign.

The colors of a large street were vibrant at dusk. Jason pulled up to a house on the Harley and checked a text on his phone. Then he buzzed the doorbell. It opened to Ashley, a plain Jane, with mousy hair in a bun and smudged mascara. She wore a tank-top and tracksuit pants. Brian's high school sweetheart, who had let herself go after she had a child. When she saw Jason, she closed the door immediately.

"Ma'am. Mrs. Maddox. Ashley, may I call you Ashley? I am sorry. I didn't mean to kill anyone."

Through a crack in the chain linked door, Ashley peered out at him, red-eyed from crying and said, "Get away or I will call the police." Then she shut the door.

Jason's face crumpled, "Can you talk to me? Please."

Ashley started crying. "I swear. I will call the police."

"Well, it would not be the first time." He sat down with his back to the door. "I am just going to sit here until you talk to me."

"What do you want to talk about? You killed my husband."

"I want to apologize."

"I do not want your apology."

Jason's phone rang. He answered it.

"You have been charged with manslaughter. They have issued a warrant," said Angela on the other end.

"Okay, I will turn myself in," he said, and then hung up. He pulled out some paper and wrote something on it.

Ashley screamed from the kitchen, "He didn't want to fight you. He said the younger guys were dangerous because they have more to prove. I will not open that door, so you can stay out there all night."

Jason, dejected, slid the paper under the door and walked away.

INK

Two prison guards held shotguns and stood vigil in the processing room at the Tucson jail when Jason entered. *How did I get myself into this?* He thought, when he stripped off his clothes. *These chemicals must be cancerous,* while they sprayed him with disinfectant. *No one better be looking at my junk,* when he showered with four other men. He didn't even finish toweling off before a guard threw him a jail uniform; orange shirt with orange pants. Once he had those on, the guard gave him a blanket, a towel, a bar of soap, and then clutched Jason's arm and directed him to a cell.

"Remember me?" Asked the guard.

Jason searched his face and said, "No sir."

"We were in the same orphanage. I am Chip Seybold."

Jason smiled and said, "Chip, you have changed. I didn't even recognize you. You see Tom?"

"No. He went off with a New York family, last I heard," Chip said, and asked, "You seen Moses?"

"Yeah, he was at my last fight."

As Jason entered his cell, Chip hit him across the head with a baton.

"What the fuck?" Jason asked, when he sidestepped the swinging baton. He took hold of Chip by the throat and shoved him up against the wall.

"What is your problem?" Jason's vision was going in and out.

"I knew I would catch up with you someday. You are going to pay for all the beatings you gave me."

"We were kids. Sorry."

"I do not care."

"I want us to be friends."

"Fuck you," said Chip. "Your ass is mine."

INK

"I could kill your right now," said Jason, and then slowly released him. Chip held his throat and gasped for air, when he stumbled out of the cell. Jason held his head in pain, even though the cut bled a little. He sat on the bed. It was not long before three large men entered his cell, and blocked the door.

The leader, who had Swastikas, Nazi SS, death's heads, and white power tattoos covering his body, stuck out his hand and said, "Sonny Stockton, leader of the Aryan Brotherhood." Jason shook his hand. "We are big fans of yours Crawford. Heard about your cowboy fights. Anyway, Niggers are trying to recruit everyone they can."

"What is up?" Jason asked.

"We are going to make a move on them. Control this mother," said Stockton.

"I just want to do my time. Not get involved," said Jason.

Stockton thought a tad and said, "We are expecting you to be with us when this shit goes down. You are part of the brotherhood, Crawford. Do not forget your roots." He pointed his finger into Jason's chest. They exited. Jason felt weary so he dropped his head into the pillow and fell asleep.

Two days later, Chip directed Jason through a corridor. Jason was concerned he was being set up to get beat-up. He scanned the hallways, and felt that at any moment he would be jumped.

Chip asked, "Enjoying jail life yet?"

"I will never enjoy jail life," said Jason, when they reached the end of the corridor and
turned left into another corridor—this one with a door at the end.

"Don't worry. You will get used to it," said Chip, when he opened the door to the visitor's room. Angela sat in a glassed-off cubical. Jason sat across from her and picked up the handset on his side. She picked up the phone.

"Ma'am. What are you doing here?" Jason asked.

"I was hoping they shaved you so I could see what you looked like clean-cut," said Angela.

"I will show you mine if you show me yours," he said.

She smiled and then noticed the fresh cut on Jason's forehead. "Why have you not posted bond?"

Jason hunched his shoulders, "These days I have more time than money."

She asked, "Would you like me to post bond?"

Jason smiled. "No, but thank you for your kindness. I got myself into this mess; I have to get myself out."

"Okay. I am preparing your case and could use some help," she said, when she pulled out a legal folder and placed it in front of herself. It was titled "State of Nevada Versus Jason Crawford," and then another folder titled "Prospective Jurors." She pulled out a list of possible jurors: Mr. Arthur Anderson, machinist, fifty-eight; Mrs. Joann Burk, homemaker, forty-two; Mr. Roger Abrams, chemist, fifty-nine, etc. Angela piled the table with books and folders.

"Who is Dick McGregor?" She asked. "He is on the prosecution's witness list."

"I don't know," Jason said, and then asked, "Who do we have?"

"We have a doctor Young, who said Maddox's heart condition means doctor Epstein should not have given him the cortisone shot. Plus, he found three different steroids in his blood."

"Doc's not bad."

"State should drop the charges just with the doctors testimony. The jury's going to love him."

"Judge?"

"That is not good news," said Angela.

"Do what you can."

"It is not you they are after."

Jason scowled and said, "Who are they after, the Dalai Lama?"

Angela laughed. "They are after the UFC. They want to ban it from the state. They say the sport of boxing is behind it. They want to convict you, so they can bring more lawsuits against the UFC. 32 states ban UFC fights." She ran a hand through her hair. "Oleg is on the witness list."

"What am I looking at if we lose?"

"They want twenty-five years."

"That kinda sucks," said Chip venomously. Chip had heard all of it and smirked at them. "Visiting time is over. Let's go, cowboy."

Chip dragged Jason out of the room. Angela wanted the guard's badge number, however, decided against it. This was a very sticky situation, and her concerns grew by the minute. The fresh cut on Jason's forehead was not deep, still, it was new—*he needs to survive not only the inmates but perhaps also the guards?* She thought.

The stock room was full of pallets of food, cleaning supplies, linen, an air conditioning unit, boilers, furnaces, and sump pumps. Jason hefted a cardboard drum of detergent off the stack and rolled it toward the door, and then he saw Chip block his way—swinging a baton. Jason stopped rolling the drum. Another guard loomed from the shadows to his right, and another on the left.

"Last man I punched, I killed. I do not wanna hit any of you," Jason said, when he backed up, and tried to maneuver through the maze.

"We will be the ones doing the hitting," said Chip, while he and the guards kept coming, swung their batons, and tried to outflank him. Jason tripped one of them, flipped another, and tossed Chip without hitting any of them; they landed in different parts of the room. The three guards stood up and rushed Jason. The same thing happened, however, Jason fell this time, and that was all it took. They pounced on him in an instant, bludgeoning, kicking, and stomping. Once the three guards were exhausted, they left the room. Jason struggled to get off the floor and to his feet. He was bloody, and struggled to catch his breath.

"Not hitting back does not seem to work," said Jason when Mohamed Elijah, the leader of the Black Panthers, entered with three other mean-faced men. Jason squared off.

"Easy cowboy. We just want to talk," Elijah said.

"This is white turf," said Jason.

"Whitey was not around when you were in trouble. Looks like Boss Seybold's taken a shine to you," said Mohamed.

INK

Jason through bloody teeth said, "What is it to ya?"

"We are all brothers in this war," Elijah said.

"Not interested in joining any gangs," said Jason.

Elijah interrupted. "No one wants to join a gang; they have to. Survival, my brother! Be with us and we will protect ya. If you want to survive!" They left. Blood from Jason's mouth poured out onto the floor after they were gone.

Four Aryan Brotherhood members showered in the bathroom when Jason purposely walked in. He washed up quickly with one eye open, and then shampooed his hair. When the steam had cleared, he was all alone. *This is not good,* he thought. With soap still in his hair, he urgently rinsed, and quickly dried himself off, however, found Hector Avila, leader of the Mexican Mafia, with three of his muscle men. They blocked the exit/entrance.

"What up, homes?"

Jason stood ready to defend himself.

"Mr. Hector Avila," said Jason, while he scanned all four men for weapons.

"I hear you are part Mexican," said Hector.

Jason smiled and said, "I hear you are part white and black."

Hector smiled and said, "Don't care if you are or ain't. You need to ask yourself, where are the Nazis, when you are in trouble. Who is setting who up? We know you been asked to join the niggers and the Nazis in their upcoming cleansing. We like you, cowboy. We heard about you. You are a good fighter, so we figure you should know that we Mexicans are going to take out both. If you are on the wrong side, things could get real bad for you."

"I see. Well, I am flattered by the offer," said Jason.

"Choose wisely," said Hector, when he exited, follow by his men.

The high stone walls of the jail were topped with snaky, concertina barbed wire. Guards held shotguns while they cruised along the walls, and manned towers loomed above. Convicts in the exercise yard, made deals, played catch, and shuffled cards, while the hot Arizona sun beat down on them. When Jason

INK

lifted 200 pounds on a bench press, one of Stockton's Aryans walked past him and nodded. He stopped pumping iron and sat up. *It is going down,* thought Jason. All the cons fell into their respective groups. The whites eyeballed the blacks, and the Mexicans eyeballed both.

Knives, grappling hooks, knuckle dusters, metal, and Plexiglas shivs came out of crucifixes, shirt sleeves, and pockets. Jason searched for the guards. They had all turned their backs in an attempt to allow it to happen. The time had come.

Whites against the blacks, and the Mexicans plan to blindside both, pondered Jason. *One wrong decision can get you killed. Which way do I go?*

A mass of cons had circled Jason, and he found himself in the center with Stockton, Elijah, and Avila who watched him.

"Get over here," ordered Stockton.

Jason considered him, then saw Elijah, who stared hard at him, and then at Avila, who had his head tilted up, toothpick in his mouth, with a "dare you to join them" expression on his face. The cons in the sunburst yard began to break out in a full-blown sweat from the heat and adrenalin. All watched, and waited for Jason's decision.

"CRAWFORD!" yelled Chip, when he entered the yard, sporting mirrored aviator sunglasses, and held a shotgun across his chest.

"Crawford," Chip said, again. The mass of cons spread out, so Jason could see him by a doorway. *Oh, no, Chip has a gun,* thought Jason.

Chip took his time and finally said, "Get over here."

Jason went over to Chip, while the gangs eyed his every step. Chip pumped his shotgun, and then said, "Follow me."

He headed for a different building, and Jason followed. All three gangs watched them, and the tension mounted with every step they took. *Is Chip going to shoot me,* thought Jason. Cautiously, they arrived at a door. Chip opened it.

"Get in."

Jason entered the dark building, followed by Chip, who shut the sunburst yard out when he closed and locked the door. Chip directed Jason through the tangled maze of rooms and corridors.

INK

Jason was on high alert. *I am going to get jumped. Crack your knuckles, prepare your fists, and stretch your neck. This corner has potential for an ambush. Stay on the balls of your feet.* Chip was very quiet. *Something is definitely going down.* He expected an ambush to come from every door and corner. Each step was nimble, tense, and ready to bounce into fight mode.

Chip opened a door to the intake room. Angela waited there with a briefcase.

Chip said, "She posted bail."

"I had to. Officer Chip Seybold here called to tell me what was happening," said Angela.

Jason thought, *ha, Chip probably saved my life. Don't make a big thing of it, even though it is. He is a man, and you are a man.* He regarded Chip. "Thanks friend." He stuck out his hand and Chip shook it. "That was nice of ya."

"Say hello to Moses," Chip said.

Jason smiled and said, "I will. Look me up if you are ever in town."

"Okay," Chip said, and then exited the room.

Jason went over to a window with a slit at the bottom where a release form waited for him. Jason signed the release and collected his possessions. Then another guard escorted him and Angela out to a tunnel. It had welded-wire, mesh-fence panels so small that no one could climb, cut, or destroy the fence. They had to cross the jail yard in plain view of all the prisoners.

"This is scary," said Angela.

"You can say that again."

"What now?"

"I need to find a job, and pay you back," said Jason.

On the high stone wall of the jail, one of Lauren's red-winged blackbirds sat perched. It watched Jason walk across the jail yard, exit the jail, hop into Angela's Jaguar, and drive off. Then it followed, from up high in the sky.

INK

INK

CHAPTER FIFTEEN

The San Francisco street was crowded with business types going to and fro. At 10:00 am in the morning, the city buzzed with life. It was a nice, warm, sunny day. Ricardo and Kiko were in the archway of the door to a pawn shop, and saw a guitar. Inconspicuous, they stepped out of the archway and followed a man who wore a cowboy hat. Not a difficult feat in a sea of city slickers. The hat stopped, and then Ricardo and Kiko could see Jason read a sign that said "Now Hiring Security" in a store window. Ricardo and Kiko scanned the store. It was called, The Branding Iron. It was a cowboy bar with swinging saloon doors, smack dab in the midst of the city.

Jason entered the establishment and walked into an empty reception area, and then continued through another set of saloon doors. He scanned the room, while the two saloon doors swung to a stop. It was a strip club with a long bar, pool tables, and three stages. Two with stripper poles. The club also had a mechanical bull.

Jason chuckled. "Oh, yeah. Cowboy up!" He saw a group on stage—a three-piece band deep in conversation, and made his way over to them. On the white bass drum, the name "The Kuss" was scripted in black ink.

Aaron shrugged, "I don't know where he is."

"Did you call him?" Mitch asked.

"Yeah! He is not answering."

Mitch picked his teeth with a fingernail, "Well, what are we going to do?"

"Hey, you guys work here?" Jason asked.

"Yeah, I am Aaron," He was a young, handsome, lanky guitarist. "This is Mitch," pointed to an older large-bellied bassist. "And Bang-bang is on the drums." A black beefy guy, the same age as Mitch.

INK

Jason nodded hello to all and said, "I am here for the security position."

"Oh, I thought you were one of Abrahams friends. Go see him through those curtains." Aaron said, and jerked a thumb over his shoulder.

"Thank you, sir," Jason said, and walked toward a hallway lined with a brown curtain.

"Why did you think he knew the Boss," Mitch asked.

"Don't know. Just did. Watch this," said Aaron to both and pointed to Jason. Aaron, Mitch and Bang-bang kept an eye on him. When Jason went near the curtain, he noticed two chairs on each side of it and stopped. *Those seem out of place. Why are two chairs there? Be careful.* Jason stepped inside, and a punch came from his right. He avoided it and seized the wrist, while another man kicked at Jason's crotch. Jason clutched his ankle and dragged both men out. He then sat them down in the chairs as if they were light as air.

Jason exhaled. "Give me a minute, guys."

Tyrone, a Denzel Washington type, and Rocco, an Italian sort, nodded. Jason eyed Aaron and his band mates. The smirks on their faces dissolved, and they busied themselves with their instruments to play it off. Jason went back into the curtained hallway and followed a light that came from an open door to a seedy, disorganized office. Abraham, a tall African American, was styling in a blue shirt with long sleeves, and suspenders which held up his pleated pants. Abraham poured from a whiskey bottle into a large water glass and downed it. Jason took off his hat and watched him for a moment.

Abraham mocked, when he glanced at his college degrees that hung on the wall. He picked them off the wall and threw them into the wastebasket. Mumbled to himself, "Wasted youth. Means nothing. The whole thing is pointless. What is the use?" Jason had witnessed enough.

"Sorry to bother you, sir," he said. "I am here for the security position."

Abraham nodded, "You startled me. Sit. I shall be right with you. First man to get past my people all week. So, who are you and why do you want to work here?"

INK

"Jason Crawford. I am good at this line of work, sir," said Jason, and he sat in a stylish burgundy Greek Key Klismos chair.

"It can get wild out there some nights," said Abraham briskly, and topped off his glass. "You have insurance? We only pay after the qualifying period of three months."

Jason did not have insurance. "I shall take care of myself, sir," he said.

Jason could sense a lot more was going on. He witnessed Abraham down another shot. *Maybe the man just has a drinking problem.* The wind blew through the office window, and furled the curtain which caused a *RUSTLING* noise. Abraham pulled out a gold-plated Glock 21 pistol from his desk drawer, and aimed it at the window.

"Nice-looking Glock."

Abraham placed the gun on the desk and pointed it towards the window.

"You ever been arrested?" He asked, when he searched through some morning mail. A letter with no return address jumped out at him, so he picked it up. Jason shifted uncomfortably in the chair and said, "Yes sir. They say I killed a man in a fight. At the moment I am in the midst of defending myself in the courts."

Abraham tore open the envelope, with a silver letter opener that appeared more like a dagger. "So you could go to jail?"

Jason ran his fingers through his hair. "Yes, sir."

"Big risk if I hire you and you go to jail. What would be the point of all this?" When he pulled out the letter.

"I understand, sir. I guess it all depends on how many people you have seen."

Abraham viewed the letter and took some time to think about it. "I like you," he said. "Start Monday."

"Thank you, sir." Jason stood up and put his hat on. He walked to the door.

"Fourteen."

Jason scratched his head and said, "Excuse me sir?"

"You are one in fourteen. There have been fourteen applicants who have tried to get past Tyrone and Rocco."

"Well, alright then, sir," he said, and then exited the office.

INK

Abraham tossed the letter on the desk. It read "Pay or die."

The two bouncers by the curtain looked at one another.

Tyrone squinted, deep in thought, and then said, "He seems familiar."

"I have never seen him before," said Rocco.

Jason opened the curtains and made his way through. "Are we okay?" He asked them. He had his arms up, palms open and was ready to defend himself again.

Rocco nodded.

"Just doing our job," Tyrone said.

Jason smiled, "Good. I will be working with you guys."

"That is great, could use some help," Rocco said.

A blues-sounding ROCK RIFF from a guitar caught Jason's attention. On the stage, a guitarist played a solo. Aaron, behind the bar, raised his hand. "Okay, thanks. I will let you know." The guitarist walked off. Aaron turned to another guitarist with long hair who waited in the wings. "You are up." The guitarist plugged in and played a rock song. Jason walked over to Aaron, and noticed the decorative cowboy inlay on the mahogany bar.

"How'd ya do?" Aaron asked him.

"Start Monday," said Jason, and bobbed his head to the beat. "What is going on?"

"I am auditioning new guitarists for my band," said Aaron.

"I play a bit."

"Bring your guitar in some time. Want a drink?"

"I will take a beer."

Mitch and Bang-bang came over while Aaron slid a beer across the bar to Jason. "He is good," said Mitch. The three walked over to the guitarist and he stopped playing.

"If you want the job, it is yours," Aaron said, when he grabbed his own guitar. "Let us do 'Drunk on X.' It is A, E, G." The band began rehearsing.

Jason drank his beer, took out a cell phone, opened an app, and then pressed the "record" button.

Within a few months, the motel lifestyle irritated Jason. Confined to the small spaces made him feel claustrophobic. He saved his money and paid Angela $100 a week for the bond money she put up. Then one day, he walked past a two-story building with a "For Rent" sign. He looked through the window. It had a concrete floor, brick walls, windows all around. It reminded Jason of the gym he was raised in, so he called the phone number on the sign. When Jason asked if he could live there, the owner said the city would not issue him a permit for the building to be livable.

Jason would not take no for an answer. The city does not have to know, he told him. And as far as you know, I would be using it for storage. Jason promised he would spend five thousand dollars in upgrades over the next year with a kitchenette, shower, and insulation. The owner asked him to sign a one-year lease to use the warehouse for storage. Jason did not have all the money for first and last month's rent and a deposit on the building, so he found a few underground fights. He employed a cleaning team that dusted and power-washed the inside of the warehouse, and then he brought in a bed. Jason installed foam insulation because the tin walls provided very little protection from the elements. He read "How-To" books from the library, and built a kitchen and shower in four weeks. Jason practiced his guitar when he could, and learned the Kuss's songs that he had recorded on his phone in no time.

Vibrant-colored rose flowers lined Arroyo Avenue in Pasadena. The streets were clean with manicured lawns, and the smallest property was one acre. *Wealthy neighborhood,* Jason thought, when he rode up to one of the properties. He parked the Harley and checked the address twice; he stood in front of a mansion. He then walked up to the gate, thinking, *"I hope she did grow up here."* The gate had a camera intercom, and Jason pressed the button to transmit.

A teenager's voice crackled over the intercom. "Yes?"

Jason nervously scratched his face, and then spoke awkwardly into the intercom. "Sorry to bother you. My name is Jason Crawford. I was told Lauren Crawford lives here."

"Jason Crawford, the UFC fighter?" The teenager asked, excitedly.

Jason shifted uncomfortably. "Yeah, that is me."

"Come in."

He heard the buzz of an electric motor when the eight-foot green-and-gold steel gates opened. Jason walked the long half-moon driveway that contained a water fountain in the center, and thought *I should have ridden the Harley up.* He made his way to the front door of the mansion and a teenager, the brash, yuppie type, held the front door open. He greeted Jason with excitement. "Jason Crawford. I am a big fan of yours. My name is Chad. You are all over the news. It sucks that the prosecutor is going after you." He spoke fast, like most teenagers. Jason did not know whether to "thank him" for being a fan, simply say "Hello" or "It is nice to meet you." He chose the simpler path.

"Hi. Is Lauren here?"

"Lauren Crawford? No. I do not know anyone by that name. My father purchased this house from the Maylors eight years ago."

Jason quirked an eyebrow. "Maylors?"

"The owner was some big scientist with NASA."

"NASA Texas?"

"No. NASA's jet propulsion lab in Pasadena."

Jason nodded. "Okay. Thanks for your time."

"Before you leave, can I get a photo?" Asked Chad, and raised a camera. "My friends are not going to believe this." Jason agreed, placed an arm around Chad, like they had been longtime friends, and made a fist. Chad snapped a few pictures, and when Jason left, the boy said, "Good luck in court."

INK

Greek revival columns? Thought Jason, when Angela and he walked through them, and into the Las Vegas Superior Courthouse. *Their presence evoked memories of the old South with its plantation aristocracy.* The oldest courthouse in Nevada catered to local ceremonies, law conventions, legal profession conferences, legal seminars, and over time, it had become the venue of choice for very public trials. Decades of taxpayers had paid for its high ceilings and decorative rooms, with some of those taxpayers sentenced to death here.

Angela was deep in thought. *How could the judge disqualify doctor Young?* She steered Jason into the very ornate courtroom, and then to a table on the left; the prosecutor and jury were on the right. When Jason sat down, a terrible thought crossed his mind—*Nevada was one of thirty-four states that had the death penalty. Common sense would be hard to find in this state.* He concluded that the citizens would have to believe that the law never made mistakes for them to allow the state to execute its own citizens.

As the preliminaries got underway, Jason noticed the obvious changes to the courtroom to bring it into the modern era—like the installation of lights and a video camera. Aside from those few items, the courtroom was the same original grandiose, somewhat imposing, room it had been for the past hundred-odd years.

Jason felt awkward and focused on the light fixtures to distract him from the enormity of the situation. When the prosecutor—Levi Miller, a smarmy, big-nosed, short man with a Napoleon complex—addressed the jury, he was forced to listen.

"You all have an enormous responsibility on your shoulders. It is a difficult thing to judge correctly, to weigh all the evidence impartially, and to be just and merciful at the same time. You must be fair to Mr. Crawford, and give justice to the victim, Mr. Maddox, his wife, and his daughter—in addition, to all who loved him. You have to make the right decision, and be able to live with that decision for the rest of your lives. I am here to make it easy for you, to help you all during this difficult time. You will be presented with facts—Jason Crawford killed Brian Maddox."

He continued, "Premeditation—he knew the punch could have deadly consequences and that is why we did not charge him with manslaughter but murder. The prosecution will show a history of violence from Mr. Crawford. Moreover, when he learned he had murdered Mr. Maddox, he fled the state of Nevada like a coward. Mr. Crawford is guilty of all those things. If it walks like a duck and talks like a duck, he must be guilty. Now that is not the type of person I want living amongst us. Do you want him living in your neighborhood? That could happen if you do not find him guilty. Jason Crawford is simply a guilty man. And you have the power to see that he receives justice. Thank you." Miller sat down.

Angela rose from her seat and walked over to the jury. She observed them and appraised their thoughts. "Good morning, ladies and gentlemen of the jury. "Mr. Maddox was licensed as a UFC fighter by the Nevada Department of Commerce, and the fight was approved by Paul Simpson of the Nevada Athletic commission, which also regulated the fight. The athletic commission officials broke several of their own rules in allowing Mr. Maddox to fight. Among the rules broken were the requirements that fighters rest more than three months between fights, have an exam conducted by a physician, and provide written certification by that doctor saying they are fit to compete. Mr. Maddox did none of these things, despite being visibly fatigued—"

"Objection, Your Honor, That is not an opening statement." Miller said.

"Sustained. Please keep your comments to the trial at hand, opening statement please," said the judge. Angela seemed out of her element, however, winked to reassure Jason she knew what she was doing.

INK

Angela turned back to the jury. "Jason Crawford is innocent because of the truth. A lot of the time we do not know what is true. Is there justice? The poor have no power and the rich win. We doubt institutions, ourselves, and our beliefs. It is in the news all the time—another government handout to bankers. We think 'there is little justice for me,' thinking like victims. Then one day, we become victims, one way or another. Jason Crawford is a victim of the system, with unlimited funds and resources, determined to cover up the state's incompetence—"

Miller shot to his feet, "Objection, Your Honor," he said. "She is doing the same thing. Mr. Maddox, the Department of Commerce, Paul Simpson, the Athletic commission or the state is not on trial here."

Angela said, "The state should be held liable for the errors it made in allowing Mr. Maddox to fight. It is the state of Nevada that should be on trial."

The judge banged the gavel.

"And that is the truth. Thank you, ladies and gentlemen," she said, and then took her seat. The judge sniffed and said, "The jury will disregard those comments. The state is not on trial here; the government is immune to such actions."

Angela pursed her lips. "Perhaps it is time to change that!"

"Please do not yell out in my courtroom," ordered the judge.

Testimony began with the prosecutor. "The state would like to call Mr. Oleg Crichenko." The courtroom doors opened, and Oleg, dressed in a gray suit, approached the stand. He stood, raised his hand, and then swore the oath.

Miller, who then stood adjacent to the jury box, asked, "Mr. Crichenko, you were Jason Crawford's trainer at the time. Was he aware that a punch could kill a man?"

Oleg nodded. "Yes, all of my fighters are aware of kill areas for defensive purposes only. A fighter must know when an opponent is trying to kill him to counteract that attack."

"Do you continue to train Mr. Crawford?"

INK

Oleg scowled and said, "No. I fired him the day after the fight. Crichenko Fighting Gym does not support that type of fighting."

Miller raised his hand. "No further questions." He sat down.

The judge asked, "Cross examination?"

Angela was about to get up when Jason took hold of her arm and made a gesture not to question him. Angela rose, "No questions at this time, Your Honor, but we would like the opportunity to question at a later date."

"Duly noted." The judge turned to Oleg. "You may leave the stand."

Oleg stepped down and walked away. When he exited the courtroom, Jason watched him, and hoped he would look at him, however, he never made eye contact with Jason the entire time. Miller rose from his seat. "The prosecution would like to call to the stand Dick McGregor." The doors to the courtroom opened. Curiosity got the better of Jason, and he peered back in his seat, to see who this person was. Jason saw an overweight, double chinned, gray haired, man enter. When he approached the bench, Dick McGregor viewed Jason with a smirk full of contempt.

Jason thought, *What the hell are you looking at? Who the hell are you? Step in the ring with that smirk on your face, I will wipe it right off. I know you, I know you, but from where?* Many years had passed since their meeting, and Dick had a bandage across his nose at the time, that covered most of his face. Miller consulted his notes, and then said, "Mr. McGregor, just so the jury is aware, you are a board-certified detective. Is that correct?"

"Yes, I am certified by the state of Texas," said Mr. McGregor proudly.

Miller clasped his hands behind his back. "Have you had any dealings with a Mr. Jason Crawford?"

Dick nodded. "Yes. Several years ago, when I was a Texas Ranger in the city of Houston. We received a call of a bust-up."

Miller smiled greasily. "A bust-up? Can you define that?"

"Bust-up is slang we use for prizefighting. We arrived on the scene to see Mr. Jason Crawford and a Billy Borden, AKA Bill Bones, fighting. We transported them both into the station."

Miller placed an index finger on the rail of the jury box. "Why is there no record of this?"

"The fighters would not press any charges against one another. The thirty-seven-year-old, Bill Borden, fighting Mr. Crawford did not want to press any charges due to embarrassment. He was under the impression that Mr. Crawford was twenty-three years old."

Miller asked, "What age was he?"

Dick grinned. "At the time, Mr. Jason Crawford was fourteen years of age."

The jury gasped collectively. Angela gave a slack-jawed expression at Jason, who whispered, "I remember who Dick McGregor is now." Angela scowled at him in disapproval, however, Jason just smiled. "I was winning that fight."

Miller spoke slowly, and made sure the jury understood this. "I do not know any fourteen-year-olds who fight thirty-seven-year-old grown men. Do you? He has state titles in boxing, karate, judo, jujitsu, taekwondo and wrestling—a history of violence, ladies and gentlemen. Is it any surprise he has killed someone? Is it? We all know in our hearts it is of little surprise. No further questions." Then sat down at his desk.

The judge glanced at Angela. "Cross council?"

Angela stood. "Mr. McGregor, on your last case for the Texas Rangers, you were under consideration for suspension due to tampering with evidence."

With his face buried in his notes, Miller interrupted, "Objection, Your Honor; the witness is not on trial."

"Your Honor, this is relevant to witness credibility."

The judge nodded. "I shall allow it."

"Again, Mr. McGregor, you were under consideration of suspension due to tampering with evidence?"

Dick scowled. "That is incorrect; I was not suspended. I resigned to pursue other interests."

"Let me put it to you another way. At the time of your resignation, was there an investigation conducted into one of your cases regarding evidence tampering?"

"Objection, Your Honor," said Miller. "Witness has answered the question."

Angela turned to her opponent. "Your Honor, prosecution council is constantly disrupting the proceedings with unfounded objections. He did not even raise his head from his notes."

The judge, his tone patronizing, said, "I believe objections are within the law, are they not?"

"Your Honor," said Angela, "defense requires clarification."

The judge tapped his fingers against the stand. "I shall allow it. Make it brief, Counsel; you are testing my patience. Answer the question, Mr. McGregor."

Dick scowled, and shifted uncomfortably in his seat. "I do not know about any suspension or evidence tampering. Once I left the Rangers, I had little to do with it."

Angela went to her desk and lifted a piece of paper. "Your Honor, I would submit to the courts evidence regarding the last arrest by Mr. McGregor, in which the case was thrown out of court due to evidence tampering."

Miller shot to his feet. "Objection!"

"Counselors, approach the bench," directed the judge. Both lawyers approached. "You are reaching, Counsel; you know this is not permissible in a court of law. I know what you are doing. Stop screwing around or I will hold you in contempt." Both attorneys took their seats.

"The jury will disregard all those comments. Strike from the record please. Would you like to redirect, Counsel?"

"Yes, your honor." Miller turned and addressed the jury. "Do not be fooled by the desperate attempts of the defense to cast doubt on this case. First, they blamed the state, and now they are questioning the credibility of a Texas Ranger—who, prior to serving the state of Texas as a law enforcement officer, served our country as a marine. Thank you." Miller sat back down at his desk.

"With no further questions, Mr. McGregor, you are excused. Call your first witness," said the judge, to the defense. McGregor left the bench.

Angela stood and said, "We call Ashley Maddox, if it pleases the court."

From the defense side of the courtroom, Ashley, dressed in black, stood up and then walked into the witness box and was sworn in.

Angela said, "I understand that once Mr. Crawford found out your husband had passed away, he drove from Las Vegas, Nevada, all the way to your home in Phoenix, Arizona, to give you something. Is that correct?

"That is correct," Ashley said.

"And that you would not let him in?"

Ashley nodded. "Correct. I was afraid, and a mess at the time. In the morning, I found an envelope that had been slipped under the door by Mr. Crawford."

Angela made her way to the jury and asked, "And what was in that envelope?"

"A note apologizing to me and my daughter and all the money he had made fighting in the form of a check—one point three million dollars." The jury murmured. Ashley continued, "I wish I had opened the door." She looked at Jason and smiled, and then turned back to the jury. "You set him free. I do not believe he meant to kill my husband. Do the right thing."

Miller shot out of his chair and yelled, "Objection, Your Honor; that is a personal opinion that has nothing to do with justice!"

"Sustained," said the judge. "The jury will disregard those comments. Counsel?"

Angela addressed the jury. "Mr. Crawford was concerned with doing the right thing, and made sure Brian Maddox's family was taken care of. In life, mistakes happen. Most people deny it or try to hide it under a rug, and hope no one sees it. Not Mr. Crawford; he tried to fix it the best way he knew how. This act of honor, integrity, dignity, and responsibility is twisted by the disgusting, degenerate slime of humanity, and they will call it cowardly; 'he fled the scene.' Is it any wonder Americans refuse to take responsibility when our culture allows the legal system"—she pointed to Miller—"to punish the honorable"—she pointed to Jason—"and it rewards the pigs!" She pointed back to Miller.

Miller shot up, standing. "Objection, Your Honor!"

The judge banged his gavel and yelled, "Order! Keep your personal opinions to yourself, missy, or I will hold you in contempt of court. Continue."

"No further questions," said Angela.

"Cross counsel?" The judge asked Miller.

"No questions at this time, Your Honor," he said.

Chelsea entered the courtroom dressed sharply in a gray suit jacket with a matching skirt, and a folder in hand. She motioned to Angela for a word. Jason saw Angela go over to her and then Chelsea whisper into Angela's ear while she passed her the folder. Angela glanced at what was in the file. Jason scanned the people sitting in the peanut gallery, and noticed a large white hat, it was Karen. She tipped her hat at him. He did what he always did with fight fans, tilted his head in a polite Southern acknowledgment.

A slow and deliberate smile came across Angela's face. She turned back to the bench. "Your Honor, can I see you and counsel in your chambers, please?"

"Court shall reconvene Monday morning." The judge banged his gavel and stood.

The courtroom slowly emptied while both attorneys gathered their belongings. Angela turned to Jason. "Follow me." They walked over to the judge, who stood by a door, and the four entered his chambers. *The judge shuffled in, shucking his robe like a corn husk,* Jason thought. Angela waited for the door to close, and then exploded.

"My office received an anonymous picture today of you and doctor Epstein. Do you know one another?"

The judge slapped his fingers against his desk. "Picture? What picture? Let me see."

Angela passed the judge the picture. The judge and doctor Epstein were pictured holding golf clubs on a golf course.

"I can see why you disqualified doctor Young from the proceedings."

The judge's expression darkened. "Young was not licensed in the state of Nevada."

Angela folded her arms. "Well?"

The judge tossed the picture onto his desk. "This does not mean anything."

She picked up the picture and stuck it in front of the judges' face temporarily. "Conflict of interest, Judge Odell. A massive conflict of interest. What is wrong with you? I have a person who could spend twenty-five years in jail. Don't you care? I am an attorney in trial for the world to see. And you are so arrogant to think that the relationship between you and the doctor immediately overseeing the event would have no bearing on the case?"

The judge stood, thumped his hands flat on his desk, and said, "Arrogant?"

Angela was furious. "Or you could use the term ignorant; you rushed me into court. You will not allow my star witness; you will not allow a continuance, and I do not care because the evidence is on our side. You knew this, so you stacked the deck."

The judge's expression softened into a look of sly, grandfatherly wisdom. "Counsel, when I was young and idealistic—"

Angela paced back and forth. "Do not give me that 'I was a lawyer too' crap. Because I know you were not a good lawyer, so you sold out. You continue selling out to anyone who is willing to pay. I know who you are."

"How dare you!"

"This is a mistrial, and I am going to request that you disqualify yourself from sitting on this case."

"For what reason?" The judge's voice tinged with concern.

"Conflict of interest. I will take a transcript to the state and ask that they impeach your ass."

The judge dropped back into his seat. "You are crazy. A picture is not cause for a mistrial. You are not going to get a mistrial, sweet cheeks. You are going back into court, and you are going to try this case. Or I shall have you disbarred."

"Do not threaten me, you chauvinistic dinosaur. The only power you have is to sell out to the highest bidder. The entire law establishment knows what you are: a joke. You are on your way out, Odell. Here is a copy of the new evidence I will submit to the courts Monday morning,—this photograph of doctor Epstein and you playing golf. My office has been offered the front page of the Tuesday edition of the *New York Times*." Angela slammed the photo evidence on his desk.

"How is that for a threat?" She stormed out of the office, and left the door open for them to hear. "Do the world a favor and retire, you old goat."

The judge and Miller looked at Jason, who smirked, pointed a finger at Angela threw the door and said, "What she said." Then he walked out of the office.

The judge contemplated the evidence, and then said, "We have a problem."

"How would you like to handle it?" Miller asked.

"I shall see what the council says. I'll let you know Monday morning."

Jason had a huge smile on his face, when he caught up with Angela in the hallway.

"That was the sexiest thing I have ever seen."

"It felt good," said Angela, with her high-heeled shoes echoed their clacking through the hallways.

"I am so turned on right now. Would you like to get a drink—or a room?"

Angela scoffed. "I would be disbarred."

They continued walking. Jason wrapped an arm around Angela's waist.

"Well, you are fired."

They stopped. Angela beheld him, puzzled. He smirked. "You know, for about an hour or two." Angela laughed and continued walking.

Jason followed. "Come on, let me fire you. We have plausible justification with a momentary loss of blood from the brain to—other parts of the body."

Angela was impressed. "You are learning how to speak like a lawyer."

"I am a fast learner; I promise," said Jason.

They exited the courthouse and stepped into the blinding Nevada sunlight.

INK

INK

CHAPTER SEVENTEEN

Aaron wiped down the bar with a rag at the Branding Iron. Mitch and Bang-bang set up the drums, checked the amps, plugged in the cables, and did a microphone check.

"Test, one, two," said Mitch.

Aaron hung the rag up to dry on a hook and then went over to the stage, removed his guitar from its case and slipped the strap around him.

Mitch grumbled, "Where is he?"

"I don't know," said Aaron.

"Do you have his number?" Bang-bang asked.

"Yeah," said Aaron.

"Do you want to give him a call?" Mitch asked.

"I will give him a call," said Aaron, and dialed a cell phone, "Voice mail. I've left three messages," he said, flipped closed the phone. Just then, Jason walked into the bar with a guitar case.

"Maybe Jason has seen him," said Aaron. Mitch exposed his gritted teeth, like a dog in anger, and then Bang-bang joined him.

Aaron hurried over to Jason by the bar. "Have you seen our new guitarist?"

"No," said Jason.

Aaron sighed and asked, "What is with the guitar?"

"I just took it to the music store to check out the pick-ups. Just like to have the pros service it. Make sure the neck is not bent. Harmonics are in place. You know." He figured out another guitarist had not shown. "I have it here if you need a guitarist."

"Aren't you going to jail soon?"

Jason shot him a threatening expression that said *do not fuck with me*. Aaron took off quickly to the stage. Jason gripped a box from under the counter, and pulled a coffee filter out of it; he placed it into the basket, took a can of coffee and dispensed six

INK

heaped spoons into it, and then switched on the coffee machine. Near the bar, alongside the wall, were steps that led downstairs. Jason carried his guitar down the steps. The dimly lit, basement where boxes of alcohol and beer kegs were kept, smelled— musky. Jason's amp was there by the kegs and he placed the guitar case next to the amp, and then went back upstairs into the bar. He grabbed a broom from the closet, and swept the inside of the bar, all the while bopped his head to the sound of the *BAND*. Abraham walked in.

"You wanted to see me, boss?" Jason asked, and he slid black coffee along the bar to him.

"Thanks. Yeah, come into my office," said Abraham.

They both walked into his office with their coffee in hand, and sat down.

"What do you know about the ABC?" Abraham asked.

"They can pull your alcohol license."

"You had any dealings with them?"

"No. Only what I have read about them."

"Could be a problem for us," Abraham said. "Shut a bar like this down."

"Will they be paying us a visit?" Jason asked.

"Maybe."

"How would you like me to handle it?"

"I want you to…be vigil this week. If you see something you do not like, let me know."

"Is something wrong, boss?"

Abraham thought for a moment. "No. Just check IDs, make sure there are no under-aged drinkers, and no drunks stumbling out into the street. If we have to call a cab for them, so be it—even if we have to pick up the tab. Keep an eye on the bar staff. Make sure they are not giving more drinks to drunks."

"Anything else?"

"No one enters the office without an appointment."

"Sure thing, boss."

Jason left the office and thought *the Department of Alcohol Beverage Control must have given Abraham a warning or something.* The band was still rehearsing when he returned back to the bar. He raised his coffee and Mitch, Bang-bang, and Aaron nodded. He poured three cups of coffee and carried them over to the band. The band stopped playing and thanked him.

"How does it sound, Jason?" Mitch asked.

"Good," said Jason. "But you need another guitarist." Jason walked off. Mitch and Bang-bang ogled Aaron as if to say, "Jason is a guitarist."

"What's up?" Bang-bang asked.

Mitch said, "What are we going to do?"

"You like him?" Aaron asked, and drank his coffee.

"What is not to like? He can play guitar. I have heard him. And he can be our enforcer if shit hits the fan," said Mitch.

Aaron sucked his teeth. "What if he goes to jail?"

"Then we will still be in the same boat we are in now. We keep auditioning."

"I don't know," said Aaron.

"What? Are we going to keep going over the same issue?" Mitch asked.

"What do you think, Bang-bang?"

"He makes good coffee."

All three laughed. Jason walked up with his guitar and amp, stepped onto the stage, and plugged his amp in.

Aaron saw him. "What's up, cowboy?"

"You guys need a guitarist today; I can help, if you like," said Jason, when he went to his guitar case and opened it. A sunburst guitar gleamed back at everyone.

"Gibson Les Paul," said Bang-bang.

"The Holy Grail of rock guitars!" said Aaron.

"Fuckin' A," said Mitch.

Aaron nodded his head at him. "Let us see what you can do, cowboy."

Jason plugged in his guitar and played "Drunk on X." The band looked impressed.

He stopped and said, "Or we can do it this way," and stepped on an overdrive peddle, that gave the riff a more rock feel. The band was impressed again, however, this time they joined in.

"Nice. Can you sing?" Asked Aaron, over the music.

"Nope!" Jason shouted.

INK

Aaron smiled. "Perfect!"

They rehearsed for a few hours, starting and stopping frequently to iron out the beats, rhythms, and solos. They had a pizza delivered for lunch, then rehearsed some more. They did not miss a beat when Abraham left. After a few hours, Tyrone entered and started fist pumping to the beat, and then danced on the way to the bar in a hip-hop robot fusion. When he reached for some coffee, the song ended.

"That was bad ass," he shouted.

Aaron said, "Do not go to jail," to Jason, who smiled.

The judge walked into the courtroom from his chambers and observed the room. Everyone in the courtroom stood. Jason saw Aaron, Mitch, Bang-bang, Rocco, Abraham, and Moses in the peanut gallery; all gave him a thumbs-up. Jason smiled at them. The room sat down after the judge. Angela sat with the new evidence in hand, tense with eagerness and nervous energy. She viewed the judge with contempt. Jason did not like seeing her this way and thought to himself, *Try to release her tension. Make her smile somehow,* and then leaned over and whispered into her ear. "If this goes bad and I go to jail, I just want to know if you would come for a conjugal visit?"

She smiled at him with a mischievous expression (contempt thoughts out of her mind now). "I guess we will just have to find out together," she said.

The judge settled into his seat. "State's Counsel, I understand you have something you would like to say?"

Miller snorted. "Your Honor, in light of new evidence that has been brought before the courts, the state has dropped all charges against Mr. Jason Crawford."

The jurors and the peanut gallery mumbled, and then cheered. Angela and Jason stood and hugged each other. Jason whispered, "Thank you."

Angela smiled against his shoulder. "You are welcome."

"Now that you are not my lawyer anymore..."

Angela looked into his eyes and said, "Yeah, I would like to celebrate."

Jason held her gaze, found Angela's hand, and briefly held it, when Moses interrupted them. "Congratulations, cowboy," said Moses. Chelsea hugged Angela.

Jason smiled. "Thanks for your support, Moses. It means a lot to me."

Moses clapped Jason on the shoulder. "My girlfriend and I have a dinner party set up for you."

Jason smiled. "That is great; you didn't have to do that. Let me tell Angela."

Jason hugged Aaron, Rocco, and then Abraham. Karen Smith waved her hand, and grabbed his attention. She flashed Jason a business card, and placed it on a bench seat, when she walked out.

Jason held Angela's hand, and led her to the exit. He stopped at the bench and picked up the business card. It read, "I can help you find Lauren." Jason felt dizzy, and then collapsed to the ground. He breathed fast, like he could not get enough oxygen. People around Jason started to panic, some ran to and fro. "Call an ambulance. Call the police. Does anyone know CPR? Get him some water. Raise his legs. Loosen his tie." Then a lady said, "Take off his trousers!" and the crowd all looked at her with a "what?" expression on their faces.

Karen changed into EMT attire in one of the bathroom stalls. A tattoo on her chest said *Whore*. When she heard the commotion, she came out of the bathroom and ran back into the courtroom to see Ricardo and Kiko. They were also in beard and mustache disguises in EMT attire, and attended to Jason. Karen's dark-gloved fingers picked up the business card and placed it inside her pocket. Then they rushed Jason out of the courtroom on a stretcher, while Karen carried an intravenous bag full of saline above him.

Angela followed them, shouting, "Where are you taking him? I have to come along!" They all exited the courthouse and navigated the thirty steps down.

Karen adopted a brusque, hurried tone. "County General no room in the ambulance. You will have to find your own way there." An ambulance waited on the street. Ricardo, Kiko, and Karen placed Jason in the back. Kiko ran to the driver's side.

INK

"Where is County General?" Angela asked.

"Sixth and Colorado," said Karen, when she closed the rear doors to the ambulance, and they drove off. Angela typed Sixth and Colorado into her phone GPS app. The message read "No Address." She typed in County General—"No Address." She turned to watch the ambulance disappear into traffic. A red-winged blackbird gave chase.

A green substance lay dormant in a test tube on a bench, and Cohen stuck a needle into it, and sucked it up into a syringe. The laboratory doors slammed open quickly. Karen entered, with Ricardo and Kiko in tow, who carried Jason in. Karen pointed to a table, and ordered, "Put him on the table, and then go to the print room and get the toner." Karen walked through a large, bloodied Ouija board on the floor with streaks of fresh blood and the heads of decapitated frill-neck lizards on each corner. In the middle of the board was a used beaker, which had dried blood residue on the sides of it.

She gave the business card to Cohen with a gloved hand and said, "It worked. Is it ready?" She pointed to the full syringe on a bench. Near the syringe was a large fish tank that contained a frill-neck lizard.

Cohen gulped. "Yes."

When she reached for the syringe, the lizard frilled its neck and lunged at her as if it was protecting its babies, however, it slammed into the glass fish tank and stunned itself for a moment. Ricardo placed Jason on the slab near Karen and left the room. With the syringe in hand, Karen went towards Jason on the table. Jason's eyes slowly opened. Karen had the needle inches away from his left eye. When the needle was about to prick Jason's skin, she peered down at him and whispered, "You will not feel a thing, my boy."

Perturbed, Jason woke and punched Karen in the face. The syringe fell to the ground, while Karen's limp body slid across the floor, and slammed into a wall.

"HELP!" screeched Cohen.

Jason stood up on the table, and tried to get his bearings. His eyes were going in and out of focus. Two scientists surrounded him. Cohen backed away, arms raised. "Take it easy, we are not going to hurt you."

Vernon fidgeted. "O-o-on the count of three, let us rush him."

Cohen swallowed. "Give up now. HELP!"

Jason's legs shook. "Who are you? Where am I?"

Vernon muttered, "O-o-one."

"It is for your own good," said Cohen. "You fainted in the courthouse; we are helping you."

Jason jumped down from the table. "I feel okay. I am leaving."

Vernon balled his fists and said, "T-t-t-two."

"You are outnumbered," said Cohen.

Vernon, "Th-th-three."

None of the scientists moved.

Jason shuffled a few steps toward the door. "What do you want?"

Vernon mumbled, "W, w, w, why didn't you move?"

Cohen fearfully said, "He is a UFC fighter."

Vernon sniffled, "D-d-d-do we even have health insurance?"

Cohen sized Jason up. "Easy. It is two against one; we can get violent if needed." *Wham.* A single blow caught Vernon on the side of the head, that whacked off his glasses and caused him to crash to the floor. Cohen beheld the broken glasses; Vernon held his head when he squirmed on the ground.

"HELP," yelled Cohen, towards the door, and then to Jason. "We are scientists. We do not like violence." Cohen ran over to a bench and pressed a red button that sounded an *ALARM*, just when Ricardo and Kiko came in with three containers of ink.

Four minion types ran up behind them. Ricardo and Kiko set the powdered ink down and surrounded Jason with the minions. Cohen stepped away.

"Get him," said Ricardo, and the minions attacked Jason at the same time. Nevertheless, Jason avoided or blocked the blows. Drowsy and lethargic, he fought like he was drunk. Jason's attack became more sluggish; his leg kicked a minion in the chest, that forced him to slam into another minion. Ricardo threw a fist. Jason had fun with it. "Oh, oh... here it comes," mocking, when he ducked the punch and kicked Ricardo into Kiko. They crashed down, dazed. Cohen, horrified now, hid in a corner with Vernon.

Cohen bellowed, "Get the Taser."

Vernon shouted back, "Y-y-you get it. I, I, I have already been kicked in the head."

"Coward," Cohen spat.

"M-m-maybe. But I plan on being a live coward."

Cohen made his way across the lab, while the fight continued. He found the Taser in a drawer, and then slid it across the floor to Kiko, who had come out of his daze. Then Kiko made his way behind Jason. Ricardo kicked Jason on the side of the head, and then Jason kicked back. They punched, blocked, kicked, and seemed evenly matched until one of Jason's punches floored him. Kiko then tasered Jason in the back. Jason turned to Kiko and stumbled towards him, struggled, while the surge of voltage dropped him to his knees. Jason fell to the floor.

Karen watched the fight from the floor. She stood and limped over to a minion who held his face, and lay on the floor. Karen sneered down at the injured man. "Unacceptable. You are fired. You are all, fired. Ricardo, find me mercenaries with military training. Now strap him down."

Ricardo and Kiko picked up the unconscious Jason and placed him down onto a gurney with restraints. They strapped his ankles and wrists down.

"You all follow me," Ricardo said, then he and Kiko helped some of the minions out of the room. Ricardo entered a storeroom, and before any of the minions asked what they were doing in there, Ricardo shot them dead. Kiko hung them up on meat hooks mounted to a wall. He stripped them of clothing, while their blood dripped onto a metal pan that directed the blood flow through to another room. By the time they returned, Karen had a bandage wrapped around her head, and a black eye was forming. She extracted blood from under Jason's toenail with a syringe, and then dabbed a drop of blood onto a microscope test slide. She placed the test slide under the microscope.

Karen scowled. "It has coagulated. That was fast. Why doesn't the serum work?"

Cohen coughed. "Perhaps we are asking the wrong questions."

"What are the right questions?"

"I am not certain at this point."

"You are an idiot, Cohen." She eyed Ricardo, then ordered, "Dump him." Then she eyeballed Cohen, "And make sure he does not remember anything."

INK

INK

A black sedan crawled into an alley; it's dash clock displayed 4:05 am. It was after a heavy rainfall so the pavement, graffiti-covered walls, and boarded-up broken warehouse windows were soaking wet. The car stopped by a pile of cardboard boxes next to a large trash dumpster. Ricardo and Kiko exited the vehicle and searched the area for any form of life—kicked at the pile of boxes to check for sleeping homeless people. Once they were sure that all was clear, they opened the rear passenger door, pulled Jason's limp body from the back seat, and threw him on the cardboard boxes. They hastily jumped into the car and drove off.

A red winged blackbird circled above and then landed on an electrical wire near Jason. More blackbirds came in, some landed near him. A light rain began to fall on Jason's face. His eyes snapped open and he bolted upright. This startled the blackbirds near him and they took off, even though they landed nearby. He also startled himself, and then he saw all the birds watching him. The cold night caused his breath to steam when he exhaled.

"Not again. How the hell did I get here? Why are those birds looking at me? This is freaken me out," he said, and took a sudden shallow breath when his phone rang. It almost stopped his heart.

"Son of a bitch." He answered it, however, said nothing. He heard a voice on the other end.

"This line is tapped so I must be brief. This is Lauren, your sister."

Jason swallowed. "Sis?"

"Go to the Foster Street Bridge." *CLICK*. Static.

Jason was unsure of his surroundings.

"Where the fuck am I? Not again." He stood up and cautiously walked out of the alley to the street. He scanned the area carefully. No people were around. Dilapidated warehouses and wreckage remains of three vehicles, lined the street. He read

INK

the street signs at an intersection—First Street and Sahel Ave. *This is not a good area to be after dark,* he thought. Then he took a right, and briskly walked up to a street with houses on it. The few people around were crack heads, hookers, johns and drug dealers. He felt like he was being trailed. And he was. The birds followed him.

He came to the fog-covered Foster Street Bridge; lights from the city bounced off the water beneath. The deserted, ominous bridge sent a chill up his spine, and he stepped cautiously to the center of it when headlights crept up behind him. A black sedan rolled up and quickly slid to a stop beside him. The back door opened to a dainty, beautiful, athletic Nordic woman with long blonde hair and extra-long legs.

"Get in," she said. Jason noticed she had vibrant red lipstick on, and did what he was told. In the front seat was a military jarhead type, who aimed a government-issued nine-millimeter handgun at Jason. Another jarhead in the driver's seat drove off.

"Is that necessary?" Jason pointed to the gun, and asked.

"Yes. It is for our protection," said the blonde-haired woman.

"From what?"

The jarhead who held the gun snorted and said, "From you. Phone."

Jason handed his phone over to the jarhead, who dumped it out the window.

The blonde-haired woman turned to watch it bounce into pieces. "Bugged," she said, and pulled out an electronic scanner.

"Take off your shirt," ordered the jarhead, and tilted his gun. Jason saw the gun's safety was on.

"What? Why?"

The gun's barrel was shoved inches away from Jason's face. "Listen, punchy! We do not have time for twenty questions. Right now, there is only one rule: our way or the highway," said the jarhead.

"Punchy?" Jason opened the door.

"No," pleaded the blonde-haired woman. "Your sister needs to see you. You have to trust us."

He closed the door and took off his shirt.

INK

"I am Ditta. That is Flanery, and Braxton is driving" she said, while she swept the electronic scanner over Jason's torso. "Nice tattoos, now the pants."

Jason smirked, "You first." Ditta smiled.

Flanery was not amused. "Get them off." Jason became annoyed with Flanery now, and his eyes were fixed directly on his.

"Try to relax," said Ditta.

Jason took off all his clothes. Ditta directed the scanner paddle over Jason's body.

"You look….cold," Flanery taunted.

Jason sneered, and then came back with, "And you look like a moron."

Flanery slapped the gun against the bench seat. "You should not agitate someone holding a gun on you. It could accidentally go off."

"By the time you took that safety off, my foot would be so far up your ass, you would think you are in boot camp again," Jason warned.

"Easy, boys," said Ditta. "He is clean. You can get dressed." Flanery's finger moved near the safety on the gun when Jason punched Flanery in the face and unarmed him. This caused Braxton to slam on the brakes, and the tires screeched to a halt.

"Freeze," ordered Ditta. She and Braxton had guns pointed at Jason's head.

He slowly raised his hands and said, "There is something sexy about a beautiful woman holding a gun. I am frozen."

Ditta blushed a little, and then looked down at his crotch; he saw his penis move.

"I can't speak for him," said Jason.

Ditta smiled, and then took the gun from Jason, "Easy."

Flanery was slumped on the bench seat.

Braxton shook his shoulder. "Flanery. Flanery."

"Visiting boot camp about now," Jason said, smirking.

"We do not have much time. Let us go," said Ditta.

Braxton drove down a deserted alley behind a dirty, dusty, forgotten building.

"Follow me," she said, and then she and Jason stepped out of the vehicle while Braxton continued to try to wake Flanery. Ditta moved a brick that exposed a keypad, and then punched in a code. Jason scanned the area. The building had gargoyle statues and a worn-out American flag on the roof.

"The gargoyles watch over us," Ditta said.

A camouflaged brick wall slid open. Ditta led Jason into a room. The door closed.

"Do not breathe," ordered Ditta. A thin mist sprayed them both, and then stopped. "The mist kills bugs that hitchhike on our bodies. Follow me."

The inner doors opened to reveal Lauren, who awaited their arrival. She was dressed in a white tracksuit and Fergus stood by her. Jason saw a beautiful woman with similar features. Her eyes began to tear up, when she smiled and ran to him. They hugged one another. "I am your sister, Lauren."

His heart skipped a beat when he said "Hello sister." He had searched for years, and now, finally, he had found her at last. "My sister!" It felt great when he said it.

"Hi, brother." She found him tall, masculine with a beard and mustache. She took a long pause, and then said, "This is our grandfather, Fergus Blackwood."

Fergus stuck out his hand, and Jason shook it vigorously. "Nice to meet you, sir."

"Tall, strong, strapping lad. Good to finally meet you, son. I am going to let you get caught up. Then I shall talk to you at lunch tomorrow," Fergus said, and walked away after Jason nodded agreeably.

"Where are we?" Jason scanned the area.

"You are at the Symbolic Sector Agency headquarters. We are in the city's deserted industrial area," said Lauren. "I teach Symbolism and printmaking to children and help scientists with ink experiments."

"Symboli-what? What are you talking about?"

"I didn't know about you," she said. She placed a small, pale hand on his larger, tanned one. "I am glad we are finally together, though."

"At last," said Lauren. She kissed both of his cheeks.

A few people in white lab coats clapped.

"You are a bit of a celebrity in here," she proudly said. "Everyone knows who you are, and we watched your fights when we could get them." Jason had a chance to look around. The facility was a place of military cleanliness, a pure host of scientific splendor. There were rows after row of stainless steel benches, with test tubes, microscopes, and Bunsen burners. Scientists worked in different areas of the warehouse. People in the background and other adjoining rooms dropped what they were doing to join the celebration.

When the clapping died away, Lauren took Jason's arm. "Follow me."

A nerdy scientist in a lab coat ran up to Jason. "Mr. Crawford, I am a big fan of yours. I run a Dojo on the fifty-sixth floor. I would love for you to stop by to enlighten us on your mixed martial arts skills."

Jason nodded. "Sure. If I get some time…"

"We are in a hurry, Harold," said Lauren, by way of excuse. She steered Jason from the door to a stairwell near an elevator. "Do you know about Mom?"

"No."

They walked up the stairwell to the floor above.

"Dad?"

"I am clueless. I do not even know where I am now. What is this place?"

Lauren laughed. They stopped outside a room, and Lauren opened the door into a clean, organized, one-bedroom unit decorated with ornaments and a poster of the fight between Jason and Maddox. They sat next to one another on a brown sofa. She would not let go of his hand.

"I wanted to contact you for the longest time, but I could not," she admitted.

"Why not? I have been searching for you for over a decade."

"Someone tried to kill me when I was younger. I was afraid they would try to get you too."

"Who would want to kill you?"

"After a few years with my foster parents, a man came to my school and followed me on my way home. He pulled out a gun and shot at me. My secret bodyguard pulled a gun on him, but he escaped. The authorities said not to contact you to keep you safe. I was under constant surveillance."

"Bodyguard? Gunman?"

"Apparently SSA was watching me since leaving the orphanage. The gunman forced my bodyguard at gunpoint into a black sedan and fled. He was never seen again."

"Oh. Now I understand," He said deep in thought.

Lauren nodded, teary-eyed. "My foster mom and dad were the best. I was their only child, and they gave me everything. I had my own bedroom, bicycle, and plenty of friends; Dad is a scientist and taught me everything about science. We would do experiments all the time. God, I love them. I had a great childhood. You'll meet them one day. And your foster parents?"

Jason shrugged. "Slight differences, but the same. You know."

Lauren smiled. "So, we both had great foster parents. That is great."

INK

Jason and Lauren spent hours catching up on the details of each other's lives. The conversation turned to their biological parents. "Where are mom and dad?" Jason asked.

"Dad died in Guatemala about twenty five years ago. Come over here." Lauren motioned Jason to sit at her kitchen table in front of her laptop. "Read this obituary while I get some files." Lauren opened some news clippings she saved on her computer. Jason began to read aloud. *Doctor Russell Crawford, of Point Breeze, died Saturday at West Penn hospital. He was 47. Dr. Crawford was born and raised in Cleveland and graduated from Western Reserve University Medical School. He joined the Public Health Service as an intern and remained active until he was a medical officer on convoy duty in the Coast Guard.*

His interest in the prevention and control of sexually transmitted diseases began when he worked as a medical commission in the U.S. Public Health Venereal Disease Research Laboratory in Staten Island, N.Y. That led to his appointment to head a venereal disease research program for the Pan American Sanitary Bureau in Guatemala. After returning to the states, Dr. Crawford continued to rise in rank until he became assistant to the Surgeon General of the U.S. Public Health Service Commissioned Corps. He worked for the Allegheny County Health Department, organizing the polio vaccination program in the Hill District. He went from assistant to deputy director of what later became the Pan-American Health Organization in Washington, D.C. Dr. Crawford was a former assistant surgeon general of the U.S. Public Health Service, and was one of the founders of the Family Health Counsel of Western Pennsylvania.

He worked tirelessly to find better ways to provide affordable reproductive health care services to women who needed them. He believed that 'every person should have access to these services, regardless of income,' said Richard Baird, acting president of the Family Health Council.

Lauren returned and saw that Jason had finished reading. She sat by him, closed the archive, and opened another file. "Here's a picture," she said, and twisted the computer back toward Jason. The picture showed a balding, pudgy man injecting the arm of a woman.

Jason viewed the screen in reverence. "Sounds like a nice guy."

Lauren shook her head. "That is what they want you to believe." She opened another file. "These are CIA files. Listen to this. _Doctor Russell Crawford and colleagues worked in Guatemala to conduct medical research that deliberately exposed 1300 people to STDs like syphilis, gonorrhea, and cancroid. It was revealed that only 700 of those infected were treated. 83 people died. They reported seven women with epilepsy (who were housed at a Guatemalan insane asylum) were put at risk by being injected with syphilis below the back of the skull because researchers thought the new infection might somehow help cure epilepsy._"

Jason's face grimaced.

"_The women each contracted bacterial meningitis, likely as a result of unsterilized injections. Taking a female syphilis patient who had an unrelated terminal illness, the researchers, curious to see the impact of an additional infection, infected her with gonorrhea in her eyes. She died six months later. Crawford's work was not unique, experts have noted. During that period of lax regulation, other researchers also used people as guinea pigs, infecting some with illnesses. Guatemalans called him Doctor Death. He was found hacked to death and the case is filed as an unsolved murder. There is suspicion of villagers conspiring, but no proof. Mom was also a part of that research team._"

Jason took it all in, however, could not believe what he heard. "So Dad was the American Joseph Mengele?"

"Yes," said Lauren. "This goes beyond just our family, of course. The United States was experimenting on human beings way before the Germans."

Jason grunted. "Were supposed to be the good guys!"

"Well, that is what they want us to believe. It is about greed. It always has been."

"What happened to our mother?"

Lauren struggled to get the words out. "When Mother came back to the states, she continued Dad's research—only she did not have any villagers to do experiments on."

In a flash, it registered to Jason who her guinea pigs were. "That is why we were placed in the foster home."

INK

"To protect us from mother, one of her researchers called Child Protective Services. Once we were placed into the orphanage, Mother was jailed, released, and then disappeared. Nine months later, the researcher was found dead with a hypodermic needle stuck in her eye."

"Holy crap," exclaimed Jason, "And here I thought we were descendants of royalty."

Lauren laughed again and gave him a blanket. "It is late. Our grandfather wants to speak with us at brunch tomorrow. Get some sleep." Then went into a bedroom.

"Sure. Like I am going to sleep after that!" he muttered under his breath, when he laid on the sofa. Lauren turned off the light and went into her bedroom. Nevertheless, Jason eventually did fall asleep.

In the morning, Jason was briefed about Symbolism, and a group of scientists and Symbolists had him do some tests. He sketched a bottle on paper, and then a flower, however, he could not draw. They had him do some printmaking of what seemed like a gun on a tile, pin pricked his finger, and dropped the blood on the gun. It did not come to life. They had him draw a bird on another tile to the same results. Lauren dropped some of her blood on it, nothing. A scientist explained what results the tests were supposed to produce if he had the power. They concluded he did not share his sister's special powers. Jason was going to mention the paintings that would come to life, however, did not think it was any kind of power. He was also slightly embarrassed that he continued to see things so he decided against it.

"That settles it then; Lauren is the special one," Jason said.

"Wait," said Nuri, a beautiful Egyptian woman, with a Cleopatra hair style, and adorned with hieroglyphic jewelry. "Look into my eyes." And he did. Her eyes were emerald green, and heavy with black eyeliner, eye shadow and thick eyelashes. She slowly blinked.

"It would seem that way," said Nuri, with a suspicious tilted head, as if not believing it.

"Let us go meet Granddad then," said Lauren, and took hold of Jason around the arm, while they walked off.

INK

"What is it?" Asked the Director, who stood near Nuri.

"His blood has a new strand. I've never seen it before."

"His test show he has no power."

"I feel something is there. I'm not certain, something new, more potent," confessed Nuri.

Lauren steered Jason through the bland, beige-colored hallways and into the food court that was full of very colorful small restaurants from all cultures of the world. They walked into an American restaurant and saw Fergus at a table, with a cup of tea. Smooth jazz music played softly in the background. The frozen ice swan in the center was gorgeous. The perfect distraction to draw attention away from the building's solid bunker-like walls, which were decorated with red, white and blue curtains, with abstract paintings of food. *Strange,* thought Jason. *None of the artwork was of the outside world. It is lunchtime, but you would never know it. The restaurant has no windows.*

They greeted each other, and then read through the menu. The cuisine was primarily classic American, however, it had dishes that catered to the vegetarians and vegans also. Fergus picked water and salmon with vegetables, while Jason requested beer, steak, and potatoes. Fergus passed Jason a picture, while Lauren ordered a chardonnay and a chicken salad. Jason saw a black-and-white picture of a beautiful, slender woman.

"Is that my mother, Mr. Blackwood?" Jason asked.

"Yes. Call me Fergus or Grandpa," he said. "That was taken on her sixteenth birthday.

We had a birthday party at the house, and all her school friends came. It was a glorious time; the SSA bestowed her with the 'Rookie of the Year' plaque. I still have it." When the server came back with their drinks, Jason asked Lauren if he could borrow her cell phone. Lauren handed it to him, and Jason handed the phone to the waiter and asked if he could take a picture of them. The server obliged and framed the three with Lauren on the left, Fergus in the middle and Jason on the right. The waiter handed Lauren's phone back to Jason, who quickly viewed the picture. He broke out in a proud smile. "It is my first family picture," he said, and showed Lauren and Fergus. "Can you send me a copy, Sis?" Lauren agreed to give him and Fergus copies.

"She was brilliant and beautiful. Then she ran off with that Pikey trash and joined the focking circus. Damn that man to hell," said Fergus.

"What happened?" Jason asked.

"She was a sweet girl, a genius with the gift of printmaking. Your father,...that Russell," said Fergus. He drank down his tea and set the cup aside. "He was a tattoo artist who had an interest in medicine, and traveled with Doctors Without Borders 'round Europe and the Isles. Well, he stole her away at seventeen, and I did not see her 'til she limped back, proud as you please—with the two of you and that bear." The waiter arrived with their food. Jason glanced down at his steak and potatoes, and then forked a potato into his mouth.

"Do you remember the bear?" Lauren asked.

"I have had dreams I played with a dog," said Jason.

Fergus touched his hearing aid. "Oh, no. It was a bear, like one of them grizzlies," said Fergus. "It grew as big as a mountain. Then it died of a cold. Your mother was distraught. Covered in them tattoo pictures, too, and your grandmother would not have none of her, so I put her up in a flat downtown. I visited her when I could, and for a while it seemed like she might perk up and take back to her studies...but not like I wanted. She started feeding her ink on others—doing it on the sly. A little bit here and there, whenever she could get away with it. Does things to a mind, it does, to feed another's blood to your own Ink. By the time I found out, she was halfway to America, and that was the end of that."

"I wish I could have known her and Dad," said Jason.

"I was dragged to this godforsaken place, once they found out her real name," said Fergus.

Lauren sensed that Jason was melancholy. He seemed like he had gotten the short end of the stick. She could see sadness in his eyes. *They should have kept us together,* she thought. *Damn those clerks who screwed up the paperwork! So much sadness, all because someone was lazy.* Lauren was deep in thought, when she ate her chicken salad. She had heard the many stories about their parents from different people, however, her grandfather refused to speak about them, shortly after he mentioned she had a brother. And here he was, that long-lost brother who sat in front of her. The whole thing felt surreal. Fergus poured himself a cup of tea and then passed another picture to Jason. It was a mug shot of his mother.

"She looks as if all the life had been drained out of her," said Jason.

"That was when we were taken away from her for child endangerment," said Lauren. "She posted bond and disappeared."

"It is a sad story," Fergus admitted.

Lauren signed the check that the waiter put on the table. Jason pulled out his wallet, however, Lauren shook her head. "Your money is no good here. Everything is done on the honor system."

"I have some of that," Jason shrugged. "Thanks."

"Come on, I shall show you around," she said to Jason. "I will see you later, Granddad."

"Come around later," said Fergus.

They stood up and left the restaurant. She held his arm, when they strolled through the food court, which was very busy.

Jason took it in. "What is this place?"

"It is a self-contained military science laboratory. You shall be safe here."

Everyone in the food court watched them, whispered to one another about the new person. They walked around like celebrities.

"Here? What are you talking about?" Jason asked.

"Someone is after you."

"What do they want with me?"

"We do not know," said Lauren. "That is why you have to stay here. At least until we find out."

"I could not stay here."

"There are two hundred and nineteen floors of stores, restaurants, workshops, gyms, and libraries. Whatever you need. It is all here," said Lauren, when she directed him to a hallway.

"No."

"Why not?"

"Because I have a job I need to get to tomorrow. I am in a band, and I do not like the idea that I am not in control of my life."

"I know exactly what you mean," said Lauren. "I have been stuck in here for years. Band, what band?"

"It is a rock band called the Kuss; one of the barmen at my job started it. I play guitar for them."

"Cool. There is a pool on the roof here. They let us out every month with chaperones," she said, and still tried to convince him to stay.

Jason did a double take. "Six months? Okay, you have to promise me you will come and have dinner with me next time."

"Okay. I promise," said Lauren, while they turned into a corridor.

"Quit working here."

Lauren whispered, "I signed a contract." They walked past a dojo where Harold was teaching kids—when Harold saw Jason and came out of the dojo.

"Oh, great. You came," said Harold, enthusiastically. "I have some students that would love to see you."

Jason shook his head. "I am with my sister at the moment."

"Go," said Lauren, smiling. "Have fun. I know you like to fight."

Jason snapped, "No, I do not like to fight." Then he stormed off.

Lauren and Harold watched him. Jason walked away, stopped, and looked around, not sure where he was, and said, "Where am I going, Lauren?" She raced up to him, grasped his arm, and they continued walking.

"We will go to my room," said Lauren, and not another word was spoken until they were inside.

"Everyone thinks because I fight, it must be what I like to do. It is not the case. I fight because it is all I was taught. If I did not fight, I would not eat; my foster parents would not feed me," Jason said.

"Tell me what happened."

"You do not want to hear it."

INK

"Yes I do, and I will not stop asking until you tell me. I am your sister. We need to be able to be honest with each other."

"I understand, but as your brother, I need to protect you from being hurt."

"The people who kept us apart believed they were protecting you and me. If you keep the truth from me, you are no better than them."

"Okay. I was shuffled through three orphanages by the time I was six. I had five sets of foster parents before I was sixteen. I was used by one set of parents for the state checks and even kept in a closet. I was hospitalized with a concussion from Catholic foster parents, who would beat me up for not remembering the words to prayers fast enough. Another mother forced me to steal. When I was nine, a redneck parent wanted me to ride bulls, and become a cowboy. So he threw me in a pen with a bull. It was irrelevant to him that the bull stomped me." He pointed to a cigarette tattoo on his chest. "That tattoo covers up a cigarette burn from two God-fearing parents, who had no problem burning the crap out of children."

Tears started to roll down her cheeks when she asked, "Is that why you have so many tattoos, because of your hard life?"

"No. One couple of foster parents could not afford to go to tattoo school, so they figured, why not adopt a kid and practice on him while getting a check from the government. These tattoos are not my choice. They are childhood scars I am forced to see every day. Those same parents said I should pay my own way, forcing me into bare-knuckled fights at eleven years old. I went to jail, and then my old caregiver, Moses, took me to Oleg, where I lived for many years. Moses and Oleg were nice to me; my childhood was different."

"I am sorry; that is why you have sadness in you." Tears rolled down Lauren's cheeks, while she sat on the sofa. "I get it now." A sad smile emanated from Lauren. *KNOCK! KNOCK!* Someone was at the door. Lauren wiped her tears away and opened the door. Braxton stood there in a blue military uniform. Lauren tried to discreetly wipe away her tears and fix her hair. *There is a spark there,* he thought.

INK

"Sorry to bother you, doctor Blackwood. Mr. Donald would like to invite you and Mr. Crawford to a karate demonstration."

"Now's not a good time," said Lauren.

Jason shook his head. "It is okay, sis. Let us go—" When he left the room, he said sarcastically under his breath, "—or we will not eat."

Ditta skimmed through some files, when she walked through the hallways, and then glanced through a store window. She saw Jason and Mr. Donald standing in a Japanese-style dojo. She knew the routine, as she had walked these halls for years and secretly admired the people in the dojo. She even tried it once herself, however, could not get over the sweat sticking to her body. She ran off through the hallway corridors and burst into a room, interrupted the scientists hard at work. Ditta shouted, "Teacher is fighting Crawford!" The scientists dropped what they were doing, and bolted for the door to follow Ditta back to the dojo.

The floor above the dojo had a round viewing area, like a medical theater, and all the scientists, along with Ditta, surrounded its ledge. Students, mostly military types, surrounded the ring. Braxton stood between Lauren and Flanery. Mr. Donald had just made a speech about Crawford and all were clapping. Flanery scowled and muttered, "He sucker-punched me, but I could take him."

Braxton chuckled. "You were facing him."

"I blinked," said Flanery, darkly.

"Shhhh, be respectful to your teacher," said Agent Decker, who had snuck up behind both.

"Which fighting style do you prefer, Mr. Crawford?" Mr. Donald asked.

"I find avoiding fighting is the best style of fighting."

Mr. Donald nodded approvingly. "That is an excellent technique. Demonstration please."

Mr. Donald assumed a fighting stance and Jason took a similar stance. They cautiously circled one another, until Mr. Donald gave a short cry and launched an attack, fists and feet were thrown from every angle, with a medium-paced attack respectfully. Jason avoided all of Mr. Donald's strikes.

"Excellent. Again!"

Jason hurled himself at Mr. Donald with his own medium-paced attack.

Mr. Donald was impressed. "Good technique and improvisation." They stopped. Mr. Donald bowed to Jason. "Thank you." Mr. Donald turned back to his students. "Now, who would like to go first?"

Most students raised their hands. Flanery stepped forward. "I will."

Jason was suspicious.

Mr. Donald nodded and said, "Go ahead, Mr. Flanery."

Flanery walked into the middle of the ring. He assumed a fighting stance. The fighters cautiously circled until Flanery launched a ferocious assault at double the speed that Mr. Donald had. Jason bobbed and weaved, however, a right did slip through to strike him. He fell to his hands and knees.

Mr. Donald shouted, "Flanery! We are sparring here."

Flanery bowed, to hid his smirk. "Sorry, Sensei. That one got away from me. Mr. Crawford, sorry." They resumed their fighting stances. The scientists viewed it from the top floor.

Ditta salivated. "Wow! That man has a nice body!"

Harold shook his head. "He ruined it with all those tattoos."

Jason head-butted Flanery's fists.

Flanery recoiled, and shook his bruised fists, hissed through his teeth. "Fuck."

Jason stepped back, hands clasped. "Do not use the same combination twice."

Flanery groaned and flexed his hands in pain.

Mr. Donald chuckled. "Good. Again."

Flanery launched an angry attack. Jason stopped a fist an inch from Flanery's left cheek. They both froze, eyed each other.

Mr. Donald nodded. "Excellent. Again."

From the frozen position, they started up. Flanery's attempted strikes were filled with malicious intent. Again, Jason stopped his right foot an inch from Flanery's left cheek. They both froze. This time a glint in Jason's eyes warned Flanery to be careful.

Mr. Donald was then concerned, nevertheless, wanted to see how far Flanery would go, and how Jason would handle it, "Excellent. Again."

Jason stepped back, and cautiously, they started up again. Flanery punched Jason in the right cheek, however, Jason knew it was coming and countered with a spinning back punch. *WHAM*. A single blow caught Flanery on the left cheek and he crashed to the ground—unconscious! There was a collective, *"DAMN,"* from the spectators.

Ditta smiled. "He is a sexy man. I am going to fuck him!"

"You should ask Lauren first if she would have a problem with it," said Harold.

"Your right," she said, "We are all adults."

INK

INK

CHAPTER TWENTY

Abraham slowly rolled his black 1967 Cadillac Eldorado into the Branding Irons parking lot. Texas longhorns were mounted on the front of the hood. Twenty-inch spinner rims were on the wheels, which were inserted with four chrome steel revolver pistols, that made the sound of a clicking revolver until they stopped spinning. *TICK, TICK, TICK.* Abraham had labeled his personal parking space "Boss," spelled in multicolored rhinestone lettering against a stark black background. When he stepped out of the car, he had two new sets of shiny spurs on his boots. While he walked to the front door of the bar, he could hear the Kuss rehearsing "Drunk on X."

Aaron, Mitch, Bang-bang, and Jason were on stage when Abraham entered. Upon seeing him, they turned their instruments down. Even Bang-bang hit the skins on the drums a little lighter. They all nodded their hellos to him. Jason noticed the new chrome spurs on his boots, while Abraham went into his office. He liked them. When a red light on the phone at the bar started to flash with an incoming call, he passed his guitar to Aaron and then raced over to the bar to answer the call.

Aaron set his guitar aside. "Take a break, guys."

Jason picked up the phone. "The Branding Iron; this is Jason speaking. How may I help you?"

"Jason, where have you been? I have been calling your cell with no answer. I was about to call the police because I was worried sick," said Angela, on the other end.

"Long story. I have a new cell phone. I can't explain things over the phone. Can you fly up and stay with me?"

"Okay, I will book a flight."

Three large men in their 50s entered and headed towards Abraham's office. Jason spotted the new shiny shoes, black hair,

INK

European features, Italian-style suits and he thought to himself, *Gangsters*.

Covering the phone, "We are not open, guys," yelled Jason. They ignored him and continued like they meant business. "Call me with the details." Jason said into the phone and then hung up.

"We are not open, guys," said Jason. Then cut them off before they reached the curtained hallway. The obvious leader had thick, dark hair and movie-star good looks. He was dressed in a navy-blue and chalk-white double-breasted pinstriped suit.

"Hey, we are not open yet, fellas. If you would like to come back at 8:00 p.m., we should be open then."

One of the bodyguards spoke to the leader in Italian and said, "This is the UFC fighter."

The leader said, "This is Pauli," and thumbed over his right shoulder. Jason quickly scanned Pauli. He had a big nose with a long face, and a single-breasted jet-black suit covered his bulky physique. "This is Frank," he continued, and thumbed over his left shoulder. He was a tall, skinny, weird-looking person, who wore a single-breasted jet-black suit also. "I am Vinny Castilforte. We run things around here."

During breaks, the band had spoken of the gangsters that ran the city, and Jason knew Vinny was one of them, however, he did not care.

"Not in here you don't," said Jason.

"We are here to see Abraham!" said Vinny.

Tyrone entered and, sensed trouble, joined Jason.

Jason crossed his arms. "Do you have an appointment?"

"He is expecting us," replied Vinny.

"Expecting is not an appointment."

Vinny then muttered in Italian to Pauli, "This guy is stupid or has some balls. Let's find out which. Show him your gun." Pauli opened his jacket and flashed a 357 Magnum pistol in his waist belt. When Jason saw it, he uncrossed his arms.

"Hey, boss," Jason shouted, over his shoulder, and kept a careful eye on all three. "I have three Italians here with guns, said you are expecting them." He eyed them sternly and took on a more serious tone of voice. "If he wants to see you, he will come out."

A standoff began. All five of them eyed one another, and waited to see who would make the first move. In the dead silent, the band faded away into the background, afraid to move. The tension tightened until Tyrone reached for Pauli's gun and said, "There are no guns allowed in here."

Wham. Vinny punched Tyrone square in the face, and he went down and out. Jason's face turned to stone when he spoke the next few lines in flawless, fluent Italian, "That was a stupid thing to do, and now you are gonna pay, because I have balls."

Vinny, Pauli, Frank and even the band were impressed. Jason delivered a devastating blow to Vinny's face, and then to Pauli. Vinny fell and began to writhe on the floor in pain. Abraham entered from the hallway with a revolver in his belt and a sawed-off shotgun at the ready. He pointed the business end at Frank and Vinny, yelling, "Freeze! Do not move or I will blow your heads off!"

Pauli reached for his gun, however, Jason seized his wrist and claimed the gun with his other hand. He quickly threw it to the floor near Aaron, and then gave Pauli a left to the jaw, which caused him to fly over a pool table. Aaron picked up the gun. Pauli stood up, snatched a pool cue from a rack on the wall, and swung it left to right, then right to left. Jason ducked, bobbed, and weaved to avoid the swinging cue. After some maneuvering, Jason caught the cue in his boot heel and took it down onto the pool table. Pauli tried to pull the cue away from Jason's boot, however, it would not budge under Jason's weight.

"Oops," Jason taunted, just before he cracked Pauli upside the head with his free boot. Pauli slammed against a wine rack and a bottle fell and smashed on the ground.

Pauli reached up behind his head with both hands and pulled two wine bottles from the rack. He swung them toward each other with Jason's head as the midpoint. Jason spun in a roundhouse motion, and avoided the bottles when they connected with each other. Jason continued the roundhouse and kicked Pauli on the other side of the head. This time Pauli crumpled to the ground in an explosion of glass and wine.

INK

Abraham laughed disbelievingly. "Nicely done, Jason!" he said, and then turned to Vinny. "You can call the ABC if you want Vinny. I am not paying. Now get the fuck out." The three gangsters picked themselves up and limped out. Jason revived Tyrone with a gentle slap to the face.

"I suppose an explanation is in order," said Abraham. "The mob's trying to force me to pay protection money. I am not paying them or any other gangsters. If you want to leave, I understand, because it is gonna get worse before it gets any better." There was a long pause while everyone absorbed it. Jason had a cigarette in his mouth, and then he downed a beer. They all looked at him.

"I am stickin' around," Jason grunted. No one else said anything.

On April 11, the day of his 49th birthday, Kiko rose at five in the morning. He dressed in a white silk shirt with long sleeves, a black suit and tie, and a pair of black loafers. He drove into the city, parked the car, and entered a diner called Hannigans. Kiko was happy to see the A rating on the window had not changed. Things like food poisoning, sickness, headaches, or hosts of other ailments could get you killed when you were a criminal. The greasy spoon was on the corner of Clark and Pacific Street, so the counter space spread to the right and the left of the corner entry. It was two-thirds full, with working-class customers.

He hunted specifically for a seat by a window and sat in a four-person booth near the bathroom. Through the window he could see a nondescript, weather-beaten gray tin warehouse until a thin, curly haired Latin waitress with dimples came over.

"Good to see you again. Can I take your order?" She asked. He ordered coffee, poached eggs, bacon, sausage, and hash browns. When she left, he continued to observe the warehouse, however, thought about what the server had said—*Good to see you again.* That was not good to hear; being noticeable and predictable was dangerous in his line of work. It was common for criminals to be killed at their regular barber or restaurant in the underworld. *Let us just hope she does not start asking questions,* thought Kiko.

The last three weeks, Ricardo sent him on the same surveillance duty every time there was little to do at the base. When his food came, he dove into his eggs with gusto; the drive to the city was forty-five minutes, a long time for him to go without breakfast. A few hours had passed before he noticed a picture on the wall that he never noticed on his previous visits. It was a black-and-white picture of a vintage convertible roadster pickup truck with a surfboard in the back and the driver's arm waiving out of the window. When he ate orange chicken for lunch, he thought, *That roadster looks good without a hood. Back in those days, the style was different. There were no seat belt laws, fewer people, and more freedom. Those days are gone.*

He noticed a few people walk by the warehouse, however, none of them were his target. He ordered more coffee when 5:00 p.m. ticked by, and he was ready to head back to the base when a black sedan rolled up to the warehouse. Two men in dark suits and glasses exited the vehicle and scanned the street, while they performed what Kiko recognized as a threat assessment. When the men believed it was all clear, they opened the rear door of the warehouse, and then two women stepped out of the vehicle and entered the warehouse. Kiko went into the bathroom and found it empty, and then walked into one of the stalls and dialed on his cell phone.

"I think we have something," he said.

"I will inform the boss. Take the painting out," said Ricardo, on the other end of the phone line.

Kiko slipped his hand into his inside custom made breast pocket and pulled out a seven-inch painting, that depicted the soul of a shoe stepping onto a sidewalk. He placed it on the ground. In short order, a shoe protruded out of the painting and stepped onto the floor of the bathroom stall. Ricardo appeared from out of the painting.

"Boss is on her way. Let us go," said Ricardo, when he stepped out of the stall. A big-bellied, gruff, bearded fisherman took a whiz in a urinal when he witnessed Ricardo step out of the stall with Kiko.

"Get a room, faggots," he said.

Ricardo produced a gun and pointed it at the fisherman. Kiko placed his hand on the hammer.

"There are about thirty people out there. You need a silencer. We are not here for him," Kiko cautioned. Ricardo considered Kiko's comment, and then put the gun back in its holster. He and Kiko walked out. The fisherman breathed a sigh of relief.

INK

On the second floor of the warehouse, Jason was in the kitchen with the oven door open, where roast beef and potatoes were cooking. He stuck a knife into the beef, and then onto his tongue to see if the inside was cold or hot.

It was cooked. Jason shunned the use of a meat thermometer; he was old school when it came to cooking. He liked to make pasta from scratch, without a pasta machine, and he would even knead it himself. The doorbell *RANG!* He stepped down the stairs to open it. Flanery and Lauren stood outside, along with Ditta and a big black man named Johnston.

"Mr. Crawford," said Flanery, "Lauren and Ditta are here to see you. This is Johnston; Mr. Braxton is on another assignment."

Jason nodded and said, "Come in."

"It is my duty to scan the premises," said Flanery.

Jason waved him in, and Flanery scanned the warehouse, with his gun lowered, while Johnston stood by the girls outside. All were smirking, and tried not to laugh.

"Hello. What?" Jason asked.

"Did you forget to dress this morning?" Lauren said.

He wore a cowboy hat, a white apron, shorts, and cowboy boots, he retorted, "This is my chef's uniform. The hat keeps my hair from falling into the food, the apron keeps the food off me, and the boots kick the shit out of the cabinets when the food tastes like crap."

"And the shorts?" Ditta asked.

"They come off when something gives me a rise," said Jason, while Ditta giggled.

"Bro!" said Lauren, and rolled her eyes.

Jason said, "Hello, Sister!" The sound of that phrase felt especially good to him while it rolled slowly off his tongue.

Lauren hugged him and said, "Hello, Brother!"

INK

Jason smirked at Ditta and then said in a flirting way, "Ditta."

"Jason," said Ditta.

Flanery returned to the door. "All clear." He touched his earpiece and spoke into his wristwatch. "Package is at one."

The girls entered and placed three full shopping bags near the door.

Jason ushered them in. "Shopping!" Flanery and Johnston stayed outside of the door. "Come in, guys. I made food for all of us."

Flanery shook his head. "Thanks, Mr. Crawford, but we are working. We have to stand guard."

"We are eating on the second floor. Wait outside that door," Jason said, and they all entered, and then he closed the door. He turned to the girls and pointed to the left at the stairs—led them up the steps, opened the door to a dining table near the kitchen. "Sit. The dining table is all set up for you. Let me get some wine." Then he closed the door.

Flanery and Johnston waited outside the door.

"Wine sounds good," said Ditta, and she sat at the table. Jason went to the fridge.

Lauren scanned her surroundings and said, "Where is Angela? I would like to meet her."

"Her flight was held up. She should be here soon. She said to start without her," he said, when he opened a bottle of wine.

"So, this is my brother's pad."

Lauren stepped around the large warehouse. *It is clean,* she thought, *the only picture in there was of her, Fergus and Jason at the restaurant.* Jason filled the girls' glasses with wine.

Lauren glanced at the picture. "Can I look around?"

Jason gestured with outstretched arms, "Go right ahead. I went through your stuff."

"You did not," said Lauren.

"Hey," said Jason, "A lady's gotta have what gets her through the night."

Lauren was horrified, and with rapid fire said, "You asshole. I am going through all your stuff. Asshole." She walked straight into the bedroom.

INK

"She would not need that thing if Captain America would lay some pipe," said Ditta.

"I heard that. Leave Braxton out of it," Lauren shouted, when she searched under the bed and found a stack of Playboy magazines. She flicked through them and took them into the dining room. Jason took two beers from the fridge.

Ditta smirked and said, "I am hoping Captain America heard that."

Lauren giggled. "Look what I found?" She raised some porn magazines. "What do you call these?"

"Sleeping pills," said Jason.

Lauren and Ditta laughed.

"You have different types of magazines," said Ditta.

"I do not have a type," said Jason, and walked past Ditta with a whisper, "I like' em all." She giggled, and liked the flirtation.

He opened the door and gave Flanery and Johnston a beer each. "I didn't see anything," he said, and closed the door. "This does not seem fair."

"Why?" Ditta asked.

"Because you have seen me naked," said Jason.

"How do you suggest we rectify this tragedy of biblical proportions?" Jason and Ditta struggled to keep straight faces.

"After much thought and many sleepless nights, I would have to say reparations were in order."

"Reparations? I think you used that word incorrectly," said Lauren.

"I do not care. I want to see Ditta naked."

"Reparations are when someone is hurt," said Ditta, straight faced.

"I was hurt. It was a cold night. My dignity took a pounding. For reparations, I propose that the poundee," he pointed to himself, "pound thee." He pointed at Ditta. She broke her straight face and laughed.

"Flanery and Braxton saw your junk, too. Do you need to see their junk?" Lauren asked.

INK

Disgust came over Jason, and the girls laughed at the face he made. "That is just wrong—wrong on so many levels. It is different. I have no interest in seeing their junk."

Ditta scoffed, "Why not? It is the same thing!"

"No it is not. Vaginas are pretty," said Jason. "I like to see pretty things. It makes me happy. Don't you like to see people happy?"

"Yes, how—"

"If you do, if you truly do, you have an obligation, not just to me but to humanity, to the entire world, to flash away," he said, with outstretched arms. The girls looked at one another and laughed.

INK

Karen sat in the back of a limo, surrounded by Ricardo, Kiko, and five large mercs dressed in black, that placed ski masks on.

Karen looked at them, and then ordered, "I want the three in the room unharmed; everyone else is expendable."

"Does everyone know what to do?" Ricardo asked. The hired guns stuck their thumbs up. Kiko drew his gun, "Let us go." Then he opened the car door, and the five mercs followed him out of the limo. One of the mercs climbed the fire escape stairs; a rope dangled from his hip. Ricardo stayed with Karen in the limo. Kiko and the remaining mercs went around the front of the building. One of them opened the front door and waved the rest in. They all stepped lightly, and avoided the girls' shopping bags. One of the mercs hid behind the post of the staircase and trained his gun-sight on Flanery, who stood at the top of the landing.

Another merc had Johnston in the crosshairs of his gun-sight. Everything happened at once in an explosion of silenced automatic weapon fire. Several bullets hit Flanery and Johnston. Their bodies slumped to the ground with a thud.

Inside the room Jason, Lauren, and Ditta ate dinner. Jason's knife scraped his plate. "Moses, the caregiver at the foster... What was that?"

Then the kitchen window was peppered with holes, and Jason shouted, "Get down!" A merc burst through, and sent the last pieces of the window frame crashing away, when he swung into the kitchen. Jason, already in motion, did a spin kick and the merc flew back out the window.

"He was not invited," Jason quipped, when he turned to see Lauren and Ditta under the table with just their eyes exposed. "Stay down."

Ditta searched for a tile from her pocket.

INK

The door exploded open. Jason threw the knife and caught a merc in the neck, and he slumped to the ground.

Jason then attacked, and kicked a gun out of another merc's hand. Lauren and Ditta crawled away. Jason drove his open palm up into an attacker's nose, and it burst with blood. Ditta pulled a tile of an arctic tiger from her pocket, however, it was broken in half. She clutched onto Lauren. "My protector's broken," she said. Lauren watched her brother in fear, and Ditta had to shake her to get her attention. "Lauren!"

"I will get mine," said Lauren, and reached into her shirt, pulled out the tile. She was about to cut her finger when Kiko stuck a gun in her face. "Freeze," he ordered.

Jason avoided a punch, and then kicked another merc in the chest. The body would have fallen backwards, however, Jason had the merc's arm in his free hand—jerked it like a rope and tore it from its socket—that caused him to drop like a ton of bricks. Jason's knee rocketed hard into another merc's gut, then his foot drove like a piston through his knee, and shattered it. When he fell away, he ripped Jason's shirt off. A gun clattered across the floor, and it startled him.

"Freeze! Or they get it," Kiko said. He had the gun pointed at Lauren and Ditta. Jason stopped. Kiko waved out the window down to the limo. Soon Ricardo walked into the room, followed by Karen. Both carried guns. Karen walked purposefully over to the girls.

"What is your name?" Karen probed.

"Amy Bennett," said Lauren. Karen suspicious, then eyed Ditta.

"Sofia Vankamp," said Ditta.

Karen raised a black-and-white picture of Lauren as a child between the two of them, and then smiled at Lauren.

"A DNA test will confirm who you are," said Karen. She turned to Ricardo. "Tie their hands behind their backs." She saw the four mercenaries on the floor in different states of injury. "Ricardo, we need more mercenaries. Find someone good! Get those bodies out of the way." Ricardo dragged Flanery and Johnston's dead bodies into the room by their feet. Kiko helped the Mercs up on their feet, while Karen kept the gun aimed at

INK

Jason. Karen gestured with the gun at the girls. "Take them away." She then squeezed the trigger and fired. The bullet hit a rose tattoo on Jason's stomach. He screamed in pain, covered the area with his left hand, and fell to the ground.

Lauren screamed, when Ricardo lifted her out of the room at gunpoint. Karen dragged Ditta out and then shut the door. The rose tattoo on Jason pulsated, and pushed a thin stream of light through his veins and arteries, which set off a chain reaction, that linked all his tattoos together. When all the tattoos linked, a flash of light exploded. All the way to the limo, Karen tried to make sense of the remorse she felt, until she saw the flash of light from the window. She shoved Lauren and Ditta into the limousine, and then she sat in the passenger seat and ordered the driver to go.

The tattoos on Jason's body became vibrant with color, linked up, lit up, and started to pulse in unison like protective armor. An hour passed before a cab pulled up to the warehouse. Angela, dressed in jeans and a white t-shirt, stepped out onto the curb with an overnight bag. She paid the driver, turned, and walked up to the door. It was slightly open. *Strange*, she thought, and after *KNOCKING!* several times with no answer, she entered. This was the first time she had been there so she took her time and glanced around. A half built Harley on a motorcycle stand, and a large tool box were the only things on the first floor.

She called for Jason; when she received no response, she climbed the stairs and noticed a trail of blood that dripped down the stairs from the landing, apparently came from whatever was on the other side of the door. She cautiously opened the door without stepping inside and scanned the room. She saw Flanery with two bloodied bullet wounds in his chest, and next to him, Johnston, with a bullet wound to his forehead that trickled blood. Angela became slack jawed and many thoughts raced through her mind. *She did not know if they were dead, whether to enter or not or if the shooter was in the room. Could Jason be the shooter? Is Jason alive? Where is he?*

Next to the window, Jason lay on the floor. Angela ran to him, checked his pulse, shook him, and then slapped him in the

INK

face to no avail. She noticed his tattoos glow with what seemed a supernatural pulse of light. The ink started to ooze out of the tattoos and pour from his skin onto the floor, and some smudged onto her hand. The tattoos stayed vibrant while the ink poured out black, red, green, yellow, and orange, as if it were blood.

"What the fuck?" Angela said. She dragged him in the direction of the bathroom in a panic. One of his hands fell from his abdomen, where it had covered a rose tattoo. It contained a flattened bullet. His skin seemed untouched.

She slid opened the shower door. Then maneuvered him into the tub. She reached up and turned on the shower then she ran out of the room. The water washed the ink from Jason's body. Angela, returned on the phone.

"911, I have an emergency…"

The water splashed on Jason's face, and his eyes opened slowly.

"Jason, you are awake! I have called an ambulance. Are you okay?"

Jason grunted, and rose up on his elbows. "I am okay. No need for an ambulance."

"What about the other two?"

"What two?"

"The two men in the living room. What happened?"

"Some men forced themselves… Where are Lauren and Ditta?" The shark tattoo ink on his calf muscle glistened.

"I don't know," said Angela, when Jason touched the shark tattoo. The shark came to life in short order, so it was in the tub with him. The shark's mouth opened wide to reveal rows of razor-sharp teeth. Angela screamed. The shark tried to bite Jason, however, he placed his hand under the shark's jaw and pushed away, that flipped the shark over so its tail then faced him. Angela screamed again, while she stretched out with her hand to Jason. He jumped out of the bathtub. The shark thrashed around uncontrollably. Several times, it went up on the rim, and almost came out of the tub. Then Angela pushed the door shut until it stuck halfway where the shark had bent the rail.

"How the hell did you do that?" She asked, in shock.

INK

On the floor with his back to the wall and out of breath, Jason said, "It was itchy. I just touched it."

Angela shuddered. "Touch your stars."

He touched a star tattoo on his right shoulder, and a throwing star slowly emerged from his skin. Jason gripped it in his hand.

"Oh my god," disbelievingly, Angela stuttered.

Jason touched another star tattoo on his left shoulder, and another star appeared. "What the fuck?"

Agent Decker and Braxton entered Jason's warehouse apartment with their guns drawn, followed by ten military troops from the SSA, dressed in swat gear.

"Freeze, SSA police, put your hands up!" shouted Decker from the doorway, and pointed the gun at Angela's back. Decker could not see Jason from her angle. Angela raised her arms slowly. Jason signaled to Angela and placed a finger on his lips in a gesture that said, "hush." He pointed to his tattoos, indicating for her not to mention what had just happened.

"Turn around and walk out slowly," Agent Decker said, and Angela did it. Decker then saw another figure on the floor in her peripheral vision; she pushed Angela towards Braxton, who held her, and then Decker spun sideways and pointed the gun at the figure. She realized it was Jason and let out a sigh of relief.

"Do not move," she said to Jason, when she heard a commotion from the tub. She opened the shower door and saw the shark while it thrashed around. Decker panicked and quickly blasted two bullets into it, killing it. The showerhead poured water onto the shark when it laid dead. Blood poured from it, while it oozed down the drain. Black ink strands streaked within the red blood.

INK

INK

A middle-aged doctor, who wore thick eyeglasses, examined Jason's arm. Jason laid on a rollaway bed, stripped down to his blue boxers. There was a table in the middle of the room and a stainless steel bench bolted to the floor. Two chairs were on the opposite side of the table. A camera was mounted in plain sight in the upper corner of the room. Jason figured the stainless steel bench was probably easier to clean up after an intense interrogation.

"Who did she look like?" Fergus asked, who wore a brown dressing gown.

"I don't know," said Jason. He reached over to scratch an itch on his right arm awkwardly, and made sure not to touch any tattoos. He was unsure of what his body would do now.

Agent Decker asked Jason, "Was he there?" And flashed a picture of Ricardo.

"Yeah," said Jason. "Ricardo Costa!" and made a mental note.

"He is bad news. Don't get any ideas," warned Decker. She was not stupid.

Fergus stuck a suspect book in Jason's face, with six pictures of females spread out on a page.

"Any of them?"

"No."

"Ricardo's trouble, so stay away from him," she said.

"Stay away?" Jason asked, when he closed the suspect book and then shook his head no.

"Ricardo has fourteen confirmed kills," said Decker.

"So I have some catching up to do."

"I know, boy," said Fergus. He placed a hand on Jason's knee. "It has been discussed. The Director sent three of his best, and he has agreed, you are to be involved."

Agent Decker abruptly cut in. "How did that happen?" She asked.

INK

"I showed him his resume," said Fergus.

Agent Decker exited in a huff. Behind a two-way mirror, Braxton watched and listened to the whole conversation.

"Guy's gonna get himself killed," said Decker.

"No gun was found, and the ambulance phone call checked out. She is clean," said Braxton.

The doctor entered the room. "He has four syringe punctures under his toenails," he said.

Braxton nodded. "Do you know what was injected?"

The doctor shook his head. "No."

"Any guesses, Doc?" Decker asked.

"Said he had not had an injection in years. Those punctures have not been there longer than three months. We have seen marks like these on drug addicts to hide their addiction from authorities, however, as Mr. Crawford does not have any drugs in his system, my guess would be that he was drugged with a substance to cause memory loss."

Decker pondered for a moment. "What do you think?"

"I do not think he had anything to do with it," said Braxton.

"If we release him, they could go after him again."

"It would not be safe for him."

"Assign some men to watch him," said Decker. "Where did the shark come from?"

Braxton raised an eyebrow and said, "No one knows."

Angela prepared food in Jason's kitchen when the door opened and Jason entered. She saw him and said, "Good, you are here. I made dinner."

"I am hungry," said Jason, when he found a pen and paper. Then he began to write.

"I have to leave for work tomorrow. Would you like me to come back next weekend?"

Jason raised the paper that said, THERE IS A GOOD CHANCE WE ARE BEING BUGGED.

"Yeah, I would like that," he said, and went back to writing. She placed some trash in the bin.

Jason raised the paper, DID YOU SAY ANYTHING ABOUT THE TATTOOS COMING TO LIFE?

INK

Angela shook her head, no.

Jason went back to writing.

Angela continued, "Prosecutor's office up here has a job opening."

"Working at Mousewitz not fulfilling?" Jason asked.

"Defending you, back in the courts, was so exciting. Mousewitz?"

"That is a nickname made up by Jewish Disney employees," said Jason.

"That is awful."

Jason raised the paper again, *DO NOT EVER MENTION THE TATTOOS COMING TO LIFE TO ANYONE.*

"Slavery's an ugly business."

"Slavery's illegal," she said.

"Between little-league baseball and Disney, they divided twenty-two million dollars last year," said Jason. "The thirteen-year-old players did not get one dime; some of the kids could not afford their own school books."

Angela was shocked. "Twenty-two million?"

"Disney's just a modern day plantation owner whose cowardly shareholders hide their faces with a company name. That is a greedy, evil company."

She took the pen and paper. "I did not know you felt that way about my job."

"It does not really matter, as long as it makes you happy."

"It matters to me. Sit, let us eat."

She placed two plates of orange chicken on the table. They sat.

"Wish I knew what happened to Lauren and Ditta," said Jason. "This is takeout from Hop Sing. You did not make this."

Angela smiled. "I ordered it and set it on the plate."

"Making it is like cooking. It gets me excited when I hear someone is cooking for me." He dug into the food nonetheless.

"Good to know." She raised the paper that read, *DOES IT STILL HAPPEN?* "I forgot the knives." She stood up and Jason took a hold of her wrist. A tattoo of a dagger was on each forearm; he touched them, and they came to life. He then handed her one of the knives. Angela admired it. Jason pulled her to him, and she sat on his lap. She pressed the dagger to his throat. She was not sure why or where this was going. Startled at first; the blade under his chin. He wrote, *LETS GIVE THEM SOMETHING TO LISTEN TO.* She raised an eyebrow, still unaware of where this was going—until Jason dropped the pen and slipped his hand along the inside of her thigh. *He did not want to make love now,* she thought—*did he?* His fingers moved on to her crotch, he was pleasantly surprised she did not wear any panties.

"Oh," she said. *That is, what he wants,* she thought.

"Forget something?"

"Not at all." She gave him a wicked grin.

He touched her naked pussy lips.

"Oh," she moaned, *does he want them to hear?*

"Feel something you like?"

"I could ask you the same thing."

He leaned forward against the dagger, and ran his nose up her neck.

"You smell so good," he murmured, a look of pure pleasure on his face. Angela was confused and excited with different thoughts. *Sex while someone is possibly listening was something new. A little kink never hurt anyone. He is gentle. Wait! Am I being raped?* His finger was inside of her, however, she held the knife to his throat, and theoretically, was in control. *You cannot rape the willing,* she told herself, and placed the knife down. Then she gave herself to him. They kissed. He picked her up, carried her to the sofa, and laid her gently on it.

"You are very beautiful, Angela," he said, and it took her breath away.

"So you are just going to use me?" She asked under his steady gaze.

"Yeah," he said, and then ripped her shirt open, that exposed her breasts. A button flew into the air, and then hit a window with a *TING.*

Down below, parked on the street, was a white electrical van. In its cargo area, an agent pointed a parabolic microphone out of the window towards the building. The sound of the button hitting the window was so loud in his headphones, he slapped them off and then held his ears in pain. Next to him, another agent, who sat at a desk surrounded with electronics, saw him grimace.

"What is it?" The agent asked, and then picked up the headphones. He heard Angela and Jason make love.

In the laboratory, Karen inspected two lines of DNA strands under a microscope.

"Amy Bennett, your DNA strand matches mine. Or should I say, Lauren Blackwood Crawford? She rose her head from the microscope, and turned to Lauren with a disturbing smile on her face. Then she walked over to Lauren, whose left wrist was handcuffed to a chair. "Are you Jessica Blackwood Crawford?" Lauren asked.

"Jessica Blackwood Crawford—I have not heard that name in a long time," she said. "Yes, I am your mother, your father, nurse—"

"You bitch," Lauren spat out.

"Killing your brother was necessary. You need to understand a male's place in the world. They exist for the use of us females. Now that you are with me, Lauren, they will pay. With my blood ink and your Durga power, we will be unstoppable. We can destroy those who wronged us."

"I will not help you, you crazy, bitch," said Lauren.

"Your destiny lies ahead of you," said Karen, and gestured with her finger. "You have seen how the rest of the worms scramble around in the dirt for what you can do as easily as spitting. You have seen what their lives are like." Her eyes were wide open, and her expression entirely mad. "You will master the gifts I have given you, and you will make this world kneel."

"No," said Lauren. She said it quietly, without inflection, as if she was offhandedly canceling a coffee date with an old friend. "I will not."

Karen grabbed a Berretta 3032 Tomcat pistol from a table and pointed it at Lauren.

"Yes you will, or you will die."

"Shoot. I'm not afraid of dying, mother. Living, and knowing I came from someone like you is what I'm afraid of."

INK

That angered Karen, so she pointed the gun at Ditta, who was handcuffed to a separate chair. Ditta had her shirt ripped down, that exposed her naked breasts; her chest was wired with four white disk electrodes to various monitors, and alternately she shivered and sweated. Cohen plugged in the electrodes to an electrocardiography machine. Ditta saw the gun pointed at her, and she looked into the dark ominous barrel of the gun. She turned her head away. Lauren could not stand to see her friend like that, so she was about to concede when she heard, "We need her," said Cohen.

Lauren, then confident she was bluffing, smiled. She was wrong.

"You idiot," Karen spat to Cohen, and then pulled the trigger; the gun went off, and the bullet ripped through Ditta's shoulder. Ditta let out a high-pitched scream.

"OKAY, OKAY, OKAY. I will do whatever you want," said Lauren.

Through the hazy smoke, while it rose from the gun barrel, "Damn fuck'n right you will." Karen warned, and then eyeballed Cohen. "Speak out of turn again and I will kill you." She placed the gun on the bench.

"Yes boss," Cohen said and then went to attend to Ditta's bullet wound. He collected blood with a syringe. Karen took the syringe from him, squirted some on a slide, and then placed it into another microscope. At her work station bench was a full 24 slot syringe rack holder. She clutched one syringe full of black ink from it.

"Bullet went in and out," said Cohen.

"Patch the bitch up," ordered Karen.

She looked into the eyepiece of the microscope. Bright red blood cells lay dormant on a slide, until a needle entered the objective lens, and punctured the cell. Black ink mixed with it and the cell reacted violently. It bubbled and spit like a volcano—tried to move away from the ink, which consumed the red cell like a wave and then it lay inactive, with black streaks through the far more vibrant red cell. Karen then opened a bag of a new clean empty hypodermic, and gently guided it to the slide. The needle pierced the contaminated cell, and was sucked into the hypodermic.

She walked over to Ditta, who had fainted from the pain. Karen jammed the needle into Ditta's shoulder and plunged down. Then she went to the diagnostic machine, where Cohen took notes. Ditta's EKG signs reacted violently.

Lauren risked another glance at Ditta; she breathed heavily. *What was in the hypodermic? Is my friend going to die? This is all my fault.* Her gaze drifted back to her mother. *If Ditta dies, I will kill you,* she thought, with intense certainty.

"That is to be expected," said Karen, and pointed to a spike on the screen of the EKG machine. "This will take some time. Keep monitoring the EKG."Ricardo ran in, followed by Kiko.

"We just saw Jason at the warehouse. He is still alive!" Lauren's heart skipped a beat.

"Keep an eye on him," said Karen.

"Can I kill him?" Ricardo asked.

"No," said Karen, and winked at Ricardo. Vernon entered and stood by the door. Karen turned to Lauren and said, "See, we can be reasonable." She un-cuffed Lauren. "Now come with me. I have a project for you," and dragged her to Vernon.

"Hhhhe's ready for her," said Vernon.

Karan, Lauren, Ricardo and Kiko went out the door.

INK

INK

Parked on the side of the road was a black sedan. Braxton and two SSA agents, dressed in dark suits and sunglasses stood beside it. They kept close surveillance on a single-story commercial building across the street, with a large neon sign on the roof that simply said "TT." A green Norton Commando motorcycle and silver Harley Davidson Fatboy were parked on the street in front of the store. By the entrance was a yellow Ducati 748 motorcycle. Braxton walked up the street to inspect the store, and he noted the peculiar name of the business they were staking out: "Tormented Tattoos." The store window had a unique design. In the four corners were red, yellow, blue, purple, black, orange, and green stained glass in the shape of spider webs. The spider web formed a clear oval, when it converged in the center of the glass. The agents had a clear view of the interior.

Inside the tattoo shop, seven customers scanned the walls like they were window-shopping. The beige walls were covered with artwork—samples of tattoos that customers could have inked onto their skin. Four workstations were busy with customers receiving tattoos. Rock music filled the room from a stereo on a mirrored Gothic armoire made from mahogany wood. A book on _Birds_ lay open on top. The page displayed the wingspan of an eagle. What was once a trade that drew in sailors, prisoners, and bikers, a business that had been considered trouble by the average citizen, and avoided by city business permit departments, had become mainstream. It was filled with the average everyday person—yuppies, business people, and bohemian types, all of who wanted tattoos. The shop rode the crest of that wave, and it came large, fast and furious. In 2012, one in five people in the USA had at least one tattoo. The old way of using photo albums stuffed with Polaroid examples of clients' tattoos was a thing of the past.

INK

Now, they used wallpaper, printed with popular tattoo images, to entice customers and save time in the selection process. Store owners realized time was money; they could have one person combing through a photo album at a time, or they could have thirty people viewing the wallpaper images. Near the bench, Jason rested in a barber's chair. He wore his hat, and read a book to himself. *"...spiders have hundreds of thousands of tiny hairs on their feet. There is an electrostatic force between each of these hairs and the surface it touches. The force is very small, however, multiply it by hundreds of thousands, and you have a charge big enough to stick to any surface, no matter how smooth."*

While he was having tattoo work done on his fingertips by Tatman, a short, skinny, long curly haired Latino was covered in so many tattoos, it was difficult to make any of them out clearly. He had piercings on his left eyebrow, left nostril and bottom left lip. Tatman's attention was drawn to the book Jason was reading. It was open to a microscopic image of the hairs on a spider's leg.

Tatman shook his head in bewilderment. "Spider hair on fingers and toes. These are the strangest tattoos I have ever done. No one's ever going to see them," he said finishing-up.

"That is the idea. The next one will not be as strange," said Jason. He rubbed his tattooed fingertips together and saw static electricity that buzzed between his thumb and fingertips. Then he pulled out $300 from his wallet and gave it to Tatman.

"Thanks. Now, I need these wings done." He pointed to the *Bird* book on the armoire, and to the image of an eagle.

Tatman saw the picture, took the $300, and stuffed the cash into his jeans pocket, and then went over to a sink and scrubbed up. "It is difficult to do eagle wings. I can do a cross between an angel and an eagle."

"That is okay."

"Something small on your chest?"

"No. Back job, from shoulders to ankle."

"Fuck dude, that'll take me a week."

"Book me in. Later," Jason said, and crossed the floor, however, stopped at a beautiful girl that swept the floor; She had long, wild, red hair, in her twenties, with an ethnic background of mixed Tahitian and European.

He tilted his hat, and said, "Ma'am."

She stopped sweeping, held the broom at the top of the stick with both hands, rested her chin on her hands, and said, "Ma'am?" slightly offended. "What do I call you? Mister, sir, or is it cowboy?" He noticed her tattoos; on her right arm were the words "Every saint has a past" and on the left arm, "Every sinner has a future."

"You can call me mister, sir, cowboy or whatever you like. As long as you call me."

"Oh, that is good," she said.

"Thank you. Nice shirt," he said, when he stepped to the door smiling. He wore the same type of denim shirt. She smiled back and watched Jason exit the store, and then she sauntered over to Tatman. She had sexy tattoos of; fishnet stockings up her legs, a dagger, wrapped in rose vine, on each hip, with Semper Fi lettered underneath it, the words "Fuck Me" between them, just above her pussy, a tribal near her heart, a unicorn on her right upper shoulder, and a butterfly on her left shoulder. She wore a sleeveless shirt knotted in the middle to emphasize her bust and expose her flat stomach, and a tartan miniskirt with black high heels. Tatman cleaned the tattoo gun.

"Who is that?" She asked.

Tatman smiled, placed the gun down, and clapped his hands. "Tatiana has a thing for our boy!"

Tatiana rolled her eyes and said, "Fuck, you are a child."

The sun had just sunk below the horizon. Its glow diffused through the atmosphere to travel evenly through more of the city. There were no stark shadows, when the intensity of the direct light was completely diminished. It was dusk; photographers called it the "magic hour" or "golden hour." The diffusion phenomenon produced vibrant, warmer color in everything photographed. Hence the nickname. The wind blew leaves off the trees onto the street. A cowboy boot stepped on a dried leaf and crushed it to pieces. Jason strolled along the sidewalk on Kearney Street, near Post, and headed for the

INK

Montgomery Street Fisherman's Wharf train station. He had a cell phone to his ear.

"No leads whatsoever?" In the reflection on a store window, Jason could see a black sedan follow him.

"Nothing at the moment," said Braxton, on the other end.

"Is that you in the black sedan, following?"

"Yeah, you are my detail."

The sedan crept slowly behind, and followed Jason.

"Well, then you probably will not like what is about to happen."

Jason walked into a small alley where a vehicle could not enter. One of the SSA agents jumped out of the black sedan and raced into the alley. He reached the end of the alley, which opened up to four other alleys and a dumpster. The agent searched around, however, could not find Jason. He punched the air in frustration, and then went back to the car. Jason hid behind the dumpster and watched him get in the vehicle and drive off. He then placed his hands on a brick wall. Jason muttered to himself, "Now, do these things work? Grab, hold, grip. Think, think, hold."

Jason's fingers clung to the wall. He pulled one hand off the side of the wall gingerly and climbed the wall to a window. He looked into an apartment window while a sexy woman exited a shower and dried off with a towel. Jason's fingers slowly came off the wall. She bent down; he lost his concentration and started to slide down the wall.

Jason gritted his teeth. "Hold, think, hold, hold!"

He clung to the wall again. Took a deep breath, he continued to climb, and avoided the window altogether. He reached the roof and hopped onto it. On the roof was a small wooden pigeon coup. He scanned the area, and the other buildings—he was alone. *PHET, PHET, PHET, PHET* – stars and knives stabbed into the wood of the coup.

Jason yelled in a victorious tone, "I am I bad motherfucker!"

A tenant in a nearby building yelled, "Yeah, so am I!"

INK

Jason searched to find an overweight, stained tank-topped wearing, ice-cream-eating man in a window of a nearby building. "Now shut the fuck up! My kids trying to sleep."

"Yes, sir," said Jason, and tipped his hat.

Moisture had started to condense in the air by 11 p.m. It had rained heavily earlier, and washed the city clean, however, the streets were wet. Out front of the Branding Iron were fifteen customers dressed in cowboy shirts, jeans, boots, and miniskirts. Some sported cowboy hats. They all lined up, and waited to enter. Some of the girls danced to the country music that thumped from inside the club, to stay warm. Rocco stood by the front door and checked a couple's identification. Jason kept an eye on everyone in the line when Dick McGregor arrived. He cut the line and snuck behind Jason. McGregor wore a black suit and tie with a white shirt. He flashed a private investigator badge to Rocco.

Jason had spied him earlier, so he was already onto him. "Mr. McGregor, the line starts here," he said, and pointed to the end of the fifteen other people in line. McGregor was a little embarrassed when the crowd stared him down.

"Here on official business," said Dick, who flashed his PI badge at Jason, at an angle that made sure the fifteen in the line could see it.

Jason walked over and took him aside. "What business?"

"Just wanted to see where you are working," said Dick.

"That is not business. That is personal. Back of the line," Jason said, and give him a crooked smile.

Dick was pissed off, slipped his PI badge in his suit jacket, and dropped it into his breast pocket. Then he walked to the end of the line under the watchful eyes of the fifteen waiting. Two customers arrived and fell behind him in line. One of them sported a cowboy hat, beard and mustache, red plaid shirt, black vest, and blue jeans with a big belt buckle and boots. The other cowboy was the same, except a little shorter, and he wore a blue shirt and brown vest. The smaller cowboy handed a knife to the taller cowboy, who slipped it into his sleeve. They kept their eyes on Jason.

"You think that is a good idea?" Rocco asked.

"Snoop's searching for something," Jason said, suspiciously.

The taller cowboy touched a Bluetooth headset in his ear. "Where are you?" The voice of Karen came through the Bluetooth, while the two cowboys stepped closer to Jason.

"Tying up some loose ends," said Ricardo, while he smirked at Kiko in his disguise.

"I need you," said Karen.

"I am on my way," said Ricardo, and then pressed the Bluetooth and the line went dead. Ricardo did not move, and then Kiko furrowed his brow at him.

"We have time," said Ricardo. Kiko thought, *Or we will make time.*

"What is the deal with the band?" Asked Rocco.

"Abraham likes Aaron as a bartender. He lets his band rehearse."

After he checked two IDs, Rocco waved two young women in. "Are you guys ever going to play a gig?" He asked.

Dick crept closer to the front of the line. Behind him, Ricardo slowly slipped the knife out of his sleeve, that exposed a seven-inch blade.

"Not sure; rehearsals are always fun," replied Jason.

"I am feeling uneasy tonight. I am glad your friends are here," said Rocco.

Jason saw the three SSA agents sat in a car across the street.

"Freezin' my nuts off out here," he said to Rocco. Dick's ID was in his hand when he arrived to the front of the line, however, Rocco did not bother with it and waved him in. He entered the Branding Iron under Jason's stare. Ricardo and Kiko, edged to the front of the line, showed IDs to Rocco.

"I am going inside to keep an eye on the Dick," Jason said, and he turned to walk into the club. Gunshots rang out. People at the door ran for cover in all directions. Rocco fell to the floor and then cried, "I am hit." Jason knelt by Rocco and saw his white shirt slowly turn red with blood from a bullet wound by his stomach.

Jason shouted, "Call 911!"

INK

Some people pulled out their phones and called. Ricardo was shot in the arm and fell to the ground. While the gunshots continued, Jason hunted for the shooter. Across the street, three SSA agents were in a gun battle with occupants in a black Cadillac. Jason could see the bullets explode out of the guns. He whispered to himself, "What the fuck?"

A bullet hit an SSA agent and went right through him. The agent went down. Braxton and the other agents ran to the downed man when the Cadillac sped away on the wrong side of the road. Out of the rear driver's side window, a black-gloved hand held a 38 special pistol, that continued to shoot at the SSA. When a motorcyclist was forced to swerve, to avoid a crash into the Cadillac. The motorcycle handlebars hit the gun out of the shooter's hand. The gun landed on the road while the Cadillac fishtailed its getaway down the slick wet street. Jason hauled ass, he picked up the gun, and then gave chase in a full-out sprint. He weaved and spun around every vehicle and pedestrian.

The Cadillac fishtailed sideways when it turned a corner. Jason stuck the gun in his pocket, leapt onto a parked car's hood, jumped off it, and landed back on the road. From the window of the passenger seat of the Cadillac, another 38 special was aimed at Jason. He ducked and slowed, when a swarm of bullets hit, and chewed into the brick wall behind him. He tried to pull the Colt Peacemakers from his tattoos, however, they became stuck in his jeans. The Cadillac hit the sidewalk, which slowed it down. It drove up onto the sidewalk, and cut across the street to another sidewalk. Jason closed in on them, turned a corner, and he ran into a crowd that surrounded a taco truck.

Screamed, and the crowd split, while he negotiated his way through. He careened through the labyrinth, out of control. Spinning, he saw the Cadillac get on the street, and race towards a busy intersection. It plowed into the intersection, neglectful of cross-traffic; horns *HONKED,* and the Cadillac just made it through—still on the wrong side of the road. Jason ran into the intersection, while a car skidded towards him, and forced him to hurdle over the hood. He clipped its solid antenna, and it was enough to spin him off balance. He hit the street on his shoulder and rolled onto his feet, without missing a beat. *I am going to feel that tomorrow,* he thought.

The Cadillac caused oncoming traffic to brake and slide all over the wet road, and forced an SUV onto the wrong side of the road. Which hit a parked Mazda RX7. The SUV went airborne and crashed onto the road on its driver side, exploded in a hail of glass and sparks when it slid down the wet street. Jason swerved to avoid it and raised an arm to protect his eyes. The Cadillac raced into an alley, and skidded to a stop at the end of it.

Jason entered the alley, and came to a halt, he sensed danger. It was pitch black, however, he could make out the Cadillac's red stop lights. He slid into the shadows on the right-side wall for its darkness, avoided the reflected specks of light that bounced off the drain water down the center of the alley. He navigated through cardboard boxes, newspaper, and trash along the wall. With great caution, he reached the Cadillac and could see smoke rise from its exhaust pipe in the cold night. *The engine must be still running.*

Careful, they could be hiding in the car ready to run me down. Through the windows he could see the car was empty. He noticed a sliver of light that came from the building's door, slightly ajar. He made his way to it and then pushed it delicately open; it creaked. From his viewpoint, he could see an indoor swimming pool. Carefully, he opened the door halfway and stepped inside. Jason heard the sound of a gun *COCK* behind him, did a spinning kick at the door, and slammed it into the assailant who had been behind it. His gun fell to the floor.

The assailant came out of the darkness, and Jason saw it was Pauli, who screamed and grabbed Jason with a football tackle. They both fell into the pool. Pauli's long overcoat tangled Jason up while they fought underwater. The other two gangsters came from around a corner of a bathroom, with pointed guns. They were unable to get a clean shot so they jumped into the pool. All three men beat up Jason. While he avoided blows, Jason reached for his tattoos, however, his clothes kept getting in the way; the three gangsters punched him, and held him underwater.

INK

When an *ALARM* from a police vehicle sounded, the gangsters panicked and left Jason there. The gangsters quickly hopped out of the water to escape out the same door. From the bottom of the four-foot pool, Jason rose slowly to the surface, and floated on his back, with no movement; it was difficult to see if he was dead or alive. He inhaled deeply, stood up and breathed deep several more times, while he struggled to get to the edge of the pool.

At the Branding Iron, Kiko held a handkerchief on Ricardo's bloody bicep. Two police cars arrived, and blocked off the street.

"Let us get out of here," said Ricardo, when he limped into the nearest alley, he held his arm while Kiko steadied him.

The police taped off the crime scene, while a crowd gathered round. Police officers started to interview witnesses. EMTs hoisted Rocco into an ambulance. Dick McGregor found an impressionable young, preppy, clean-cut police officer, who was egger, and seemed like he just came out of the academy.

"...everywhere he goes, there is trouble."

"And you say his name is Jason Crawford?" Said the young police officer, Barney, while he wrote in his notepad.

"Yeah, I followed him from Texas. You can reach me here, if you have any questions about him." Dick gave the officer a business card.

"Okay. Thank you," said Barney, impressed by his private eye moniker on the card.

INK

INK

WINGS 'N GILLS
CHAPTER TWENTY-FIVE

Angela opened the door to the warehouse. A deliveryman stood in front of her. He might have been thirty-five or forty-years-old, however, he showed the boldness of an adolescent, when he scrutinized her from head to toe. He made Angela uneasy.

"Well hello. I am Todd Spencer, Dart Deliveries. And you are?" He said, while he leaned up against the door with his right hand in a cool, flirtatious manner. He was very handsome and knew it. He was short, slim, sleek, and wore a perfectly pressed brown uniform. His black hair was cut short and combed with care. Angela was immediately frightened of him. Perhaps because his brashness and self-assurance seemed a little out of character with his appearance.

"Angela Murray," she said.

"I have a large package for this address," he said. She paused, on an irritated edge. The package in his hand was small; this could easily escalate into a confrontation, so she waited, annoyed.

"Sign here," he said, and she took the stylus and signed on the electric note pad.

"Would you like me to bring it inside? It is heavy, and large." She snatched the package and slammed the door in his face.

"Your jeans have arrived," she said to Jason, who was stretched out on a brown sofa. He was dressed only in his shorts, with a cell phone to his ear. He tilted his head in acknowledgment to her, and then Angela went into another room. The large space echoed with the buzz of two tattoo pens. Tatman worked on Jason's lower neck, while Tatiana worked on his right hand.

"It's the Italians." Jason said, and spoke into the phone.

Dominic Carr   Page 195

INK

Braxton's voice crackled through the phone's speaker. "They have alibis. We have news on the agent. He is going to make it. I heard Rocco's going to be okay as well."

Jason saw a tattoo on Tatiana's chest. "That is good news."

Braxton cleared his throat. "The vehicle was registered to a pizza shop owner. I gotta go. I will call you if we get anything," said Braxton, and hung up.

Jason put the phone down. Then stared at a tribal tattoo on Tatiana's chest.

"Tatiana, is that a Maori tribal?" He asked, and pointed to the tattoo.

Tatiana nodded. "Yeah, you know your tattoos."

"No, I know cultures."

Tatiana raised an eyebrow. "Yeah, prove it. Where is the Hawaiki?"

"Trick question. They say the legendary Maori homeland was flooded by the Pacific Ocean due to a rise of the global sea level a thousand years ago."

Tatiana stopped tattooing. "Impressive. I like intelligent men."

"What a coincidence," said Jason. "I am an intelligent man."

"Well in that case, remind me to bang you."

"Oh, I will." The smiles gave way to sexual tension.

Tatiana capped her tattoo pen, "Fingers 'n' feet are done."

Tatman asked, "Work on the wings?"

"Can I start on his butt?" asked Tatiana, with a devilish smile.

Jason's skin stung by now. He stretched. "Let us take a break—" Jason stood up and walked past Tatiana "—and a cold friggin' shower."

Tatiana smiled. Angela entered the room with jeans and a T-shirt in her hands. She saw the tattoo from Tatman. "Nice job on the gills. You can barely see them."

Tatman flexed his long, thin fingers, "Finesse in my art is what I strive for."

"Looks good. Try these." Angela handed Jason a black body shirt with sewn slits and blue jeans torn at the left knee. He tried them on while the tattooists sat on the sofa and finished their beers.

Tatman plunked his empty down. "You like the torn stuff?"

Tatiana wriggled. "It is a sexy look."

Angela's cell phone rang. "Hello. Yes...that works for me. See you then." She hung up and addressed the whole room. "I have a job interview tomorrow."

"That is great," said Tatman. "So you are going to be a prosecutor?"

"I hope so," said Angela. "Do they fit? How are they?"

"Jeans need to be lower at the front."

"If the jeans go any lower, they shall show your junk."

"Go lower. T-shirt is too tight."

"It shows your muscles," said Tatiana.

"I do not care about that. I need to be comfortable."

"It is late to start on another shirt. Just try it," said Angela.

"It needs a slit here." Jason pointed to his back at the lower neck, where the handle of the sword tattoo was.

Angela inspected the T-shirt. "Okay." Jason held Angela around the waist and guided her into the kitchen away from the tattooists.

Jason spoke quickly and in a low voice. "I have to warn you; from now on when you are bad, you will not get spanked. You will get paddled." Jason raised his hand. In the middle of his palm was the scar from a rope burn he received as a kid. When he spread his fingers, they were webbed, and formed a paddle.

Eyebrows raised, and flushed with excitement, Angela said, "I gotta try those. Get them out of here."

A round frame supported five spreaders that kept open a bloody, fleshy arm wound. At the submarine base, Ricardo laid on a table, topless and sweating, when Karen dug into his arm with long forceps, gently pulled the lodged bullet out. Vernon stood nearby with a metal pan. With a *DING!* Karen dropped the bullet into it and then handed the forceps to Cohen. She took off her gloves and facemask.

"Patch him up," she ordered Cohen, and he rolled a tray with bandages closer to Ricardo.

INK

Karen pulled Ricardo's hair. "I want you to go to the ship and get it ready for the Adriatic, understood?" He agreed.

Kiko hovered by with a phone to his ear and said, "He has arrived."

"Bring him in," said Ricardo, and Kiko went out the door. "Bring who in?" Karen probed.

"You have been annoyed with the quality of people we have been employing. So when you told me to get someone good, I made some inquiries."

CREEEEK went the door when it opened. Kiko entered followed by Oleg and they both walked over to Karen.

"I understand you are looking for a professional," said Oleg.

Karen smiled. "Let us talk," she said, to Oleg and placed her arm in his, and then directed him out of the room.

"Kiko?" Ricardo said. "I want you to stay here and protect her."

Karen walked down one of the cavernous hallways a short distance, opened a heavy soundproof door to the print room, and let herself in. Lauren sat at a table and worked on a tile, while Frank Burns sat and watched her.

"Is she finished?" Karen probed, while she took off a ruby broach from the lapel of her jacket. Lauren set the final touches of carving and coloring to the tile.

"Almost," said Frank. "She is actually a very good artist, very talented."

"Thank you, Mr. Burns," said Lauren, and offered the tile to Karen. "There you go."

Karen saw the image on the tile; it was her Beretta 3032 pistol. She raised her actual Beretta pistol, which Lauren had used for an example, from the table. Karen examined the gun artwork in the tile for discrepancies and found none. She was amazed at the detail, still, did not show it. She stuck the gun in her pocket, placed the tile on the table and then grabbed Lauren's finger and forced the pin of her broach onto it. The finger bled and dripped onto the image. The Beretta slowly appeared on the tile. Karen gripped the gun, turned, and shot all its bullets into a human cadaver, that hung on a hook and dripped blood into a barrel. The *BOMBASTIC* sound echoed in the room, and forced Lauren and Frank to cover their ears.

"Works," said Karen, then placed the gun on the table. She pulled out the picture and placed it on the table in front of Lauren. "Make two of these."

Lauren saw the picture was of a bomb. "That is the anatomy of an atomic bomb; it is illegal for Symbolists to make bombs," she said.

"If you do not, I will kill Ditta, and then you," said Karen, smugly. "I will make you a deal; you make these two bombs, and I shall allow you to choose which target one of them is dropped on, as long as it is the SSA headquarters." She exited the print room, closed the door, and locked it.

Karen walked down another hallway to the laboratory. When she entered, the bright fragmented light from the electrodes, flashed and sparked in the laboratory, caused the animals to stir in their cages. They scattered for shelter and paced in circles—some of them hid behind one another, as if they sensed danger. Vernon tried to calm them with fruit and vegetables.

"Something strange is happening," said Cohen standing over by Ditta, who laid on the workbench. Karen walked over to him, and then witnessed the bullet wound in Ditta heal itself to smooth skin, with no evidence of a wound.

"Interesting, but that's not what we are after," said Karen. She went over to a table, sat in a chair, and then examined some slides with blood on them.

"We can sell this and make a fortune."

"I have a fortune."

"It's a discovery that can change the world, we…"

Karen turned from the slides and eyeballed him with daggers in her eyes, annoyed that he interrupted her research. Cohen, already on thin ice, saw that expression, shut-up and hastily placed white disk electrodes all over the unconscious Ditta. Karen went back to the slides, confident her message was received. Vernon, who witnessed the exchange, slowly made his way to Karen. When she peaked into the viewer of the microscope, Vernon stole one of the syringes from the 24 rack

INK

full of black ink. Cohen was writing notes on a pad, and saw Vernon stuff the syringe in his pocket and walk towards him. Karen raised her head from the microscope and noticed one syringe missing. Cohen announced to all, "EV nine firing in five." Karen paid attention.

He walked over to a machine that had wires connected to Ditta and placed his finger on a toggle switch, and then said, "In five—four—three—two—one." He flipped the switch. Vernon stood near the bed. Ditta's body jerked, shuddered, and twitched when electricity passed through it. The flow of electricity stopped. There she lay, with her mouth and eyes wide open. Nearby, a heart monitor flat-lined and the *ALARM* sounded.

"Damn it," Karen cursed, and threw up her arms. Then she peaked into the microscope again.

"We have a problem." Cohen pressed into Ditta's chest.

"So I heard," Karen said, nonchalantly, and continued looking into the microscope viewer. "It is the same as Jason's dosage," she said, when she stood up, and watched Cohen. "Does not make sense."

"Help me save her life," Cohen begged, frantic.

She noticed that Vernon had a glazed expression on his face, shocked. She promptly slapped him with a left to the face. He snapped out of it and saw the word *Slut* tattooed on her forearm. He ran over and breathed into Ditta's mouth, timed his duty with the heart massage from Cohen. Karen just stood, deep in thought.

The flat line jumped when Ditta's heart started pumping. Cohen backed up, staggered a bit, and out of breath. "It makes perfect sense if Jason has developed an immunity to it. How long did you say you have been experimenting on him?"

Karen considered this. "Good point. Let me see." Karen stepped closer to Ditta, who then vomited on her. "I am going to kill the bitch." She raised an electric bone cutter. Cohen stepped in front of her, blocking access to Ditta.

"Do you want to go back to experimenting on animals and Jason?" Cohen said. Karen lowered the bone cutter while it continued to buzz.

INK

A tattoo pen buzzed, while feathers were drawn on the back of Jason's leg. Rock music from the radio played in the background of the warehouse. Jason was face down on the sofa, and just wore shorts. His legs were raised, relaxed on pillows. Tatman sat in a chair, and worked the pen. "Tatiana was pissed when I told her I was coming here and didn't need her."

"You hit that?"

"I wish," said Tatman. "If she weren't such a good tattooist, I would have fired her ass."

"What for?"

"Not putting out. What the fuck's the matter with you?"

"Yeah, right," said Jason. "Beautiful woman."

"She likes ya. Give her a jump."

"Sure, Angela would love that."

"Throw her into the mix."

"Then I would have no need for heaven."

"You two an item now?"

"I have no clue," said Jason.

"Women touch your dick and they think they have property rights."

"It is not property rights. They do not pay any property taxes. Its squatter's rights." They both laughed.

"Done." Tatman raised his arms in victory, like he had scored a goal in a soccer match. "Fuck, dude. I thought I would never finish those fuckin' wings."

"You and me both. What do I owe ya?"

"Last payment is eight hundred."

Jason went over to a chair with a pair of jeans flung over it. He delved through his pockets, took out $500, and gave it to Tatman. "I am short three hundred. Can I owe you?"

Tatman took the five hundred. "Yeah, sure. I know where you live," he said, with a smile. "Gotta run. Have another customer."

Jason saw him out. "I will swing by with the three."

Tatman paused in the doorway. "I will say hello to Tatiana for you. Later," he said with a devilish grin.

Jason closed the door, touched his wings and they came to life—then expanded a foot above his head. Jason smiled. He craned his stiff neck to look over his shoulder and almost blacked out at what he saw. The wings grew out of his back. They were huge and white, speckled with gray, and they stirred like vast feathered arms. His muscles felt strange, like they had been twisted into a new configuration to anchor the new additions. Turning was awkward, even so, he managed it. His wings twitched and shifted spastically.

"Motherfucker," said Jason, when the wings extended, "Cowboy up."

The wings flapped as fast as they could. He went straight up like a rocket. His head smashed through the plaster of the second floor. Jason howled and shook his head, which sent out a cloud of powder dust.

"Wow. Okay, that is the wrong word to think. There is a learning curve here. Hover." The wings flapped like crazy however, then settled into a hover. Jason pulled his head out of the ceiling and descended from the roof. He had a hard time mastering his new appendages, he hit the walls, and collided into hanging lights.

"Easy, hover, easy." He descended to the floor, while he slowly acquired the hang of it. He focused on the entry door and said, "Cowboy up!"

He blasted through the air across the room at lightning speed and stuck to the door like a spider. Jason smirked. "I am a bad motherfucker." The door opened all the way, and Jason panicked, hit the wall then crashed to the ground.

Angela walked in. "Jason? I'm home!"

"I gotta stop saying that," he said, slumped on the floor, and then flew off. "Hey!"

Angela searched around, however, could not find him.

"Up here!"

She looked up and saw at first what she thought was a large bird, yet, quickly realized it was Jason with wings spread, holding onto the roof. "What the hell?"

Jason dropped to the ground. "Check this out!" He spun around to show off his wings.

"What, are you a fly now?"

He turned so the feathers at the top of a wing, tapped her in the face.

"Stop—did you just slap me?" She asked.

He raised his hand and said, "That was not a slap. That was a love tap, reminding you not to be disrespectful to flies."

"What? Wait, I am not banging flies, so keep those things away from me," she said, and stormed off into the kitchen. Jason went after her and pinned her against the fridge.

"Come on. We can bang in zero gravity."

"I am afraid of heights."

"Oh, my scaredy-cat." He kissed her on the cheek, and then took off and flew around the warehouse.

He landed heavily, held onto the roof, and peaked through the tinted windows. On the street, he saw the SSA agents vehicle. Cautiously, he climbed out of the skylight and retracted his wings. He walked to the edge of the building and looked down to the street where the SSA black sedan was parked. An agent had stepped out and light up a cigarette, while he kept watch at the front of Jason's building. On the roof of another building, he spotted another agent that spied him through binoculars. The clear moon hung above him. Jason observed it deep in thought, and his eyes narrowed. *I need a disguise.*

INK

INK

Long, lustrous hair was manipulated by a brush. Jason entered the bathroom, and sniffed the air, to find Angela with a brush in her hand.

"What is that smell?" He asked.

"Jasmine perfume," she said, and continued to brush.

"I like it. Gets me horny."

Angela pointed her ass away from him, "Well don't come sniffing around here. I'm still sore from last night."

He thought for a bit, and said, "I need a disguise. You have any ideas?"

"Yeah. I have an idea. Give me your hat and thirty minutes," she said.

He did, and then left her company. He lit a cigarette, and went down stairs. The tool box and motorcycle had been pushed to one side. A wooden board hung on a wall had throwing stars, daggers and an axe stuck into it. He moved a bunch of chairs into the center of the warehouse, and stacked them high. Then he placed a tall ladder near them, and slipped a broom, mop, 2x4s, and scrap wood through the chairs and ladder. He took flight, using the makeshift construction as an obstacle course—bobbed and weaved, dipped and soared, stopped and hovered. He clipped the broom and mop handles a few times, however, practiced repeatedly, doing different combinations and then heard the bathtub water running. Angela called for him.

Jason was up on a section of exposed wooden beams on the second floor.

"Let us try INK Time." He blasted across the room, the chairs and ladder scattered around the room in a crashed cacophony. He smashed through them like a bowling ball and ended up tangled in one of the chairs.

"Jason?" Asked, a concerned Angela.

"I am coming. Some chairs fell"—he yelled—and then pulled his face off the leg of a chair and muttered, "Into my face." He untangled himself, saw the mess he created, and mumbled to himself, "Jason Crawford was here!"

Angela had worked on Jason's hat for twenty minutes. *This is my chance,* she thought, and then decorated the bathroom with strategically placed candles for a sexy and inviting mood.

The bathtub overflowed with bubbles. Angela stepped into the tub naked. She sat on the ledge he had built on the right side of the tub to hold soap and shampoo. When Jason entered, he saw Angela posed with one leg propped up on the bench. Her legs were spread, and she showed her pussy.

"Can you help me?" She said, and held up a razor between her fingers.

Confused, he thought, *she said she was sore, now she's showing me her...— don't look a gift pussy in the mouth. Just eat the damn thing!*
"Sssuracalp." He mumbled, and believed he said, "Sure I can help."

He dove into the tub fully clothed, took the razor and slowly lathered her pussy with soap. It was the first time he had shaven a vagina, so he took his time, with short strokes, lathered it up frequently. He was gentle, careful, and delicate, constantly stopped to admire its beauty. *"There must be a God to create such beauty,"* he thought. Angela slowly took off his clothes. In the tub, the water became cold so she would empty out some of the water and refill it with hot water. He built a precise landing strip, Jason couldn't help himself and kissed it several times, however, then Angela stopped him. She clutched his hair in one hand, took the razor in another, and pulled his mouth off her pussy.

"My turn," she said.

Jason felt tongue tied, still, furrowed his brow with a "What?" expression on his face.

"Your face. We need to finish the disguise before we play."

"Oh," erectly, Jason said.

On him in no time, Angela's strategy was in effect, and working; she held the razor to his face, and shaved Jason's beard off.

"Is this going to take much longer?"

"Stop complaining. You shaved me."

INK

Jason smirked. "That was fun. Gillette should market that razor. The new face and puss, when you are on the go, or trying to get something going. Twin blades for twin lips. His and hers. Show your women you care."

"Jason!" said Angela, laughing, "You will make me cut you."

She had told Jason she would like to see what he looked like without a beard and mustache, and when he answered that maybe one day she would, she left it at that. She knew from experience nagging men never worked. And the men that nagging did work on, she found spineless and boring.

"Twin blade for twin lips!" muttered Jason.

"Stop. You are terrible." Angela set down the razor; her mission complete. She looked at him like she saw him for the first time. Jason's beard and mustache were gone. She created a new version of Jason, clean-cut and unrecognizable. She savored the moment and took pride in her handiwork.

"You look ten years younger," she said.

He felt his chin, with a finger. "I feel naked."

"You are naked." She said and raised a hand held mirror from her bag beside the tub. He saw his reflection. Shocked, he did not recognize the man in the mirror. His appearance never meant anything to him. And he had never shaved. He looked at her, and remembered reading somewhere, "that some women will bring out the best, or the worst in men," *"This is the bitch to my yang,"* he thought.

"You know what I like to do when I am naked." He came near her.

"Wait." She held him back, reached for a makeup bag on the floor of the bathroom, opened it, and pulled out a beard and mustache she had made. "This will work. I barely recognize you." She peeled the paper off the sticky back.

"Try this; it has a strong adhesive that can be used many times."

"Where did that come from?"

"I had it made a while ago. I like to be prepared."

Angela stuck the beard and mustache on his face. Jason then became suspicious and realized this was her plan all along; from when she had said she would like to see him clean cut in the Arizona jail. That was a long time ago, and instead of being angry, he discovered a newfound respect for her being patient.

"Wait a minute, did you plan—" Before he could finish his sentence, she sensed trouble, cut him off and stood up.

"Does this mole look cancerous?"

She placed her leg on the bench. With her pussy in his face, she pointed to a very small brown discoloration on the left side of her vagina.

"I should take a closer look. (He placed his left eye onto the mole so close, he could not blink) Hmm. Not cancerous. But I should kiss it to make sure." He then proceeded to do so.

What does that even mean? Angela thought. She took his face off her pussy by the hair and said, "See if the beard is waterproof." She forced Jason's face underwater, and then back out. The beard and mustache became soaking wet, however, stayed on.

"The facial hair works. You can just stick it in your jeans pocket, or in your hat. Take it off," she said, and reached outside the tub for his hat. He handed her the fake facial hair, while he kissed her pussy. Angela stuck the beard and mustache inside the hat. "I glued a pocket in here; you can just stick it in like that. Pay attention."

Jason's eyes lit up. "Oh, yeah. Impressive." He pulled her down into the tub and leaned over to kiss her.

Angela pulled away. "I want to discuss our relationship."

"Now is not a good time."

"Why not?" She said, and could see Jason's pupil's go up to his eyelids, gazed hi right, and then hi left, considering an answer. Then both his eyebrows rose.

"Because I have an erection, and the law states a verbal contract is null and void if made under duress or in a state of erection. Or at least it should." Jason said.

Angela cracked up laughing. "You are so full of it."

"Yeah, and now you are going to be full of it."

They kissed.

Lauren sat at the table, and viewed her empty tile with concern. Karen stormed into the print room with Fred.

INK

"Having trouble?" Karen probed, and slapped Lauren across her face.

"I will not build a bomb," said Lauren.

"Then give me the location of the SSA." She pulled out the Beretta pistol and pointed it at Lauren's head.

"No," said Lauren.

"Then you die," said a vexed Karen. Lauren slapped the gun out of her hand. Karen picked it up and fired at Lauren.

Lauren's right and left hand deflected all ten bullets. One of the bullets ricocheted and hit Fred Burns in the forehead, that killed him instantly. His head landed on the table with blood oozing from the bullet wound.

"You bitch," said Karen, and snatched Lauren by the hair and then dragged her out of the room. She marched hastily through the hallways. Lauren stumbled to keep up when they entered the laboratory. Cohen and Vernon were examining Ditta on the table. She smiled when she saw Lauren.

"I will not build an atomic bomb," said Lauren, out loud, for Ditta to hear. *Maybe it will help her prepare for the worst.*

"Cohen, Vernon, get her on the slab, and wire them both up," said Karen, and pushed Lauren to them. Lauren tried to fight them off, however, they overpowered her and tied her down to a stainless steel experimental table. Karen wired Lauren up with the electrodes, while Cohen and Vernon wired up Ditta. Karen eyed both girls and said, "The first one who gives me the location to the SSA, I will keep alive." Both girls looked at one another.

"Goodbye, friend," said Ditta.

Lauren smiled. "Goodbye."

"Wait," said Cohen. "What about the experiments?"

"Forget the experiments. Kill them both," she said, and went to an electrical board.

Then Cohen placed a wire on Lauren. He hesitated, and then he placed another wire on the metal table. Vernon gawked at Cohen, stretched his eyes open in a what the hell you doing motion. "She has gone crazy," whispered, Cohen to Vernon.

"They are both wired," said Cohen.

INK

Karen flipped a switch. Lauren and Ditta's bodies jerked when electricity blasted through them. Both screamed in pain. The lights in the room flickered.

INK

Back in the bathtub at the warehouse, Jason kissed Angela passionately. He climbed on top of her when Jason recoiled with a shout of pain.

"Ohhhh. She is dying!"

"Who?"

"Lauren," said Jason, and scrambled out of the tub. "I know where she is."

Angela slipped out after him, took a robe, and belted it. She was afraid. "How?"

Swiftly, Jason dressed in his torn jeans and slit shirt that Angela had made for him. "Not sure. Give me five minutes, and then call Braxton and tell him I know where Lauren is. Have him track me through my cell phone's GPS."

Jason pulled out his fake beard and mustache from his hat and stuck them on his face. He slapped his wings tattoo, and they unfurled. With one beat of his massive wings, he flew up to the skylight. Through their binoculars, the SSA agents witnessed Jason, without wings, walk to the side of the building, step off, and disappear. A flurry of communication broke out between them. Jason descended the building, his cowboy hat flung behind his neck. He slapped at his wings again; they came to life and he flew through the air. Then he removed his beard and mustache, and shove them in his jeans pocket. He went up into the cloudy sky, when the new dawn broke on the horizon, he headed toward the ocean.

Morning mist had smothered the tranquil beach town of Saint Leonards when he approached. A few surfers made their way to the beach, while he flew stealthily overhead. Seventy-seven red-winged blackbirds were on the roof of a building walled in mirrored glass. Jason landed on the roof retracted his wings, effortlessly and descended from the first floor of the building to the street in silence. He placed his hat on his head, and walked to the front of the building. There were cameras on the front corners of the building, and a revolving-door entrance. When he pushed through the doors, building security guards dressed in blue shirts, badges, noticed him, and shot trespasser stares towards him. There was only sunlight that streamed through the windows, with no lights on in the building; two guards inspected a circuit board.

A third burly guard cut Jason off and said, "Holt. You cannot come in; we have a power issue." The guard clutched Jason's shoulder, however, Jason pulled a knife from his arm, turned on the spot, and stabbed the hapless guard in the throat. The lights flicked on for a moment, and then off again. He moved without breaking stride. The guard slumped down to the floor, and ripped the t-shirt from Jason's torso; it hung from his jeans. Two other guards went for their guns, when Jason, now bare-chested, reached for his shoulders. The security guards were met by the razor-sharp whistles of throwing stars, which hit both of them in the face. They fell to the marble floor in cries of pain.

Jason saw a pair of nonoperational descending escalators, and started towards them, when he noticed a camera in the corner. He tilted his head down and threw a star at it. The camera smashed into pieces and crashed to the floor. Once he reached the escalators, he stopped and crouched down for a better view. A flashlight beam caught his attention, and he followed it to a pair of boots that stood guard on the lower floor. With one flap of his large wings, he floated down the escalators like a glider. At the same time, he stuck his hand in the hole at the knee of his jeans.

Jason's boots landed on the tiled floor with a CLACK. The sound gave him away and the guard illuminated the darkness with his flashlight to expose Jason while he threw the axe. The light bounced of the flying axe, that was steered by the heavy-weighted, sharp steelhead, flying out of the darkness into the light, it swung horizontally, spun fast, and sliced through the air towards the guard. With a THUMP sound it slammed into the chest of the security guard with such force, it lifted him off his feet. The guards flashlight flung into the air, and tumbled. The guard hit the ground with a THUD, followed by the metal flashlight with a THUNG sound. It illuminated the guards face.

INK

"Mama," Jason heard the security guard say, when he walked toward him.

Jason stood over him, surprised at how young he appeared. He was a kid, that looked 18 years-old. Then he saw the guard struggle to raise his hand towards his chest. Jason admired the fight in him. The kid eventually press the talk button on the microphone, hooked on his shirt. "Code three. I repeat, code three, (blood came out of his mouth, as his lungs filled with it.), Mama." He said while he eyed Jason. The guard chocked on his own blood, jerked and then died, with his eyes open.

"Stupid fuck'n kid," Jason said out-of character. Like the kid had found a new nerve in Jason. And the kid did, however, Jason would find out why much, much later. Jason felt awful, and closed the kids eyes. "Rest in peace."

A geared MECHANICAL sound made him scan a powerless, stainless steel elevator,' near it was a black, rough-iron, spiral staircase that descended below. Cautiously, he stepped down the first dark flight of stairs until three flashlight beams lit up the connecting second flight. More flashlights flooded the area; there stood ten mercs on the floor in the dark, they held flashlights, guns drawn, and surrounded the staircase. They knew someone was on the first flight of stairs, and they were armed to shoot. Kiko stood behind them.

Jason went back up the stairs and onto the first floor. He ran up, jumped into the air, and slapped his wings, and they extended out. With one flap of the wings, he flew from the first floor into the stairwell, where he did a U-turn, and then blasted towards the mercs on the second floor. Before the mercs could react, Jason decked the nest of mercs, their flashlights mounted on guns flung into the air. Light beams tumbled disjointedly, while Jason's flying fists, elbows, knees, kicks, throat jabs, and temple punches effectively ended the fight before it began. He retracted his wings, while he skidded to a halt. His fists, elbows, knees, and boots were slick and dripped the blood of his enemies.

Kiko applauded, slowly and sardonically. "Impressive!" There was ambient light from the tossed flashlights on the floor for Jason to find him standing in a corner. In a reflex motion,

INK

Jason raised his arm to his head, and covered half of his face with his right hand. Then he thought, *This would be a good time to see if the disguise worked,* because Kiko would recognize him, and there was a good chance Kiko would not leave the building alive, so he dropped his hand from his face. Kiko said, "But now you die." He then realized the shaved beard and mustache had worked, because Kiko did not recognize him. *This time you will not have a Taser gun to help you,* he thought to himself. Kiko pulled a samurai katana sword from a display on the wall.

"Son of a bitch," said Jason, and then realized he also had a sword. He reached behind and pulled the large INK fantasy sword from his back. Kiko blinked in surprise.

"Cowboy up, motherfucker!" Jason sneered, when Kiko dashed forward. Iron swords clashed violently, and caused sparks to illuminate the darkness. Constantly on the defense, Jason struggled with the sword's weight and size. He had no experience, technique, or footwork with the sword, which made him seem clumsy. His sword swings were sloppy and slow. In contrast, Kiko fought swiftly, nimble, and ran around; his ultra-light katana jabbed and poked Jason, who bled from a host of little cuts on his shoulder, waist, and brow. Unexpectedly, the lights came on and stayed on.

Kiko slid to a halt, and grinned from ear to ear. "You are no match for my speed."

They fought all over the floor, the furniture, and the walls. Steel hammered against steel. Kiko flung Jason's sword across the room. Jason, on the sofa, flapped his wings, to evade Kiko's lunge, and landed near his sword.

"Oh," said Kiko, and stroked an imaginary Fu Manchu. "Clever."

Jason picked up his sword and blocked Kiko's slice, however, he followed his weighty sword's momentum, and then swung around. Kiko blocked the sword briefly, because the weight, bulk, and momentum of Jason's sword cut through Kiko's sword in a shower of sparks and metal fragments—just before it sliced through Kiko's waist, and cut him in half. Kiko fell away in two pieces.

INK

"Sushi, anyone?" Jason muttered. He dropped the sword and searched the two rooms that branched off the staircase. They were empty, so he walked to the elevator and stepped inside. He noted that it went down to the fourth floor, and it was currently on the second. He touched the 1873 western Peacemaker tattoos on his abdomen; they came to life in his hands. They were beautiful, with ivory grips, oiled hammers, six-round chambers, and barrels as long as his hands. He spun them, and then cocked both guns. Jason pressed the elevator button for the third floor.

Six machine-gun-carrying mercs on the third floor watched the elevator descend. The two nearest the doors nervously perspired and anticipated, while the elevator moved from the second floor to the third. When it stopped, it took its own time for it to DING softly and slide open. It was empty. Two mercs eased to the edge, and then peered inside, however, did not see Jason on the roof until it was too late. The powerful wings rocketed him past the mercs at blinding speed. Jason turned back onto them with his guns blasting. The classic Peacemaker pistols blazed, while bullets exploded from their barrels into two of the mercs' heads.

He shot three mercs in the chest, when they turned towards him. When Jason ran out of bullets, he dropped the spent six-shooters aside, and he yanked two more from his tattoos. Another merc shot at Jason with a stream of machine gun bullets. Jason plunged, darted, swooped, zigged, and zagged all over the room, with his wings retracted to lower his target profile. Jason shot, and hit the machine gun shooter in the chest twice, and he slumped to the floor. Another merc came from around a corner with a Mossberg shotgun at his hip. The weapon blasted both barrels of buckshot at Jason.

Lead metal filled his flight path, when he twisted, spun, and bent, even so, some lead clipped him in the left wing. Feathers fell to the floor, and dissolved. Jason crashed to the floor, and his wings retracted. The merc tossed his spent shotgun aside, pulled out a .45 Browning pistol, and ran at Jason, firing with a deafening scream. Jason picked himself up and touched his wings again, and a fresh new set sprouted out. He darted across the room between the bullets and drove a boot into the merc's chest, that sent him airborne. The elevator doors opened on two hapless minions, shocked to see the flying merc headed straight for them. The corpse slammed into both of them, and knocked them unconscious. Jason breathed heavily.

INK

There was silence for a moment. Then Jason heard footsteps and turned in the direction of the staircase. Oleg stood at the top of the stairs. The old man cracked his knuckles.

"Well, well, well," said Oleg. "You shaved."

Surprised and disappointed, Jason asked, "Turn to the dark side, Mr. Crichenko?" They circled one another.

"After your disgraceful display, the town would not renew my business license," said Oleg. "My business tanked. No one would let me coach."

"Maybe it had something to do with you throwing your fighter under the bus?"

Oleg scowled and said, "Security is the only thing I can do now, thanks to you."

Jason sadly said, "Sorry about that, friend."

"Foe," said Oleg.

"We don't have to do this."

"No," said Oleg, "We do not, but I want to." They dispensed with the small talk. Oleg's face was warped with rage when he attacked, and opened Jason's forearm with a hidden knife. Jason stepped back before the cut went too deep. Oleg threw the knife, and Jason dodged it easily. He ducked just under a follow-up punch that smashed into the wall; sheetrock chunks exploded around Oleg's fist like shrapnel. Jason pirouetted around him and hit him with a reverse roundhouse. Oleg hit the wall with a grunt.

Jason let him turn around. He attacked with a vicious series of blows, however, Oleg seemed to absorb his punches and kicks. This time Oleg's attack was an unrelenting fury, fists pounded like jackhammers. He grabbed hold of Jason, and hurled him like a rag doll into the elevator, which a leg from a merc had kept open. Oleg lunged at Jason and seized an arm while Jason got to his feet. Jason shoved Oleg out of the elevator, gripped his collar, and twisted him around. Oleg seized

Jason by the throat. Jason broke the hold and fell onto a chair. Oleg jumped onto his back and grabbed him around the neck in a chokehold.

Jason darted his right hand, seized Oleg's wrist, and held the chokehold at bay. His left hand was under his body. Then he noticed his right arm was bloody near the knife tattoo on his forearm, and he tried to reach for it with his left hand, however, it was stuck. Oleg tightened his grip while Jason leaned his body to free his hand. Oleg continued to strangle him. Sweat built up fast on Jason's forehead in the struggle, and then he freed his hand, approached the tattoo. His finger stretched for the knife, and Jason made contact with the tattoo. The dagger handle protruded out of the skin. Oleg witnessed it, and loosened his grip.

Jason gripped it and plunged the knife into Oleg's shoulder. He screamed in pain and released his hold on Jason's throat. Jason whipped around, slung his arm around Oleg's neck, and strangled him. Oleg gasped. Jason pulled his arm tighter. Oleg finally slumped in Jason's arms and dropped, lifeless, to the floor. Jason backed away, and breathed heavy. Oleg's wallet fell out. Jason saw a few hundred-dollar bills inside. *Do not take it— I owe Tatman three hundred,* he thought, and took the bills, stuffed them into his jeans and said, "Old habits die hard." *Bad karma. That will come back to bite you in the ass.*

The elevator doors bounced off the dead man's leg. The stairwell near the elevator was enclosed on this floor, with a door access. Jason opened the door cautiously and heard *TUNG, TUNG, TUNG, TUNG,* the sound of footsteps. So he pulled out another pistol from his tattoo. Vernon stepped up the stairs and then froze, at the sight of a gun barrel pointed at his face. Jason held the pistol on him. "Where are Lauren and Ditta?" Vernon raised his arms, peed his pants, and pointed downstairs. Jason motioned with the pistol for him to lead the way, and Vernon walked down the stairs.

"Why are they not dead?" Karen inquired.

Karen and Cohen stood by Lauren, who was on the table near an unconscious Ditta. The animals started to stir wildly in their cages.

"Electrocuting both girls overloaded the circuits. We should try the truth serum before we kill them," said Cohen, as if he had abruptly turned into a mad scientist.

"Kill that one," she said, and pointed to Ditta. "We do not need two."

"I do!" yelled Jason, from across the room by the stairs, and pointed a gun at both of them, while he held Vernon like a shield.

"Is that what was wrong with the elevator?" Karen questioned.

Vernon swallowed. His voice trembled. "Y-y-y-yes, ma'am."

Karen raised an eyebrow. "Ma'am?"

"Move away from the girls," said Jason.

"S-s-s-s-sorry," said Vernon.

Karen whipped her Beretta out from inside her coat and shot rapid-fire at Jason, however, she hit Vernon three times in the chest instead, while Jason dived narrowly out of the way. Cohen shot with his gun along with Karen, and test tubes, griffin beakers, Erlenmeyer flasks, droppers, rods, pipettes, and a host of lab hardware disintegrated in sporadic explosions of glass and plastic. Jason tried to get a shot off, however, Karen was near Lauren and Ditta. He placed his back against a concrete support column. The animals spasmodically flinched at the sound of *GUNFIRE*, growled, and showed their teeth.

Karen shot continuously, until her gun was empty. The bullets chewed into the concrete support. Jason saw his opportunity and took cover behind a solid workbench. Cohen shot at Jason, however, missed. Oleg entered through the stairwell, and limped into the room. He desperately wheezed, with a knife still jutted from his shoulder. He saw Jason behind the bench and placed a boot on it, pushed it so the bench slammed into Jason. This caused Jason to crash onto the floor, slide, and before he could deploy his wings, he was pinned against a wall.

An *ALARM* sounded. Karen and Oleg turned to a television monitor in unison; it showed SSA agents Decker and Braxton with a police escort hastily arriving outside of the building. Karen cussed. "…Get her into the sub." Cohen picked Lauren up and carried her to the submarine. Karen opened the hatch and untied the mooring. Cohen stepped into the submarine and sat down with Lauren on his knee. Karen took the pilot's chair, and shrieked "Kill them!" to Oleg. She closed the hatch and coasted out of the cave in the submerging vessel.

Jason shoved the bench aside just in time to see the submarine depart, and then limped over to Ditta and picked her up. Oleg, bled and stood unsteady, cut them off from the elevator and stairwell. He cracked his knuckles, scowling. "Now you die!"

Jason adjusted Ditta in his arms. "Can I take a rain check?"

With a *DING*, the elevator door opened, and the two minions inside saw Jason extend his wings and blasted into INK Time. They shot at Jason, however, they hit Oleg, and he crashed to the ground. They exited the elevator, and peppered the room with gunfire. Jason felt the bullet trails chased him.

Even though, he was shot in the same arm that had the knife wound, Oleg stood up. He found a gun. "Kill them both!" he shouted, blood ran down his mouth. The guns thundered through the underground lab. Jason moved at impossible speeds, like a human rocket. Bullets ricocheted off the roof, walls, animal cages, electrical boxes, workbenches, and computers. Oleg realized the only way out was through the winding staircase that led upward, so he targeted its supports with his pistol. *PONK, PONK, PONK,* sparks exploded. Both stair supports riddled with holes. Jason flew Ditta into the stairwell when he heard the staircase creak and shift to one side. It blocked half the exit.

"Oh fuck," said Jason, and spiraled up fast through the fourth floor. He hugged Ditta tightly to shrink their collective profile and enable them to pass through the ever-closing opening. Third floor. His wings scraped when they went through and up to the next floor. Second floor. No sooner were they clear of the stairwell onto the first level, when a powerful explosion sent a flame up the ascending stairwell. The percussion of the explosion spun Jason out of control, that bounced him up through the escalator walls to the street level. He wrapped his tattered wings around Ditta to protect her as they crashed to the ground, flipped, and then slid across the floor to a stop in a tangle of limbs, feathers, and blood.

Jason retracted his wings, and released his grip on Ditta, that made her slink to the floor. He held Ditta's wrist, felt for a pulse, and started to do CPR.

"Do not die on me! Come on. I haven't even seen your junk yet."

Decker and Braxton entered the foyer through the revolving doors. Jason saw them and tried to cover up with what was left of his t-shirt. The two ran at Jason, guns drawn. "Hands up! Identify yourself," said Decker.

Ditta coughed up a red and black liquid, and Jason jumped back. "You are safe," Jason said to Ditta. He looked up at Decker. "A friend." Braxton was near her, and squinted to focus on Jason's face, and then his tattoos, when Braxton's eyes became large. That was when Jason realized Braxton recognized him. Therefore, he watched Braxton to see if he would say anything, however, Braxton said nothing.

"Find and block the exits and entrances. (she said to an agent) Where is the other girl?" Said Agent Decker.

Jason wiped his forehead. "Taken away in a submarine. I am going after them. There are a bunch of mercenaries down in the escalators." Not sure if Decker recognized him.

"I will come with you," said Braxton.

"I have to go alone," Jason said, when he stood up and headed for the revolving doors.

"Gather round," said Decker. Braxton turned to Agent Decker.

"Get some ambulances in here and radio for a helicopter," she said. Jason stepped out of the building. Police cars and military vehicles, which drew a crowd of beach-goers, blocked off the road. If he took flight it would draw too much attention, so he walked away through the crowd, and searched for a secluded spot. Jason went up the street, found an alley, saw a power poll, and scanned the area to see if anyone was around. No one was.

He climbed onto the wooden pole and started to scale it. He then leapt to the balcony of a building, climbed the wall to the roof, and leaped from one roof to another to get his bearings. He scanned again and saw no one, so he touched his wings to life. In INK Time, he flew vertically, and the speed made him nearly invisible against the sky until he disappeared into the clouds.

INK

A clean-cut male EMT, along with his partner, a perky brunette, were crouched by Ditta. One felt her pulse, while the other stuck an IV drip needle in her arm. Braxton entered from outside, cut through SSA agents and police that surrounded Decker.

"Chopper's here," said Braxton.

"Take no risks with these mercs. If their arms are not up, shoot to kill. Cantinar will take over," Decker said, and gestured to a tall, black marine with a mustache.

Cantinar stepped up. "You heard the captain," he said. "If I see any one of you taking risks, I will shoot you myself. None of you are dying on my shift."

An army green Bell 212 helicopter with its rotors spinning was on the street. Trees shook and leaves tumbled in the streets from the propeller turbulence. Decker and Braxton stooped when they ran into the helicopter, hopped in and then it took off. They put on helmets that were equipped with built-in headsets.

"Agent Decker, Do you have a destination?" Asked the pilot, through his helmet microphone, while the rotors beat loudly.

"We are searching for a submarine." Decker said, into her microphone.

"USS Alabama aircraft carrier is ninety-eight miles off the coast, with a team of navy seals on it."

"Let's go," said Decker, while the helicopter skimmed the surface of the ocean. Braxton hung his legs over the side of the copter. With his headset on, he seemed like he was in his element. Although comfortable in the chopper, he urgently searched the ocean.

The pilot, copilot, Decker, and Braxton heard incoming radio traffic. "Wind Walker one-one-nine, this is Stingray.

Whiskey X-ray two hundred. Half-mile visibility with heavy rain. Final inbound bearing two-one-seven. Deck is moving."

The pilot looked at Agent Decker and said, "Stingray, this is Wind Walker, request code seven, repeat requesting code seven." Agent Decker gave him a thumbs-up.

Braxton searched the ocean until the helicopter landed on the massive aircraft carrier. Decker and Braxton were led to the radar room where they met Admiral Jennings, a portly type who shook hands energetically. "We found something on the sonar," he said.

The XO (Executive officer in the military) and three other officers watched and listened. The XO, had a thin, clever, bookish, appearance, that sat at a radar display.

"We have an object there." He pointed to a green blip on the radar.

Decker squinted. "Could it be the sub?"

"Hard to say," said the XO, "But my guess is yes."

Decker nodded, determined. "Let's go."

The admiral shook his head. "US Navy cannot. They are in international waters."

"They have a hostage," said Braxton. "An American citizen. We cannot let them go."

The admiral placed a hand on Decker's shoulder. "Let us take a walk, Captain," he said. They walked out of the room, followed by Braxton. "I have ten navy seals at the ready. Would you consider a black-ops extraction?"

Decker thought for a moment, and hesitated, however, Braxton did not.

"I shall take full responsibility." Braxton said.

"They are waiting for deployment in the ready room." The admiral said, and they turned to walk away. Decker grabbed Braxton's arm.

"You have a thing for this girl?"

"I have a thing for all the people I am supposed to be protecting."

Decker admired Braxton's response. So she warned, "Be careful," and they walked off.

INK

Jason flew over the ocean and it was not long before he found something. A large black submersible traveled north underwater, out to sea. He took a closer inspection and was able to make out the sub while it headed for a black ship on the horizon. Jason removed his torn shirt and dropped it into the ocean as a signal, however, it was so small. He took off his boots, dropped them in as well. Then like a pelican, folded his wings back. Dove in with arms outstretched to protect his head; plunged underwater, grimaced, until he touched his gills, and brought them to life. It took a minute for him to get used to breathing the oxygen in the water.

Then, webbed fingers appeared and a whale tail ripped through his jeans. Jason waved his whale tail once, it speared him through the water faster than a sailfish, and he slammed his head into the sub, which dazed him. "Son of a…" he muttered, while he held his head. The impact alarmed Karen, while she guided the sub. She took off her lab coat, clutched a two-way radio microphone and spoke into it. The stern doors opened on the black ship ahead. A flotilla of eight jet skis and underwater scooters deployed from the ship's stern and raced towards the sub. Each vessel was equipped with spear guns, knives, and nets. Ten scuba divers, dressed in black wet suits, powered forward in two Zodiacs.

The eighty-two-foot M-K-V Navy SEALs craft looks tiny compared to the aircraft carrier, Braxton thought, when he stepped aboard with a white wet suit in hand. The carrier raced across the ocean with Decker at the helm. She stripped naked to change into a wet suit, and the ten Navy SEALs looked away. They were already suited up in scuba gear, scattered in different positions on the boat, and searched the ocean. Braxton was the bashful type, still, when he saw that the SEALs gave Decker and him privacy, he also stripped naked, and pulled on the skintight white wet suit.

Jason held his head, and tried to get his bearings, when the divers fired upon him. He realized six spears were headed his way and waved his tail in a panic. He was out of the danger zone and blasted through the surface, high into the air over the flotilla out of control.

In the SEAL boat, Braxton yelled "THERE!" and pointed, when the strange figure plunged back into the ocean. The boat's helmsman turned the wheel and headed to the area, at full speed. It raced across the ocean, and bounced over the waves. Then Braxton with his wet suit on, was amped up and ready to go, because the boat's rapid bouncing annoyed him.

"You see that?" Decker asked.

The black ship on the horizon came into Braxton's view. "Yeah."

"We are going to be outnumbered," said Decker.

"I like those odds," said the number one SEAL.

Braxton smiled at the remark, however, Decker did not.

Jason swooped in behind the few divers at the end of the flotilla, pulled their face masks off, and ripped the air hoses off their tanks. Then he whipped a knife from his arm and slashed their air hoses. Scuba divers did not see him come or go. Jason was as fast as a Phantom. The flotilla made a formation around the sub to protect it, and escorted it to the ship. One by one, divers disappeared.

Dead Divers floated on the surface leaving a popcorn trail. When the SEALs approached the submarine, another lifeless diver flew out of the ocean like a rag doll. Decker, Braxton, and the SEALs dropped into the ocean from the boat. Underwater, the white wetsuits joined Jason to fight the black wet suited scuba divers. SEALs and divers exchanged shots from CO_2 guns, and then closed in for hand-to-hand combat with knives. Decker and Braxton went after the sub. Streaks of red clashed against the marine blue ocean water, as blood from the divers slowly smothered the area. Sharks chewed on dead bodies, while water scooters and equipment sank into the depths, and littered the sandy bottom.

INK

Two divers were about to ambush three SEALs with a net. Jason came from beneath the SEALs. He gripped the net and forced it to the surface, which tangled the divers in it. One broke free of the net, while Jason pulled the other diver out of the ocean. He used his wings to leverage himself. He spun the diver round and around and threw him into the distance, like an Olympian hammer thrower. The diver flew through the air, slammed into the side of the ship, and fell into the ocean under the observant eyes of Ricardo and four clueless sailors on the top deck.

Decker and Braxton were caught up in the melee, which allowed the sub to race away. A diver with a knife, crept up behind a SEAL when Jason torpedoed through the water, and punched the diver in the head. His knife drifted down to the bottom, followed by the diver. Jason and the SEAL turned around to see the sub enter the ship. Decker and Braxton were not able to catch it before the ship's doors closed. Then Jason sliced through the ocean en route to the ship, he broke the surface of the water and went airborne when he snapped his wings into action. One swoop of his mighty wings, and they stretched wide like a glider.

"Look out," said Ricardo, when he ducked.

Jason took four of them out with his wings, like a bowling ball takes out pins. Ricardo dived under a tarp. Jason landed on the ship's deck, retracted his wings and then lifted the tarp. To see a gold, framed painting of a weeping willow tree, next to a stack of two-by-fours and paint buckets. Ricardo disappeared.

"Motherfucker's a Houdini," said a frustrated Jason.

Two of the sailors staggered to their feet, and Jason took out his frustration on them with a pair of neat roundhouse kicks, which sent them overboard. When the other two sailors stood up, they were met with punches and kicks, which also landed them in the ocean, one of them almost landed on Braxton. They had swam for a few minutes when Braxton, Decker, and five SEALs reached the ship. Jason crouched by a ventilator.

Now he had time to survey his surroundings. He eyed the navigation deck's windows, there was no sign of the captain or any more sailors. He scanned the ship's deck. It was a cargo ship with a 240 foot-long deck, strewn with construction scaffolding, hanging painters' boxes, wax paper, drywall, tarps, paint cans, skylight, and a shipping container painted industrial gray near the bow. He also saw a customized hull for the submarine to enter and exit near the stern. He cautiously entered a door with a stairwell that only led down, steadied himself on the railing.

In the water below, Braxton put a knife through the heart of the last sailor discarded overboard by Jason. Decker, Braxton, and the five SEALs stealthily made their way to the anchor chain and released their tanks, weight belts, flippers, and goggles. They tied all the gear together with weight belts then it all sank to the bottom of the ocean. Braxton and Decker climbed first, wrapped their arms around the chain, dampening it and left it slippery for the SEALs. The SEALs had far more experience, though, and only needed to use their hands to pull themselves up. Even though the SEALs' climb was more difficult, they were faster than Decker and Braxton. Once on deck, they concealed themselves behind a shipping container.

Jason continued through a hallway with many doors. He opened one of them abruptly, poised and ready for anything. It became apparent after he opened a few doors, that this deck had sleeping quarters. He found another set of stairs that led down to the lower deck; there was a maze of rooms and stowage areas. He could also see the skeleton of the ship on this deck.

"Bulkheads," he said, like he made a mental note.

Two mercs came out of a cargo hold with Lauren and dragged her to the front of the ship. Jason slapped his shoulders, and two throwing stars became airborne. The stars razored toward the mercs, however, they saw them and ducked, as the stars banged into a steel door with a feeble *TING-TING* and fell to the floor. The mercs dragged Lauren away, and Jason gave chase. They ran through empty stowage areas. The mezzanines above seemed empty. Unfinished swaying chandeliers hung like iron skeletons from the ceiling. He entered another room and came to a sudden stop.

Paintings and portraits covered the walls and floor of the large room. An intravenous bag full of blood hung from its stand near a table in the center of the room. A brush connected to a tube extended from the IV bag lay on an unfinished painting. He took a closer look at the paintings; some were of an English fox-hunt, a bunch of top-hatted lords and dandies on big, high-stepping horses, their hounds milling all around them. The odd thing was that one of those British top-hatted was a short, slim dark Brazilian man in a dark suit that was running out of the oil-based countryside with a katana in his hand.

Sensing danger, Jason stepped back just when Ricardo exploded from the painting sword first. The would-be assassin's sword caught Jason across the chest, which opened a long, shallow cut. At the same time, Jason brushed his hands against the pistols tattooed on his hips, raised them and fired both. Jason missed, and rolled over the dusty floor. Ricardo quickly stepped into another painting and vanished. Amazed, Jason figured out how Ricardo disappeared under the tarp, and then picked himself up, and breathed heavily. Every breath stretched the cut with tiny, tearing jabs of pain. He stood in silence, only broken by the CREAKING of the ship around him.

He heard the fast *PAT-PAT-PAT-PAT* of footsteps, spun, fired again, and cried out as Ricardo slashed his left arm. He just managed to keep a grip on his pistol, held the cut with his other hand, which also held a gun. Jason closed his eyes for a second. The *CREAKING* of the ship grew louder. In a painting of a large, sleeping clown, the eyes came to life, and saw Jason, who concentrated on the sounds of the room. Ricardo did not dare to step out of the painting.

Jason could hear his *HEART* beating in his chest. Then he opened his eyes, raised his pistols up, and blasted away at all the paintings with a pirate yell—"Arrrrrrrrr!" He spun in the center of the room, to shoot up every painting, picture, and sketch he could see—Horses, seascapes, cities, skylines, and portraits; Jason shot them all without discrimination. Dog hunts, country fairs....there! Ricardo burst out of a sickly sweet painting of a mother that led her son towards a Ferris wheel. His face was a mask of rage. Ricardo crossed the room in two huge bounds, sword held over his head, and then jerked back when Jason's Peacemakers spoke.

One bullet caught the assassin high on the right arm. The next hit the Kevlar vest he wore under his tank top. The bullets whacked Ricardo onto his back and then flipped onto his chest. He scrambled like a crab on all fours for the nearest painting. "Mother loved me best!" he screamed, nonsensically. "Me! Me!" Jason raised the pistol in his left-hand to take aim, though, Ricardo dove into one of the urban landscapes. When he leaped in, he transitioned from flesh to paint with a weird shimmer of motion. Jason shot at him, however, his pistols were empty. Then he thought about what Ricardo had said when he watched him race down a street to a hospital. He held his arm and vanished through the emergency room door.

Jason dropped his empty pistols. "Mother…" he said, and spat a glob of bloody saliva on the floor. He turned and limped out of the room, and wondered if he had just shot his brother. When he reached the base of the staircase, he looked up, and saw the men carry Lauren onto the top floor. He touched his wings and shot straight up. He passed the engine room, crew deck, passenger deck, stateroom deck, and lower mezzanines, flew his way up toward the wax-papered skylight. Jason threw his arms up to shield his face and crashed through the wax-paper cover into the outside air. He landed on the deck, rolled, stood up, and drew new pistols, while his eyes adjusted to the light. A few yards away, Decker, Braxton, and the SEALs were startled at the sight.

"Did you find her?" Braxton asked. Decker stood closely, held a Doberman on a leash next to her—the one from her protector tile. She seemed exhausted.

"Yeah, I saw them carry her up here. She up here?" Jason asked. He let his pistols hang down by his sides. The wood floor beneath his feet was dry and hot.

"We have not seen anyone," said Braxton.

"Did you see anything else?" Decker asked, and breathed heavily.

"Did you know Ricardo can escape through paintings?"

"That is how he has been able to elude the SSA," realized Decker. She checked her Colt special combat gun's clip, and then slapped it back into place, and disengaged the safety.

INK

Neither the gun nor the Doberman was able to save her when the bear came out of a painting beneath a heap of tarps and two-by-fours. It rose up like a titan from the bowels of the earth. Its fur was black as shadow, and its eyes were red as burning coals. It slapped Decker aside like she was a rag doll. The massive claw opened her from navel to neck. She hit the ground and lay there, jerked and twitched like a squashed bug, her guts slid out of her torn stomach.

The Doberman dissolved into the air, the huge bear hurled itself at Decker, and tore her remains into pieces. The SEALs rushed Braxton and flung him over the bow into the ocean, and then followed. Jason raised his two pistols and then felt the cold, hard pressure of a gun barrel against the back of his head.

"Drop the pistols." It was Karen Smith's voice, a rough and broken croak.

INK

INK

The pistols made a loud *THUMP* sound when they hit the wooden deck. Jason watched in frustration while his friend Decker lay there and bled, while four mercs chased the SEALs to the side of the ship and shot at them with rifles and hand guns. The SEALs dove deep under the ship to avoid the bullets and headed for the stern. Jason started to feel lightheaded from the blood loss he suffered in combat.

"Killdor!" she shrieked, to the bear. Its claws and muzzle red with blood, ponderously, it stood on its feet and lumbered toward Karen. It bared its teeth. "Evaporate!" she said. Bellowing, the bear vanished in a cloud of ink particles that the wind dispersed in seconds. Karen jabbed Jason with her hand gun and he turned around to Karen and saw Lauren behind her, held by Kiko and Ricardo, who had a bandage on his arm. They both pointed guns at her, and held her arms. Her long, brown, beautiful hair was tangled and matted with dried blood. Jason's heart beat like a *DRUM* with elation. *She is alive!*

"You are hard to kill, Jason. Celtic sea captain now," Karen ordered, the captain—a tall, slim, bearded Australian in his 50s. He and two sailors hastily went to the bridge.

Karen seized Jason's shoulder in her hand, and pressed her hand gun hard against the his head.

"Move," she ordered, and pushed Jason forward, "A family get together." She laughed maniacally when they walked to the stairs. *If that is a sane person's laugh, I will never ride motorcycles again,* Jason thought. The laugh was whipped high and wild, and shrilled with hysteria. Karen was dressed in high heels, pants and a t-shirt, which left her tattooed arms, exposed. When she stepped past him to led the way, Jason noticed the tattoos of lettering, chains with skulls, ravens, grinning masks, and a peacock's fan on her right arm. Her gun dangled loose in her wrinkled, tattooed hand. They made their way below deck. "It should not be too long now. Nothing is stopping us," Karen said, while they navigated the halls of the ship.

Jason, in pain, asked, "How did you know Lauren was at the apartment with me?"

"We were watching the warehouse," Cohen said, when he pointed a gold-plated gun.

Karen smiled fiercely. "Shut up, Cohen! Who do you think gave your lawyer evidence on the judge? We have been keeping tabs on you since you were born. I have been your guardian angel. I saved your life at least once."

"We should be best friends," said Jason, and rolled his eyes.

Karen shrugged, nonchalantly. "We were keeping you alive until you could get us to Lauren."

"It is brilliant," said Jason. "Go on, I am fascinated." He clenched his hand all the way, so the blood dripped from between his fingers to the ship's floor, like a popcorn trail. Jason knew that if Braxton was alive, he would not be too far behind. They came to a room that had an armed minion and entered. Jason scanned the room; in the center was a grimy, balding, skinny, frail man, whose pants and tank-top fitted too big for him—like they were hand me downs. He adjusted his spectacles to see them clearly. Near him, an unconscious man lay on a stainless steel gurney with a needle in his arm. The frail man held the needle in the unconscious man's arm, while the man's blood dripped into a large IV bag that was under the table.

"There are four gallons of blood ready, madam," said the frail man.

Ten stainless steel gurneys were at the end of the room, with dead people on three of them, who had bled out. A chemical and biological torture console was at one side, and near it, was an electrical console with two stainless steel chairs. They forced Lauren and Jason to sit in the chairs. Ricardo, Cohen, and two large mercs held them by the shoulders.

"You have squandered your life brawling in saloons and fucking whores." She walked in between Lauren and Jason and sat down on a heating duct. She eyed her children with apparent frustration. Her eyes lingered on Lauren, who trembled in fear, when she noticed the reflection of the bear in Karen's eyes.

INK

"You have done better," she said approvingly. "You know your way around the Ink. I made a bargain with the Painted King." She spoke more to herself than to either of them. "What I had to work for, scrabble, and kill for, you were born with. You could have crushed master Symbolists at six with the proper training." She pulled a disgusted face. "Training I would have given you, if not for the interference of the insects. They caught me unprepared, took you away from me..."

She looked up, her red-rimmed eyes wild. "Never again! I suppose I should expect this ingratitude from you," sneered Karen. "I made you a god, and you have squandered yourself at the SSA. With nothing to show for it!"

Then she clasped Lauren's head and eyeballed her. "Your destinies lie ahead of you," said Karen, she gestured with her hand gun and then placed it on a console. "With me. I paid the blood price for your power, and struck the bargain that made you the colossi you are. I spent decades rooting through forgotten libraries, sleeping my way through the greatest Symbolists in the world, prying and poking for information, for the right books and scrolls to make you what you are." Her eyes widespread, her expression was entirely mad. "You will master the gifts I have given you, and you will make this world kneel." She gazed into Lauren's eyes. "Where is the SSA headquarters located?"

"FUCK YOU, MOMMY DEAREST!" screamed, Lauren so loud everyone tried to protect their ears. Karen punched Lauren in the face so hard it cut her lip and whacked her unconscious.

In the water, Braxton and the four SEALs escaped unscathed and made their way to the stern of the ship. Braxton gripped one of the SEALs by the wetsuit.

"What the fuck?" Braxton asked.

"We were outnumbered. It is best to get out and live to fight another day," said the SEAL.

"Today is another day. We are going back," said Braxton, and thought, *you were the one that said you liked the odds.*

INK

They saw a merc at the top of a gangway, that patrolled the waters. He was high up on the ship and difficult to reach.

"Volco," said the SEAL. The other SEALs nodded. He turned to Braxton. "Do what they do." Stealthily, they made their way to the platform where the merc stood guard. Members of the SEAL team dove deep down into the water, formed a pyramid and two men held each foot of the one at the top of the formation. They swam as fast as they could to the surface, and launched the top SEAL out of the water some eight feet. The airborne SEAL snatched the merc from behind, placed a hand around his mouth, stabbed him in the chest, and dragged him back into the ocean in one swift move. No one saw that merc after that. Braxton and the SEALs climbed the cleared gangway.

"So you are our mother?" Jason asked.

"Tell me the address or I will kill you both," warned Karen.

Jason took a moment, and then said, "Okay, it is on the corner of crazy bitch and fuck you, Mommy dearest."

She stuck out her hand and said, "Gun," Cohen gave her his gun, and she shoved it in Jason's face. "This time I shall make sure you are dead. Goodbye, my son."

Karen pulled the hammer back, placed her finger on the trigger, paused then turned the gun on Cohen, and fired— shooting him dead.

Braxton and the four SEALs surrounded the two doors of the ship's bridge. With military precision, they entered with an Indian YELP sound from different directions, that effectively confused the occupants, while they drew their hand guns. Swiftly, the SEALs disarmed the captain and two officers before the men knew what hit them. At gun point, Braxton said, "Tie them up." He turned to the captain. "Turn the ship around and head back into US waters."

"Found a trail of blood," said one of the SEALs near a door.

Ricardo and two large mercs, who stood behind Jason, were stunned. Karen slipped the gun into her pocket. "First things first. I no longer need him, never liked him," she said with grit in her voice.

Jason was also in total shock and disbelief. "No wonder they took us away from you. You are a lunatic." Karen slapped his face hard.

"How I kill you can be fast, or slow and painful." Jason stared at her. She glanced down, smirked, as if thinking of something devious. She reached over to a table, snatched something, and shoved it in front of Jason's face. It was a hypodermic needle, filled with red and black, striped liquid. He flinched, and Ricardo and three large mercs held him in place.

"Remember this?" Jason had an expression of fear on his face now. "When you were a baby, your nanny Chelsea and I would have to hide them before injecting you, or you would cry at the mere sight of one."

She pulled over a table with syringes. "Because you are so ungrateful for all that I have done for you, your death will be slow and painful. The first one will not kill you. Nor the second. Not even the third. Because I know how much you love needles."

Jason's face twitched. "How about a smoke?"

"Not a chance. That stuff will kill you," Karen believed, and raised a syringe. She tapped out the air bubble, and adjusted it for injection.

Jason gritted his teeth. "Fuckin' whack job!"

"You served your purpose," Karen whispered. "You men are tools used by females for our happiness, and when we have no more use for you, we discard you."

When Jason saw the syringes, he started to sweat profusely and tried to squirm loose from those who held him. Karen moved closer. He faced away from her while his eyes focused on the needle. The sharp tip oozed its poison when it inched closer to his neck. Blood dripped from Lauren's lip onto her shirt, which seeped onto a tile that hung around her neck. When Lauren's eyelids slowly opened, she saw Karen about to stick Jason. From the tile, a huge *ROARING* lion lunged itself at Karen, and bit her wrist that held the syringe. Its fluid squirted into the air like a rainbow stream.

"Killdor," screamed Karen, while the lion crashed her to the ground.

The bear came out of a dark corner with a deafening ROAR, and knocked the men that held Jason to the floor. The bear swiped its huge paw, which whacked the lion off Karen and into a corner. Jason was free.

INK

Once he saw the bear go after the lion. Jason slapped his hands to his stomach, drew his Peacemakers, and came to his feet firing. *BOOM*—he shot Ricardo in the left shoulder, which caused him to crash to the ground. *BOOM, BOOM, BOOM*—he shot the other three mercs in the chest, that took them down. The lion and the bear went at each other, in a tumbled roar of tangle of fur, claws, and blood. Karen flew to her feet like nothing had happened, and bled from her wounded arm. Her back was to Jason. She raised her gun to point behind her at Jason.

BOOM—her shot went wide, however, caught Jason's attention. He shot back at her while she turned to face him. *BOOM*—His bullet hit the gun out of her hand, and her shot went astray. "Killdor." Karen yelled. Jason punched her in the face, that pitched her over face-first, and crashed her to the ground. The bear roared in a hellish fury, and threw the lion across the room again. It charged at Jason, and bumped Lauren aside like a toy. Ricardo saw the bear approach and leapt into a painting of the Eiffel tower in Paris at night, which stood by a wall.

Jason stood his ground, and fired methodically at the bear—*BOOM, BOOM, BOOM, BOOM, BOOM*—however, it had little effect. Jason ran out of bullets. Then the lion jumped on the bear's back. As it struggled with the lion on his back. Jason turned his back on the bear, pulled the sword from his tattoo, sunk it into the wood floor, and pole-vaulted over the sword with all his strength. The bear threw the lion off. It landed near Lauren. Then the bear swung its massive paw at Jason with its razor-sharp claws. It hit the sword at the wrist, and sliced its own paw off. It flew towards Jason, who was face-up on the floor.

Jason raised an arm to protect himself, as the claw ripped a little flesh off of it and bounced to the ground. Blood mixed with ink poured from its veins and arteries. The bear growled in pain when it lumbered closer to the downed Jason. He drew two more Peacemakers and fired from the floor at the bear's head. Braxton entered the room with the Navy SEALs. A sudden blaze of furious gunfire ensued. Bullets hit the beast from all directions, and it slammed into the ships side. Jason slapped out two more Peacemakers and continued shooting.

The bear's head, became a ruined mass of broken bone and oozing blood, slid across the floor from its own momentum. The bear's limbs jerked feebly when bullets entered them, and then it burst apart in an explosion of gore and rotten Ink. A peaceful silence filled the air, along with gun smoke. It was over. Jason wasted no time, and immediately picked up his search for Lauren. He found her safely protected by her lion, in a corner. Jason went towards her, and waded through the morass, and past his mother's prostrate body. Karen's hand rose up, which clutched an empty syringe, then slammed it down, and stuck it into Jason's foot.

He dropped his pistols when a sharp, shot of pain went through his body. He kicked her in the face with his other foot and Karen stumbled up to her feet. Jason punched her until the plastic surgery in her face came apart. He finally saw through a bloody pulped face who had kept him away from his sister and, like a man possessed, he destroyed her. He pulled Karen downward, then slammed a knee into her face. "Happy Mother's Day." Jason held her by the collar, twisted her around and gritted his teeth. "I never did thank you for using me as your guinea pig."

He punched her in the face. Karen flew backwards and crashed through a half glass door; shards flew everywhere. She was bent over the door, and her shirt was raised to reveal a tramp stamp that said *Spank Me*. He also noticed a great mad, batlike creature that stretched its wings across her back. The door opened and she stumbled, and bounced off an electrical board full of flashing lights, and fell to the floor. Jason and Braxton cornered her. Karen's plastic-enhanced face fell apart, and revealed the wrinkled ugliness of her true skin. She smiled grotesquely; her lips scarred and her teeth were full of blood.

INK

Her eyes were a deep, wild blue with branching lines at their corners and heavy purple bags under them. She placed a finger on a button.

"Do not move or I will press this button and blow us all up," she threatened.

Jason pulled the needle out of his foot.

Braxton, face sweating, asked, "What do you think?"

Jason focused at what her finger was on—it was on the "Play" button of a compact disc player. "Bitch is crazier than an outhouse rat."

Karen grinned through bloodied teeth. "That is it. We are all going to die," she said, and let out a cackle. She pressed the button. Over the ship's loudspeakers, a Frank Sinatra song began to play.

Jason went over to her, squatted down, and said, "Your bomb is a dud, just like you, Mommy."

The crew, of a two-mast 220 foot high, endurance coast guard cutter did not take long to board the ship's deck. Two body bags were zipped shut near the impromptu triage area. A tall, redheaded man and a chubby, muscular, black woman tended to two wounded SEALs. Lauren sat on the stairs to the bridge, when Jason wrapped a blanket around her and sat.

"Ricardo could be...dead," said Jason, and caught himself before he said to Lauren that Ricardo could be their brother. Lauren had been through enough today, and it was not the time or place. He would need to confirm it with a DNA test before he said something about it. A medic had just wrapped Jason's foot when a medevac helicopter hovered by the ship.

"Good. Do not need a killer coming after us," said Lauren.

"What is the cost of DNA analysis?" Jason asked, and pitched his voice just over the *THUB-THUB-THUB* of the helicopter blades.

"I can get you a free test through my work," she said.
Jason watched a medevac helicopter land near the bow.

"I wish she was not our mother," she said. Her voice trembled. "Why us?"

"Are you kidding?" He smiled bitterly. "You are an intelligent, beautiful, gifted Symbolist; I am a handsome nut job." He saw her smile. "Who cares where we came from? What matters is the people we became."

She placed a hand on his arm. "You're right, brother."— With emphasis on brother.

He placed something in her hand—a fat, leather journal closed with a brass clasp. "This is for you."

She saw the ragged book. "What is it?"

"That woman's journal." Jason smiled, wickedly. "It fell out of her pocket when I was...thanked her."

"That woman?"

"Well, she may have given birth to us, but she is nothing like us."

A smile appeared on Jason's face, when Angela stepped off the medevac helicopter. She ran to the nearest coast guard crewmember. The crewmembers pointed in Jason's direction. While people went to and fro on the busy deck, she spotted Jason by the stairs and ran over to him.

"Are you okay?" Angela asked.

He was beaten, bruised, bloody, and shirtless. He took a step towards Angela, limping, and she could see the bandage on his foot.

"Had better days," he said.

"You look like you could use a rest."

"Yeah, I only have one muscle that is not bruised—care to guess which one?" Jason asked. She kissed him softly with care. They separated.

"Wrong muscle!" said Jason.

She smiled and they kissed passionately for a minute or two. Then they broke free and that is when Angela noticed Lauren.

"You must be Angela," said Lauren.

"Yeah, I am guessing Lauren?"

"Yeah."

"Nice to meet you. Your brother's hot," Angela said, and went back to kiss Jason.

"Sir. I hate to interrupt," said a helicopter crewman to Jason. "Sir, we are looking to get underway."

INK

"Where will you be taking him?" Angela asked.

"To the SSA for a debriefing. You will also be riding with us."

Angela's eyes narrowed. She disentangled herself from Jason, and glared at the crewman. "Under whose legal authority?"

"Cole Braxton, ma'am." The crewman pointed over his shoulder. Braxton had sat on the stairs with Lauren. She rested her head in the hollow of his neck. Angela deflated somewhat.

"I like her, Bro," said Lauren.

"Can we go in the coast guard cutter? I hate heights, Mr. Braxton," asked Angela.

"It is not my call. I'm following orders," said Braxton, then stood up, and led the way. Lauren, Angela and Jason followed him to the helicopter. *I need a vacation, a naked beach, and sleep for a week,* Jason thought, when he ducked the blades and stepped onto the helicopter.

They sat together in the back of the helicopter, when it left the ship behind. *I have my two favorite girl's right here,* thought Jason, while he closed his eyes and drifted off. Lauren's head nodded with the subtle turbulence on one of his shoulders, and Angela's was on the other. Angela could see bodies and debris floating, when the helicopter flew over the battlefield. Spear guns, air tanks, jet skis, and bodies littered the ocean and sandy bottom. Four men in a boat, were pulling the dead bodies into it.

"Tell Braxton I will catch up with him," said Jason.

"Why?" Lauren asked.

"Do not want the SSA knowing who I am," he said.

"You're leaving?" Angela asked.

"We are," he said, and pushed Angela out of the helicopter, to hers and Lauren's shock. Jason turned to Lauren, and said, "Later." Then leapt out of the chopper, and flew after Angela.

Angela screamed all the way down to the surface of the ocean, where Jason scooped her up in his hands—his large wings flapped them out of danger.

"You asshole," said Angela, and slapped him in the face.

INK

"Keep talking to me like that, and you won't get me in bed," said Jason and let go of her. She held onto the back of his neck with both hands, her body dangled in the air.

"That is assault. I could have you arrested," said Jason, with outstretched arms.

Angela held on for dear life when Jason flew higher and higher, however, her hands were slipping, "Jason! Hold me! I will not hit you again. I am sorry," pleaded, Angela.

He held her and she stopped panicking.

"Sorry is not good enough," he said. She kissed him. "That is a start."

"Take your panties off." She heard him say, while they flew into the sunset.

"Jason. Don't be silly."

"My arms are getting tired."

"Hold me. Okay, okay."

Intimidating, blue stonewalls stood thirty-five feet tall fortified the Fullmore Psychiatric Hospital. Fletcher Fullmore, a slave trader turned owner from Charleston, South Carolina, started to build it in the 1850s, however, died before its completion. Due to property taxes, it had fallen to the state, which turned it into a prison; then, with an increase of mental illness in the Southern states, it had become a psychiatric hospital. The city folks considered it a monument of greed, and believed the land that it rested on was cursed. Indians originally occupied the land until Mr. Fullmore's employees slaughtered them.

Then he forced slaves to work the land, until the Civil War broke out and his own slaves hung him. The president of the hospital was a man named Jack Shneb, a portly type in his fifties, with a little grey hair left in the classic shoehorn pattern of a balding head. He walked through the hospital halls, followed by Lauren and Jason, their footsteps echoed. The doors were colored lime green. The walls of the hospital were blue stone rock bonded with concrete, interior hallways painted white, and meagerly decorated, however, a hung painting of kids playing soccer in a city park caught Jason's attention. He took the painting off the wall, and then placed it face-down on the floor.

"Cannot have any paintings in the building," said Jason, then scratched his stick-on beard and mustache.

"Why?" Mr. Shneb asked.

"Well…um…how do I put this?"

Lauren could see Jason struggling, so she said, "That is where she gets her powers from." Lauren gave Jason a ribbed smirk.

"I shall take care of it," said Mr. Shneb, and unlocked a jail door with his master key. The group continued to walk down another hallway. When she followed him, Lauren could feel the cold generic walls, and she shivered. She rubbed her arms, and tried to warm herself up. They stopped at a solid metal door at the end of the hallway. Mr. Shneb opened a slide viewer on the door.

"Maximum security. Here she is. I shall leave you to it," said Mr. Shneb, then left Lauren and Jason. The two peered through the viewer. Their mother was inside, strapped to a bed, and talked to herself.

"She looks oblivious," said Lauren, distraughtly.

Jason swallowed. "Yeah, sometimes it is best not to know where you came from."

"I was hoping she would get better."

"They say the apple does not fall far from the tree."

Lauren slapped him across the shoulder. "I will not end up insane."

"Who says we are not already?"

"Shut up. You are pissing me off," Lauren said, while Jason smiled at her. She furrowed her brow. "What?"

"Nothing…Just… you are sounding more and more like a sister every day." They laughed, and Lauren hugged him and he hugged back, while they watched their mother. Karen raised her head, and saw both of them. She smiled and flashed her yellow teeth. Both of them jumped back in shock.

"I have seen enough."

"Yeah, I am with you."

They left.

"I feel awful turning my back on her," said Lauren.

Jason responded without a second thought. "She turned her back on us many, many years ago. What goes around…"

"…comes around," said Lauren.

INK

An elegant crystal chandelier, lit up an old, wood ornamental, classic restaurant. Blue, velour drapes that framed the windows, matched fine linen tablecloths, redwood floors, and beautiful wood-paneled walls surrounded the restaurant—however, no paintings. Two darkly dressed SSA agents with earpieces stood guard by the door and surveyed every move around Lauren, Braxton, Ditta, Angela, and Jason, while they enjoyed lunch.

"I was interested in law before I went into the SSA. What case you working on?" Ditta asked.

Angela said, "It is a murder case. I am not at liberty to discuss it." She stroked Jason's fake facial hair. "I love his beard."

"I prefer him clean-shaven," said Ditta, and then she poked Lauren in the arm. "Did you tell him what we found?"

Lauren drank some water, and then shook her head and turned to Jason. "Tests came out. All fine, but we found something strange in your DNA."

Jason ate, and paid more attention to his food than to what Lauren was saying. "If you found money in there, I will split it with you."

"Jason, this is important!" Angela said.

Jason looked at the girls.

Lauren set down her fork and knife and said, "We found a DNA strand from the chlamydosaurus kingii."

He rolled his eyes. "English! English!"

"The Australian frill-necked lizard."

Angela seemed worried.

"He is fit and healthy," said Lauren. "No need to be concerned."

Angela smiled mischievously. "That would explain why he is good at...at talking."

INK

Ditta said, "We also found a DNA strand that only comes from the Humboldt squid, native to the Eastern Pacific Ocean. It is the most aggressive of its kind."

"Would you like some squid in you?" Jason asked Angela, seductively.

Angela rolled her eyes and said, "Not at the moment."

Jason raised a fork with fried food on the end of it. "It is calamari." And brought it near her mouth. Everyone at the table laughed.

"Oh, I thought you were talking about your—Angela glanced down at his penis—

tentacle." Then she opened her mouth to accept the calamari.

Jason pulled the calamari away from her mouth and put it in his mouth. "I was!" Again, everyone at the table laughed. "That is my penis's nickname from now on." He continued to eat. "Squid DNA would explain why my urine is black." The girls were concerned, and scowling. Jason groaned, "It is a joke. Are you done? You are upsetting my tentacles and my calamari." Braxton was the only one laughing.

Lauren interrupted with concern, "We did find ink in the DNA also. We are not certain if it is yours or the squid's."

"I am sure it is the squid's," said Jason, and drank some beer from a bottle.

"He is not interested," said Ditta.

"So are you and Angela boyfriend and girlfriend now?" Lauren asked. Braxton made sure she knew he was not pleased with a stern look out the corners of his eyes.

"That is not very sister-like," said Jason.

"She does bring up a good point." Angela jumped right on it.

"I just found out I am part lizard and part squid," said Jason.

Angela relented. "Me moving in, my new job. I want a commitment."

"When are you moving in?" He asked.

"I have been living there for two months," she said.

"Does the landlord know?" He asked.

Braxton laughed and said, "You did not even know."

Jason shrugged, and then cut into his steak. "See, I am not good boyfriend material."

Lauren frowned. "Why not?" Braxton furrowed his brow. "Oh, stop it, Braxton. This is one of the pleasures of family, being in their business, whether they like it or not."

"Yeah," said Ditta. "Why not?"

Angela smiled a little. "Can I get an explanation?"

He hesitated, and then said, "I tend to be unfaithful."

"I do not mind sharing," said Angela.

He spoke before she finished, "That is why I...ha, what?"

Angela shrugged, uncaring. "You can see other women."

Jason squinted suspiciously. "Wait, what?"

Angela said, "I am not the jealous type. I am bi."

Ditta jumped in. "I am bi too."

Jason looked at Lauren. "You?"

"No, straight as an arrow," she said.

Jason took it in and said, "Ha—I—I—I see."

Angela bit her lip. "I am not talking about monogamy. We can share the ladies."

Jason was taken aback. "Have you two—?" He pointed at her and Ditta.

Ditta laughed. "Not yet."

Angela said, "Could be fun."

Braxton said, pointedly, "He did save your life, Ditta."

"I guess I do owe him one," she said.

"You the man!" said Jason, and gave Braxton a fist bump, "Bro!" Jason paused in thought. "Are you girls fucking with me? 'Cause that would be a cruel thing to do to a person."

Both girls shook their heads.

"You mean like threesomes and stuff?" Jason asked.

Angela shrugged. "If that is what you like, as long as there is honesty. That is important to me."

Lauren looked at Braxton and said, "You need honesty in a relationship," with concern in her voice.

Jason thought it over. "How? You mean, when you are not around I could—? This could work."

Lauren smiled and raised her glass. "Congratulations to the boyfriend and girlfriend." The five raised glasses and cheered.

Lauren and Braxton stared at one another with a mischievous twinkle in their eyes, and she placed her hand on Braxton's thigh.

Angela smiled. "I have a boyfriend."

Jason leaned back in his chair. "And I love modern women. Check please." He waved for a server. "Well, I guess we should go back to my place and make it official. Ditta should come along."

Ditta chuckled. "Some other time. We have to get back to work."

"I have to get back too," said Angela.

Angela, Ditta, and Lauren stood up and each kissed Jason on the cheek.

"Hey, it is not official until its…official!" said Jason.

Braxton stood up. "Better luck next time. Later," said Braxton, and escorted Angela, Ditta, and Lauren to the SSA agents. They exited.

Jason blew out a disappointed breath and thought, *I have a girlfriend and a bi chick, and I go home with my dick in my hand.It's just wrong.*

A beautiful girl walked into the restaurant. "Nice. I wonder if she is bi."

A server with long hair in a ponytail gave him the check. Jason searched for his wallet, however, could not find it. He checked his pockets. No luck. He waved the server over.

"I seem to have misplaced my wallet."

The server smiled. "This has happened before. Would you like to work it off in the kitchen?"

"Sure," he said.

"Let me have a word with the manager," she said, and went to find the manager.

I will just work it off cooking, maybe learn something, he thought, when she waved him over. He met her by the kitchen, near two large silver doors with viewing glass. They stepped inside; it was a white-tiled commercial kitchen with its own pizza oven. A chef was plating at the pass, while he directed four cooks, one over a steaming pot, one on a stove with a frying pan, and two chopped up food. Servers exited with food and returned without. The server handed an apron.

"If you clean those, the manager says he will comp your table," said the server, pointing. Jason turned around to a mountainous pile of dirty dishes spread all over a stainless steel sink. *All that?* he thought, when he put on the apron, rolled up his sleeves, and went to work. He rinsed the dishes, and then placed them in the large commercial dishwasher. When a white light exploded all around him, the retinas in his eyes adjusted abruptly. He turned around, and searched for the origin of the flash. Dick McGregor stood there, with a camera aimed. He snapped three more photos of Jason washing dishes.

Dick laughed. "I knew you would end up a nothing, Crawford. And with these pictures, I am going to let the world know."

Jason asked, "Did you ever ask yourself why your parents named you Dick?"

"Never gave it much thought."

"I think your parents knew, throughout your entire life, you would always be a dick." Dick showed Jason the preview picture on the back of his camera, and Jason slapped the camera into the sink full of water.

"Oops," said Jason.

"That is a thousand-dollar camera, you asshole."

"There is a blood sucking mosquito in here." Jason threw some jabs inches from Dick's face. Dick grabbed the wet, sunken camera, and ran out. A kitchen helper entered with a pile of dirty dishes and placed them near two other piles. Jason continued washing.

Rock music played in the background of the tattoo studio. A twenty-dollar bill and a boom box tattoo displayed on the wall, caught Jason's eye. He sat back in a barber's chair, and talked with Tatman.

"Dude," said the artist, "You hit the jackpot. Who is it gonna be?"

"That is what I said," replied Jason. "Tatiana."

Tatman nodded. "I will let her know." Tatman went over to Tatiana. She had just finished a tattoo, and the customer just paid her. A few people looked up on the wall, at the tattoos.

Jason's cell phone rang, and he answered it. "Yeah?"

Aaron was on the line. "Yo, cowboy! The Kuss has a gig." Tatiana walked over and pointed to a tattoo on the wall, and Jason gave her a thumbs-up.

"That is great. When?"

Tatiana gripped her tattoo pen, laid the chair back, and straddled him. She began a tattoo on his shoulder.

"I can't talk," said Aaron, "I am at the bar. We are gonna be rehearsing soon. I will tell you then. Can you make it?"

"I will be there in"—he glared at Tatiana—"in about an hour."

Tatiana pouted disappointment, while she rubbed her crotch on his. Jason hung up.

Tatiana sulked prettily. "I was hoping it was time to pay the piper."

"Did you say pay the piper or play with the pipe?"

Their faces were inches apart. Tatiana smiled. "As long as Angela's okay with it. I heard you and she were an item."

His grin was huge. "You would not be bi, by any chance?"

"They say all women are two drinks away from a bi experience."

"In that case, what are you drinking?"

She leaned in close to his ear and whispered "Rummmm," in harmony with the tattoo gun's humming. The sound of a *GONG* came out of the radio, and continued to fill the store.

While he read the newspaper, Jason on the rooftop of a building, heard a similar *GONG*. He looked to his right, where half a mile away a church stood. The church bell *GONGING* continued to chime out across the city. The church had a pitched roof, brick vaulting, and stained-glass clerestory windows; it was a Gothic cathedral, with two spires on each side of an entrance that led into the sacred precinct. Jason saw the architectural symbolism—the two spires were female legs; the sacred precinct was her pussy.

INK

I gotta get laid, he thought.

He went back to read the paper. Jason used an American flag to keep warm when it began to rain lightly. He was perched high up the building on a gargoyle's head. He lit a cigarette, while rain dripped off his cowboy hat onto page six. It was an article titled, "Cowboy Down," and featured the picture of Jason washing dishes in the restaurant. Another article read "INK: the Tattooed Superhero" and had a blurry picture of Jason, topless, by a revolving door, and stabbing a guard. He was done with the newspaper and placed it on the roof, and then scanned the city below.

A few people rushed around to avoid the rain. Then, Jason saw Pauli walking behind Vinny and Frank along the street. Jason flicked the cigarette, and its orange glow descended into the night. The *GONGING* faded into AC/DC rock music, and he turned up the sound on the new boom box tattoo on his shoulder. He dived off the building and held the American flag when he descended. It billowed, showed its 52 stars, stretched out and then he let it go.

As Jason dove towards the city streets, his cowboy hat fell back into position. His black t-shirt, which he had converted into a poncho, flew over his shoulder like a cape. He slapped his wings tattoos, they jutted out, and he angled for Pauli. Jason swooped one foot away from Pauli's face. When he passed, he reached out, snatched a burning cigarette out of Pauli's mouth, and placed it in his own. It happened so quickly that Pauli thought that the cigarette simply fell from his lips. When Pauli searched for it on the ground, he became puzzled when there was no sign of the cigarette.

Jason soared upward while he took a drag from Pauli's cigarette. Smoke poured out of his nostrils. Jason flipped the cigarette into his mouth with his tongue. His wings swooshed, he came down again, and plowed into Pauli's chest that sent him crashing through a large automobile dealership window. Pauli landed between two shiny new cars on the tiled floor, showered in broken jagged glass.

The load sound of shattered glass *KSHHH* caused Vinny and Frank to turn around. All they saw were broken glass pieces on the sidewalk. Vinny asked, "Where the fuck's Pauli?" Jason landed amidst the broken glass, music blaring. The alarm from the dealership went off, however, it was not very loud. Jason retracted his wings and flipped the cigarette out of his mouth, to uncover it.

"What the fuck is that?" Vinny asked, over the music.

"John fuck'n Wayne," said Jason, and placed his hat on. Vinny and Frank pulled back their long overcoats, to expose guns. A smirk full of confidence appeared on Jason's face. He had practiced for this his whole life and finally, he would see if he was, a gunslinger. He took another drag and smoke poured again from his nostrils. He dropped the cigarette to the sidewalk, snuffed it out with his boot, which sported one shiny new spur, tilted his cowboy hat, flipped his poncho, over his shoulder, and exposed his tattooed Peacemaker pistols.

Vinny and Frank snickered in amusement. Because of the music, Jason could not hear what Vinny said, however, his lips took the shape of "Look at this fuck'n guy." Vinny and Frank stepped away from one another. Jason smiled. Frank's fingers edged closer to his gun. The men eyed one another. Jason's fingers were calm and steady. If Vinny and Frank were nervous, they did not show it. They were stone-faced, like they had been in this situation before. Nevertheless, Jason saw a tell; Vinny's fingertips twitched. He would be first.

"Fill yer hands," declared Jason.

Vinny and Frank reached for their guns at the same time. Jason had already pulled the Peacemakers from his lower abdomen and shot four times before the mobsters were able to get their guns aimed at him. With two bullets in both Vinny and Frank's heads, they hit the sidewalk, dead along with their guns. Jason rose the guns to his lips, and blew away the smoke from the gun barrels.

"INK is in the house," he said, spun the Peacemakers in his hands, and then shoved them back into the tattoos, and they disappeared. He finely had conformation he was fast, and a satisfied, confident crooked smile appeared.

"Help me," Pauli said. Jason turned to Pauli who was on his back, and straining to lift his head to see out into the street. All

INK

Pauli could see was the silhouette of a man with smoke that poured from his nostrils like a dragon.

"Nice." Jason entered the showroom and stepped past Pauli, however, not before he dropped a gun that landed on his chest with a note that read, "Check the bullets from this gun with Rocco from the Branding Iron." Jason ran a finger across the fender of a car, in admiration. An abstract painting of a race car hung on a wall. It caught Jason's attention and he walked over to it, pulled a knife from his arm and slashed the painting to pieces. He checked the walls for other paintings, however, could not see any. He left the knife stuck in the painting's remains, and flew out.

Behind a counter on the floor was a small painting of two romantic lovers in a gondola, cruising through a canal in Venice, Italy. The gondola rower came to life, and Ricardo emerged with an oar. He dropped the oar, and then saw the painting with the knife in it, and walked over to it. He pulled out Jason's knife from the painting with his gloved hand. Pauli had noticed him.

"Can you help me? I can't move." begged Pauli.

Ricardo turned from the painting to see Pauli cut up, bloodied, and covered with the glass that surrounded him. "Sure," Ricardo said. "Hold this." He threw the knife at Pauli, and it stuck in his eye, killed him instantly. Ricardo picked up the gun that lay on Pauli's chest, and then walked out of the store and looked up into the night sky. He raised his arm and shot the gun into the sky at Jason's flying silhouette, when it crossed the moon.

THE END